Coming

A NOVEL

Susan Marting

Integro Press

**St. Louis, Missouri
USA**

*Dear Father Pio —
God is Good!
Thanks for all you do!
Peace*

*"God is not coming to scare the hell out of us."
Pio Jackson, OFM
10/24/10*

Published by Integro Press, LLC
St. Louis, MO
http://integropress.com

Copyright © 2007 by Susan Marting
All rights reserved, including the right
of reproduction in whole or in part in any form.

Cover design by Jessica Blanset
Editing by Christine Frank

Library of Congress Control Number: 2009911913
ISBN 978-0-615-27670-0

First Printing 2009
Printed in the United States of America

Lightning Source Inc.
1246 Heil Quaker Blvd.
La Vergne, TN USA 37086

In loving memory of Richie Greene

❦ 40 Days Ago ❦

"Coming," I mumbled as my feet scooted my slippers across the floor, toes scrunching through the fleece lining. I wrapped my bathrobe around myself and rubbed the grit from my eyes. Running my fingers through my tousled hair, I wiped the mascara from under my eyes with my knuckle and carefully hurried down the steps. Again, a knock at the door.

"I'm coming, I'm coming."

I had slept as if I were in a vegetative state for the past seven hours after burying my father and accepting condolences from what seemed like everyone my father had ever met.

"He was so funny."

"He was so loyal."

"He helped me get my start in the business, you know."

"I loved the way he walked your cat on a leash… it always cracked me up."

"He was the most respected guy in the office."

"If it weren't for him, I don't know where I'd be."

"I'll never forget the time he…" and on and on it went. I appreciated the kind words, the stories. Everyone

40 Days Ago

seemed to have his or her favorite that required disclosure.

Dad had been killed by a slap shot at the professional hockey game on Tuesday. The puck sailed over the Plexiglas and hit him square in the forehead. The doctors think that the blunt trauma caused his heart to stop, but in any case he was dead within the hour after repeated attempts to revive him. He had been so excited about the great seats his brother had gotten for the game, and my uncle was overcome with guilt over what happened. No matter how many times people tried to console my uncle with the fact that it was just a freak accident, he could not help but feel partially responsible, and he was devastated.

Because of the suddenness of my father's death, I was completely exhausted, not having had a second to brace my psyche for the tragedy. The news of his death was like a puck to the gut for his family and friends, and my poor mother was not doing well at all. The funeral reception at my house was lovely, and I'm sure my father would have had a great time if he had been there, but for me, there had been hardly a chance to breathe in five days.

Finally, at midnight, I had been able to flop in my bed with the exhaling force of a popped air mattress. The kids were asleep; the kitchen was somewhat clean. Well, the food was put away. The dirty dishes could wait until the next day. My husband and I whispered a few words of need, dependence and love for each other and fell sound asleep wrapped in each other's embrace.

It was barely seven in the morning when the knocking started. Who could be here so early, I wondered.

Coming

Maybe a florist delivery. Or a well-meaning neighbor with another ham. At the risk of seeming ungrateful, I rolled out of bed and with dizzy steps headed toward the front door.

Again, the knock.

"COMING," I half-yelled, half-whispered so as not to wake the whole family.

Opening the door a crack, I found an empty-handed man. He was young, maybe in his late twenties, early thirties. He was taller than me, but not tall by any means, maybe five-seven or -eight. He was not lean, not fat, but solid. His short brown hair was cute, clean, but a little shaggy, and his face sported a day's worth of beard growth. Too early to shave? Or maybe just a look he was going for, I found myself wondering. I looked beyond the young man and saw in the driveway an old VW Beetle. Not the reinvented Bugs but an old one, maybe from the early 1970s. It was orange, slightly dulled from decades of solar abuse, with some visible scratches and plentiful small dings.

My eyes returned to the man's light-brown eyes. Long, thick lashes. Cute, I thought. His eyes twinkled as he smiled and said apologetically, "I'm sorry it's so early. I see I woke you up. I just wanted to stop by because I knew your father. I didn't come yesterday, but I have something to talk to you about."

"Come in, come in." I opened the door fully and with a sweeping motion of my arm ushered the man inside my home, tightening up my robe. "I'm sorry I'm such a mess. Can you give me a moment to run upstairs and get dressed?" I asked.

40 Days Ago

"Oh, I don't plan to stay," the man replied with his hand waving in front of him. "I'll just be a few minutes and then you can go back to bed."

"Well, I'm sure I won't do that, but can I put some coffee on for you? We have some delicious muffins and sweet rolls from the reception yesterday," I offered.

"Sure, that sounds great," the man said, following my lead down the hall and sitting at the kitchen table. He gazed around the kitchen as I puttered about, filling the coffee maker with grounds from the freezer. I realized I had no more filters and, turning my back to him, reused the filter that was in the coffee maker. From the refrigerator I pulled trays with haphazard piles of muffins, bagels and sweet rolls. I still was not quite awake or I most certainly would have rearranged the pastries into an appealing array as my mother had taught me. I carefully moved dirty trays and dishes, taking great care not to create a cacophonous porcelain concerto and wake up the rest of the house.

As the coffee brewed, I sat, rolling my head around the back of my neck in an effort to wake up a little more. "So, how did you know Dad?" I asked of the stranger.

"I've always known him," the man replied, with a slight grin.

My brow frowned, but my mouth smiled.

"See, I knew your dad when he broke his arm ice skating backwards."

I smiled and nodded, remembering how Dad once was showing off at the rink just before he splayed himself across the ice and broke his forearm.

"And I knew him when he saved that neighbor boy who got hit by a car while he was on his bike."

Coming

I squinted slightly as I thought this guy must be older than he looked, because that was probably thirty years ago. Maybe he was that kid! I waited for him to continue.

"And I remember when you were born he had a couple martinis with his buddies at the office and ended up staying at the office celebrating your birth until your mother had to call a cab from the hospital to send him home. Boy, was she ticked!"

"Wait, wait, wait...you've *heard* these stories. You don't *remember* them," I said, trying to make sense of his words.

"Oh no," the stranger went on. "I was there for all of it. I was even there when he was a boy and taught himself to play the guitar. That was awesome."

Suddenly, an extremely uneasy feeling sunk down into my gut. My heart began to pound, and I felt like I might throw up. I stood up from my chair. "Um, you'll have to go now," I tried to say in a calm voice. I didn't want to upset this disturbed young man, no matter how well he knew my father. "Who *are* you?" I demanded.

"I know, it all sounds weird," he said. "But if you sit back down for just a minute I can explain."

"You have five seconds." I barely sat.

The man filled his lungs deeply before he began to speak. "Do not be afraid. I am Jesus of Nazareth."

Petrified, I pushed my chair back and stood up, putting my hands over my mouth as I gasped. What did he say? What? Oh God, no.

Seeing my alarm, he went on calmly. "I can prove it to you. Just don't faint on me, okay? Ready?"

40 Days Ago

Of course I'm not ready, I thought, but no words came out. I was stunned. Frozen.

"Please, take a breath. You're going to faint if you don't breathe," the man said with a slight grin. "Okay, here we go. C'mon, Joe."

With that summons, my father was standing next to the man, not four feet from where I stood. I sat slowly back into my chair, as my legs could no longer support me. Dad looked great. There was no gash in his forehead from the puck that had caused his demise. He was handsome and vibrant. His hair was dark and full, unlike the gray, balding father with whom I was familiar. He was thinner than recently, looking overall as I remembered him when I was a little girl. My father was smiling as he shook his head slowly back and forth at the sight of his daughter.

But I was not so calm. I was freaking out completely. My hands began to shake uncontrollably. Tears welled up in my eyes. Then my whole body began to tremble.

"Don't be afraid," the young man repeated. "No one ever really leaves you. Your father has been with you since he died. Death is not the end. It is a continuation. But after death there is no passage of time. Everyone lives in the moment. One day is like a thousand years and a thousand years, like one day."

But I thought people went to heaven, I tried to say, but again, nothing came out.

He seemed to hear me anyway.

"Heaven is a reality not confined by space or time. Heaven is life. Heaven is full of souls, souls fully alive. They are completely in tune with each other and with the Spirit, just as the strings of many violins vibrate when the strings of only one are played. Everything sparkles with love. Everyone in heaven feels God's energy and feels the connectedness…it is as if they are marinating in the spirit of God. Yes, they are alive, but their perception of reality is different than yours. They can see you, but they don't usually interfere with your life. You have your own lessons to learn on earth. But they hear you if you call on them."

I started to imagine what it would be like to live in heaven with my dad. I forgot my fear. I spaced out for just a nanosecond, but then whipped my head around towards this Jesus character, mad at myself for letting my guard down. I refocused. "So," I asked shakily, "what exactly are you doing in my kitchen?"

Jesus smiled broadly. "On earth, people mostly take care of themselves. Love is a delicate balance. Sure, you must love yourself and take care of your needs, but once we forget about others for the benefit of ourselves, the scales tip, and suffering begins. There is so much suffering in the world now. I want heaven on earth. That is the way it was designed."

"But c'mon, we're human. We're naturally selfish," I found myself arguing and couldn't believe I was speaking to this hallucination.

"Au contraire! You are naturally loving. You were born with the breath of God, the breath of compassion, within you," Jesus said joyfully.

"Then why do we consume our hours desiring things we don't have…a new car, a young face, a nice kitchen, cool parents…?"

40 Days Ago

My dad frowned and dropped his jaw in disbelief as he glared at me.

"I'm talking in generalities here, Dad. Not me…you know, other people, who have rotten parents. You really were the best, Dad." I couldn't believe I was talking to my dad.

Daddy smiled. He probably knew what I meant all along. He was just messing with me.

Jesus spoke again. "People are not living in love. I tried so long ago to teach about love and compassion, forgiveness and humility, justice and acceptance. But people get so easily distracted. For some reason, they just don't believe in The Way that I spoke about. They think there is a better way. I tell you, *I AM* The Way. Love is The Way. But so many people won't believe it. Everyone wants joy in his or her life. Yet people dwell on the things they *don't* have, the things that they *think* will bring them happiness, rather than realizing that they are already whole and blessed with a deep peace. People have The Way within them. And when you believe in the power of love and live in The Way, healing flows.

"But how can I be bold enough to live in love, knowing others do not and taking the chance that I will suffer as a result?" I asked, unconvinced. "What if I let go of everything that I hold dear, but no one else does, and I just end up losing everything? It's every man for himself here."

"And that's why the world is a mess. That is the mentality…every man for himself. I spoke so long ago of faith. Not just faith in God but faith in love, faith in compassion, faith in The Way. You must have faith that love works, always and without fail. You know there have been many people who took the chance to live in love, knowing the balance was not yet there, but living as if that balance depended on them. Siddhartha Gautama, Giovanni di Bernardone, Jalaladdin Rumi, Mahatma Gandhi, Rene Cassin, Martin Luther King, Jr., Agnes Bojaxhiu, and many others. And there were also millions of so-called 'average' people who did ordinary things, but did them with love and therefore lived a sacred life. They took a stand and lived in love and found a joy in life that others cannot know. When your only desire is love, miracles happen. Justice happens. Beauty happens. And joy never ends. There are many people today living in love."

"But I don't think most of us are that brave," I offered.

"Courage comes with prayer. God is like a giant magnet…as soon as you turn towards God, towards love, you get sucked in, and you can hardly turn away. And the closer you get, the greater the grip, the easier it is to live in love. God remains. Let God know you are turning, and your selfishness is instantly forgotten. God's power will give you the courage to turn one hundred-eighty degrees if you need to, and the healing begins. The more sincere the desire to live in love, the easier it is," Jesus explained.

"But others will ridicule me and call me a Holy Joe (sorry again, Dad) or a Bible Thumper or whatever …they'll think I'm a freak," I said.

"Blessed are you when they insult you and persecute you and utter every kind of evil against you because of me."

40 Days Ago

"Oh yeah, the Beatitudes. You really meant them, huh?" I asked, slightly sarcastically.

Jesus smiled and said, "Yep, I meant them. Believe it or not, I mean everything I say."

Then the reality hit that I was sitting in my own kitchen, having a conversation with "Jesus," and I became uneasy again.

"Are we finished here?" I asked, wanting to go back to sleep and pretend the whole thing hadn't happened. I tried to calm myself but kept at a distance from the kitchen table as my mind was trying to believe, understand, accept…all the while doubting everything I was seeing and hearing.

I looked over and Joe, my ghost dad, was now smiling broadly at me. My heart ached to hold him and have him comfort me. I began to move closer to give him a hug. The young man interrupted my motion, putting his hand out in front of me. "No, you can't touch him. Not yet. The time will come. That's what I'm here to talk to you about."

I sat back down on the edge of my seat, frowning and taking my gaze from my father back to the young man. "What?" I asked, but it was barely audible.

"I'm coming. I'm coming back. This is it. This is the moment that's been spoken of for so long. I am coming."

I went limp. I plopped back in my chair, and my jaw dropped. I looked to the floor then slowly back to the man as if to see if he were really there. He was. But my father was not.

"Daddy?" I called quietly.

"Soon," was all the man said.

Coming

I sat bewildered.

"Listen, I need your help," the young man began to explain. "The way situations in the world are escalating, there is going to be a global disaster. I just can't let that happen to creation. Things are a mess. Two thousand years ago I spoke of the Kingdom of God. People understood what I meant, because they lived in kingdoms. They knew that a kingdom was more than a geographic territory…it was also a sphere of influence. But somewhere along the line, many people came to think that the Kingdom of God was only a place you go after you die to be with the omniscient old man in the clouds. Many years ago my followers understood that the Kingdom was within them. God was within them, *always* within them. The sphere of God's influence was in and around them. But now, people act as if God is a reward in heaven for doing good…that they will only know God after they die. They don't treat others with dignity, as if God dwells within each person.

"So I could redefine the Kingdom of God as the State of Love. The Kingdom of God, the State of Love, is within you. You can live in the State of Love, and if you do, you will know great peace. You are an infinite soul, and you will continue in the State of Love after you die. If you don't live in the State of Love, if you pursue selfishness and oppression of others, fearfully clinging and hoarding, you too will suffer and live in terror or loneliness. The fear in your heart will block the love within, and the effects are disastrous. You will not know the peace of God.

"Too many people are living in selfishness and fear rather than love. They don't honor the dignity of life.

40 Days Ago

Things are a mess. Many people get it. Many people are loving. But so many...so many are not. Things are a colossal mess," he repeated, hanging his head, looking totally dejected. "It is time for me to come before all beauty is destroyed."

"I agree. Things are a mess, a big scary mess, but back *way* up for a second. What do you mean when you say you need my help?" I asked, suspicious that I could do anything to change the world.

"I need someone to forewarn the world. Like John the Baptist did a couple thousand years ago. You know, let people know I am coming. Try to get them to shape up. Try to get them to listen to their hearts. Not the human desires of their hearts, but the love in their hearts. Deep in their hearts. Below the desires, below the distractions. That is where God remains, and that is where love is. When it is time for me to come, I won't be able to bear to lose anyone to hatred and evil. Each and every one of you is so beloved and cherished, and I want every person to feel the freedom of my coming. Can you help me?"

"But wait," I said, backing up the conversation again. "What do you mean you're 'coming'? What are you actually going to do when you come?" I asked. "Are you going to suck the good people up to heaven and drop the bad ones through some sort of trapdoor down to hell?"

Jesus tried hard not to laugh. He tried to turn down the corners of his smile, but I was being serious.

And I said to him, "I'm being serious! I don't get what will happen!"

Coming

"I know you are, sorry for laughing. The image is just—I hate to use the word 'ridiculous'—" And I got his point. "Actually, when I come, I'll be coming to a new earth. It will really be more like the old earth."

"*What?*" I asked, totally confused.

"What I mean," said Jesus, "is that when I come to earth all will be like paradise. Right now there is plenty of everything for everyone. There is no need to hoard anything. But people panic and are greedy. When I come, people will feel the abundance and share freely. The more you share, the more there is to share. It is a natural law of love that humankind just cannot grasp. When I come, the earth itself will become like a garden again. No terrible storms, no bad air, no polluted streams. This will come to pass because all of the people will be living in peace with each other and naturally living in harmony with the earth. Everyone will be living in relationship with all of creation. It will once again be a Garden of Eden. This is love. This is The Way. Love heals everything."

"How's *that* going to happen?" I asked, with serious doubts that our planet could ever be restored or that people could happily share the resources.

"Like I said before, people will begin to love. People will begin thinking outside themselves. They will not be focused on what they want, but on what is good for everyone. People will have respect. People will work together to find solutions to every problem and do so with an expectation that harm to anyone or anything, is harm to all. People will live in awe again and be humbled. This is my passion. Can you help me?" Jesus requested, as if asking me to help him with a stuck zipper.

40 Days Ago

I was again back in shock. "You said that soon I could be with my dad." Weakly I asked, "Does that mean I'm going to die?"

"No, no, you're not going to die," Jesus assured me. "Not now. But with the new heaven and new earth, people will be connected in love with those who have passed on and share in their peace."

I had no idea what he meant by that so I focused on something more tangible. Again, I had serious doubts that our world would ever be restored to the paradise that Jesus spoke about. We couldn't be further from it. But how was I supposed to make a difference? I was so shocked and confused.

"C'mon…me? You've got to be kidding. What can I do? I don't have connections all over the world. I can't change anything. I can hardly change my vacuum bag. Why me? How about a president or pope or something?" I begged. The young man let me rant a bit with a kind smile that was both captivating and unnerving. Apparently, he'd heard it many times before from prophets.

I began talking, almost to myself now. I was lost in my thoughts and ignoring Jesus' presence. I looked down and rubbed my forehead as I spoke. "C'mon, not me. Clearly, I'd love to help you, but I'm a mother. I have to take care of my kids. I can't be running all over the world saving souls. I have to do the dumb stuff mothers do. That stuff that keeps us busy all day long but nobody can tell you exactly what it is." I began to panic and said, "C'mon. *Jesus Christ*, not me!" As I cursed emphatically, I looked up nervously to catch the man's reaction to using his name in vain.

Coming

His eyes twinkled. A smile slowly crept across his face, a smile which seemed to say, "She's in."

39 Days Ago

The day before had been a long day. After the stranger left my home, I had quietly made my way back upstairs to my bedroom. My whole family still slept soundly, which puzzled me since I had just been through what seemed like the force of a typhoon. I had gently climbed in bed beside my husband and held him. As he came into consciousness, he realized that I was trembling, but he assumed I was still upset over the loss of my father.

"It's okay," he said. "He's in a good place now."

"Oh, you have no idea," I said quietly. "He just might be in the kitchen."

My husband pulled his head back and looked at me quizzically. "What did you say?"

"Oh, man, I don't even know where to start," I said, sitting up in bed and beginning to fidget.

"What's the matter, hon?"

"Well, there was this knock on the door about an hour ago. Nobody else heard it but me, and I thought it might be someone coming over with condolences, so I got up. When I went to the door, this nice young man came in and told me he was Jesus. Then he made my dad appear next to me in the kitchen. Jesus said I needed

Coming

to warn the world that he would be coming back, and then he just left."

"Uh, sweetie, I think you were dreaming." My husband chuckled.

"No. I know I was not. I wasn't. I considered it myself, but everything was real. As real as you and I are here now. Don't tell me it wasn't real. I know reality. I'm not nuts," I said, getting more agitated at the whole situation.

"Okay, okay, let's hear the story again, and we'll see what we can make of it," my dear husband reassured me patiently. I loved him.

So I went through the whole scene again, as if reading a screenplay with lighting, props and movements in place. At the end of the story, complete silence.

"Well?" I asked.

"I don't know. It's really weird. It's kind of freaking me out. I don't know what to think. I guess it's possible. Anything is possible. But what are you supposed to do? I mean, why you....not that you're not a wonderful person. But why you? Why us? Why now?"

"I know nothing. I know what you know. I don't know what to do. I'm scared, no, more like absolutely terrified. What should I do? Who can I tell? Anyone will think I'm having some kind of mourning-meltdown. No one will take me seriously. No one. I don't want this job. I did not apply for this job. Other people would love it. Not me. Damn it....not me!"

I had spent most of the day in my room, panicking.

~

39 Days Ago

So on this day my husband called into his office and told his boss he needed one more day off work. He said his wife was still in pretty bad shape, and he thought he ought to stay with her. I'm sure the women of the office appreciated his sensitivity. Little did they know how bad "in bad shape" was.

My young children woke and got ready for school, going about their morning robotically. My mind swirled until I had a pounding headache. As they went out the door, I closed it and leaned against it, afraid that I might faint. I don't think I have the energy for my family *and* the whole world, I thought. I began to cry, and my husband walked me over to the couch and just held me and said absolutely nothing.

For the rest of the day, every time my husband and I got near each other, we would just look into each other's eyes with a stare that seemed to say, "I don't know either." I did not attempt to tell the kids anything. They were so sweet and innocent. I could just see them jumping up and down and cheering that Jesus is coming. "Yeah, Mom saw Jesus," they would chant, and then they might tell all their friends, and I was just not ready for that. I just didn't know what I was supposed to do.

I decided to keep a lid on it, and maybe Jesus would come around again with a little more direction. I waited up in my bedroom most of the day. Then my husband and I went to the park. I looked closely at each person and strained to look down the street trying to see if Jesus were watching me. I looked for that orange VW. It was nowhere. Would he be disappointed? Did he expect me to get right on the phone to the president? Would he fire me? That would be okay. No, probably not. Who wants

Coming

to be fired by Jesus? I had absolutely no idea what I was supposed to do. Finally, at eight o'clock when the kids went to bed, I cried. I sobbed harder than I had when my dad died. I couldn't stop. My husband held me. I think he was crying too, but it was hard to tell, because at that moment it was all about me.

38 Days Ago

I woke up at six-thirty to the sound of my husband showering before heading back to work. I jumped out of bed and woke the kids for school. They all went to the same elementary school in grades one, two, and four. Yes, they were close. Yes, we did have electricity right after we were married. Yes, I'd do it all again the same way...well, ask me again when they are all in college.

As the kids headed out the door for the bus stop, and my husband went off to work, I began to clean up the kitchen from breakfast. I'm alone, I thought. Now what? Just me and my relentless thoughts. But I thought of my dad, and remembered Jesus saying that I would see him again soon. That was something hopeful. I decided to just wait for further instruction. Surely, Jesus was not finished with me. God is omniscient. God knows if I need help. Jesus will be back. No need to panic, I tried to convince myself.

I began gathering up dirty laundry, shuffling from room to room, emptying hampers into a pile. I sat on a little footstool and began sorting. Whites...why me? I do laundry, I drive carpools. Permanent press...I know about fifty people, tops. Darks...I don't want to be famous, I like my life. Permanent press....maybe I can talk

Coming

my brother into doing this job. He's got thousands of connections in his business. Whites...Can I say no to Jesus? I don't think so. Colors...I've been taught to trust him my whole life. This is the acid test. Yes, I'll trust him.

At that moment, Jesus was standing beyond the soiled pile of permanent press clothes, as I flung a dirty button-down shirt, hitting him in the kneecaps. I flew to my feet and leapt to him. I threw my arms around him and held tightly. I had never been so happy to see anyone in my life.

Jesus laughed and embraced me. "Did you think I would abandon you?"

"No, of course not," I lied.

"C'mon," he said, pulling the truth right out of the depths of my being.

"Okay, yes. I thought I would flunk the test, and you would be sorry you picked me, and the whole world would suffer for it. I'm not sure I'm the right one for the job. I tend to worry. I tend to second-guess myself. I think you need someone who is more confident. I never know for sure what to do about anything. I never am quite sure of the solution."

Then Jesus said calmly, "The solution is *love*."

"But then why do I pray if the solution is always the same?" I asked.

"Because you forget the solution. A thousand times a day, you forget. Love is like a bar of soap in your shower. The more you set it down, the more likely you are to drop it when you pick it up again. You just have to hold onto it. Or better yet, cover yourself in it."

38 Days Ago

"That sounds easy. But how do you cover yourself in love? Do you mean we're supposed to love all the time?"

"Absolutely. Love has dimensions. Love might be the knowledge that you are perfect and cherished, so that you feel a deep sense of calm within. Love might be acceptance of differences, so that no one is excluded. Love might be forgiveness of hurts hurled upon you, so that you can move on and live. Love might be compassion and mercy, so that others are comforted and strengthened. Love might be justice, so that everyone has opportunities for a decent life. Love might be humility, that the ego takes a back seat. Love might be respect for creation, so that you have gratitude for her gifts. Love might be unity…bigger accomplishments are made with cooperation.

"See, with love, you feel a deep connection to each and every person and even to every living thing. Others' trials are your trials. Others' joys are your joys. You realize that you are each an instrument in the orchestra, beautiful when played alone, but incredibly awesome when you all come together to create layers of sweet, glorious music," Jesus explained.

"But the world is a mess. You said it yourself. How can I fix it by myself? We have world leaders working on all the problems, and still the same troubles exist for generation after generation," I said with frustration.

"God is big. Tell everyone the solution is love. The solution is not power. It is not land. It is not the natural resources. It is not control. It is not winning. Tell everyone to honor life. No more famine. No more terrorism. No more crime. No more killing. No more war. No one wins a war. Tell everyone to seek unity. Share the resources. Share the wealth. Trade with services and resources. Stop letting the accumulation of money be your goal. Isolationism divides, trade unites. Tell everyone to let go, to stop hoarding, to stop thinking only of themselves. The solution is love."

"But what about countries who have nothing to share?" I asked, thinking of countries in terrible civil war and tribal strife or desert countries with cracked earth and dying livestock.

"Love is the solution."

Here we go again, I thought.

Jesus continued, "There will be no peace on the outside if there is not peace within. Make sure each person has what they need, physically and spiritually, and they will have peace within. Once individuals feel at peace, their whole community will be at peace, and the world follows. You are designed to work together. The collection of humanity is like a puzzle. Each person is a piece. The bumps on a puzzle piece represent the things you have plenty of, things you can offer to another. The dents in the puzzle piece represent what you are lacking, those things which someone else can offer to you. You must figure out how you fit together, freely giving and accepting. You know the joy of fitting puzzle pieces together, don't you?"

I did. I loved puzzles. I was one of those obnoxious kids who hid the last piece in my pocket so that I could have the complete satisfaction of finishing the puzzle. Did he know that about me? I felt a bit embarrassed by my juvenile behavior.

38 Days Ago

Then I pulled back into the present moment and thought about getting every person what they need. A big order, but I thought Jesus had a point there. I mean, it seemed to me that living in peace should be easy, but then I'd never really suffered. Once, when I was twelve, I wanted a jean jacket from a swanky store, but my mom gave me one from the discount store that looked exactly like the one I wanted. It just didn't have the tiny pink tag on the pocket for all to know we overpaid, and I never wore the jacket. I thought I suffered. Another time when I was seventeen, we had an ice storm and lost power for several hours. My parents wouldn't let me drive to my friend's house because the roads were slick. There was no television, no radio, no lights, no heat. I really suffered then. In fact, I was insufferable. After six long hours, power was restored, and life was happy again. My poor parents.

I realized that I had never suffered in my whole life. Not deeply. Not to the point of despair. Not to the "it doesn't matter what I do, life sucks" point. And I agreed that if people reach that point, and apparently millions around the world reach it daily, there cannot be peace. So simple, but how to give every person what they need? There are so many needs: food, medical care, clean water, housing and education, not to mention hope and a sense of purpose. I snapped back into the conversation. "Every person in the world?" I almost yelled. "That's impossible!"

"Not if you look at what they are lacking and help them find it. Forgive their debts. Help them get on their feet until they have a commodity to share. Every person has dignity. Therefore, every society has dignity. If a country has little water, solar power may be its biggest resource. If a country seems too mountainous, too flat, too forested, look at the bounty of the earth, and with respect, gratitude, and conservation, take from her. Each individual, each country, has an offering to world prosperity. And remember, there are plenty of resources for everyone. When people work together, amazing things happen.

"Have no tolerance for self-serving leaders," he continued. "They undermine their country's dignity. They steal from their own people. They destroy civilization by eating the poison fruit of power. Every community needs a group of wise leaders who are willing to trust in love and the fruit that love brings. Every community needs to work with every other community for strength. If one community tries to rise to the top militarily, that community must dismantle their leaders who have lost their wisdom. Never meet force with force. Balance force with yielding, and know when to push your agenda. The only true agenda is love. The only true power is love. Any other agenda will sicken the world."

"But how do I tell this to world leaders? I'm not even six degrees of separation from anyone important. I've been trying to find someone....I'm just not," I whined.

"Well, I'm somewhat important. And you know me," Jesus said with a smile.

"True. And no offense, but I'm not sure even you can set this up. I mean, well, I don't want to sound sarcastic or disrespectful or anything, but last time you were here they *killed* you, remember?"

38 Days Ago

Immediately, I regretted that comment. "I'm so sorry, I shouldn't have said that," I admitted, recoiling.

"No problem. I am still here, aren't I? You can't kill love. You can knock it down, even bury it for a while, but love always rises," he said with a grin.

Wow, he could not be shaken. But I was a different story. "I'm just so petrified. How am I supposed to just move from being a mom and wife and friend to a world leader?"

"Love."

"Oh yeah. I get it. 'The solution is always love.' But *how*?"

"You need confidence. You need to know that you are filled with love. All the time. Every soul on earth is filled with love...you just need to spend some time tapping it, like syrup from a maple tree, until it flows freely from you. Here," Jesus said, "sit down in this chair for a minute."

As I sat, he had me close my eyes. He repeatedly told me gently to relax. To breathe. He was quiet for several seconds while I took long, deep breaths. He spoke softly, saying, "Listen and feel. Breathe. God is love. The spirit of God is within you. Love flows through you. Tap it. Feel God's spirit flowing through you. Feel the energy of love touching your whole being. Feel the power of love. Let the love flow through your mind until all you know is love. With every breath you take, you renew the spirit of love within."

An electricity, like goose-bump electricity, coursed through me at the speed of light.

"Whoa. Is that it? I'm ready now? Did I get charged up?"

Coming

Jesus laughed out loud. "You always have the charge. That's my point. The power of love is in you and everyone else. You need to still yourself occasionally and feel it and remember it. When you are still, then you can hear God moving. There is nothing more powerful than love."

"Okay," I said, "I'll be still, but I don't think that will change the world. I think I'm going to have to *do* something. But I'm terrified, and I have no idea where I'm supposed to start."

Jesus reassured me. "When you feel that nagging idea that just won't leave, that's me. Follow me. Get some rest for the journey. We're going to have some fun."

Jesus reached out and embraced me, and I had never felt so completely content and joyful in my entire life. He made everything sound so simple, so peaceful. He brushed my hair from my face and slowly faded from sight. I didn't reach for him. I just stood there, knowing that he would be with me, nagging me. Others might call it *inspiring* me, but he said it would feel like nagging. Jesus said I had better rest, so I forgot the laundry and went to the couch and sat peacefully. My mind was blank, my body calm. I just sat. Probably for an hour. I did not weigh my options. I did not plan ahead. I did not think back. I just sat and somehow felt so relaxed.

37 Days Ago

After finishing the chores started yesterday, my head in another world, darks in with whites, white underwear now pink, I occasionally would still feel sick to my stomach. With each wave of nausea, I would sit in the chair in which Jesus had put me and breathe and relax until I could feel the love and peace flowing again. I stumbled around my house, almost doing the breakfast dishes, almost making the beds. As I turned on the shower to let the hot water warm up, I looked into the mirror. Staring at my face, I tried to see what Jesus saw in me. I just stared. I didn't judge the wideness of my nose as I usually do. I didn't curse the hopelessly shapeless eyebrows. I didn't suck in my cheeks to make myself look thinner. I just stared until the steam blotted out my vision, and I turned to the shower, unsure of what it was that Jesus saw when he looked at me.

As I stepped into the shower, it instantly felt fabulous. As I lathered up with soap, I recalled Jesus' metaphor about love and smiled. I stood under the hot water, letting it rinse me clean for probably a full ten minutes. It felt so good, so warm. With each breath of steam so healing, I didn't want to get out. I rolled my neck around

Coming

in the heat, and then I heard it. Right in my head, not in my ears. I knew his voice.

"Everyone will have a dream. Everyone. Same dream. Pay attention."

I threw my arms around myself to hide my nakedness. I looked in all directions.

With my heart pounding, my breathing shallow and quick, I reached for the faucet and turned it off quickly as if the voice were coming out of the shower. I reached for a towel and wrapped myself. I grabbed another for my hair and twisted it up in a turban on top of my head. I stepped out of the shower, closed the toilet and just sat down on the toilet lid, trying to catch my breath. Jesus did say we hear God when we relax. I was very relaxed in the shower. But, Jesus, I was naked. How embarrassing. Jesus likes to have fun, I decided. I thought that if he ever visited me again, in person, I was going to have to give him some trouble for this one.

I began to loosen up and smile at our friendship. Our relationship. I realized I had never really had a relationship with Jesus. He was someone who had lived a couple thousand years ago that I admired. I loved him. I prayed to him. But this was a real relationship, and I was beginning to enjoy it.

Okay, what did he say, I asked myself. What did I hear? I was so freaked out that I almost didn't take notice of the words. But then my memory was as clear as could be. *Everyone will have a dream. Everyone. Same dream. Pay attention.* I knew those were the words verbatim. Even through my panic, my head was clear enough to know without a doubt what I heard. I thought about the words over and over. What do they mean, I

37 Days Ago

wondered. I began talking to myself again. I guess it means just what it says...that everyone - everyone in the whole world? I guess so. Everyone will have the same dream. That's crazy. How weird. I knew God talked to people in their dreams in the Bible, but I didn't think that still went on today. I thought dreams were just subconscious thoughts that never found their way into the wakeful brain. So God's talking to everyone in their dreams. Interesting. This will be weird, but interesting.

So now what? I moved from the toilet to my bedroom, undoing the turban and towel-drying my hair. I looked in my drawers and closet for something to wear, routinely, as if it were just a normal day. I was no longer panicking. I was not anxious about anything. I was just moving through my room with the knowledge that I had something to do, and I had the confidence to do it. I didn't need to give myself a pep talk. I was going through some options in my head of how to tell the world that everyone would have the same dream. It was as if I were going through options of what to fix for lunch. I dressed in jeans and a knit shirt and put on a little mascara. The magnitude of the job was no longer overwhelming. I was even looking forward to it. I slipped on some clogs and headed downstairs.

As I clopped down the steps with the cadence of a quarter horse, I stopped dead in my tracks with three steps left to go. That's it! I said to myself. I'll hang a sign. I'll climb a tall building, and I'll hang a sign. It's brilliant! That will get many people's attention. Maybe even media attention. If I wanted to get the message out, I would have to do something crazy enough to catch media attention, I realized. I can do crazy. I can do this. It might even be fun.

I decided to call my teenage nephew, who was totally into climbing. He had upper-body strength like you wouldn't believe and no fear of heights. None. That was a bit of a problem for me, I suddenly remembered. I got dizzy as I ascended. But I dismissed my fear as if it were just a fleeting thought. I could do this if I had to. Once.

The worst part of the day was waiting until Tommy got home from school. Okay, Tom. He was seventeen now and "Tom." I puttered like nobody's business all day, about to explode with excitement for my master plan.

At three o'clock sharp, I called my sister-in-law and asked to speak to Tommy. *Tom*. She told me he had basketball after school until about five-thirty or six. Dang. She asked how I was doing, and my mind went haywire trying to decide whether to tell her or not. She was my sister-in-law. We were close. But what a ridiculously weird story to try to tell someone. I decided to wait and tell her later.

"Oh, I'm hanging in there," I lied. I told her I'd call back after dinner, but she told me Tom had to work until ten-thirty. Dang again. Why are kids so busy? Can't they just hang out and watch *Leave It To Beaver* and play *War* in the neighborhood? I asked her if she would please have him call me right after basketball because I had a quick question for him that I would explain to them both later. I thought maybe the intrigue of it all might be my insurance that she would have him call me. She tended to be nosy.

37 Days Ago

It worked. At five-thirty-five the phone rang as I was browning ground beef for tacos.

"Hey, this is Tom," I heard in an unnaturally deep voice from the other end.

"Tom! Thanks for calling me! Hey, I was wondering if you could take me to the climbing gym and show me how to climb."

"Sure, why?" he asked with a cynical chuckle that I didn't like at all.

"Oh, I just need to get some exercise, and it looks like so much fun. I can't run unless someone's chasing me, and I can't bike unless it's all downhill. But I thought that that climbing stuff looked fun. And I can stop as often as I want and just hang out until I'm ready to climb some more. I can act like I'm enjoying the scenery and not wimping out with total exhaustion."

"You got a point there," Tom admitted. "But not that *I've* ever done that," he said jokingly.

"How about tomorrow?" he asked. "Basketball is cancelled, and I don't have to work until Monday."

"Oh perfect! Tom, you're the greatest. What do I need?"

"Just dress comfortably, maybe sweatpants and a long-sleeve shirt so you don't scrape your elbows and knees, and I'll bring the rest."

"Great! How about I pick you up at three-thirty tomorrow? Does that give you enough time after school?"

"Actually, I have an early dismissal tomorrow, and I get out at one-twenty-five. Can you pick me up at one-forty-five from school? North entrance?"

"Even better," I said. "I'll see you then. Thanks, Tom."

Coming

How in the world do parents of teenagers keep track of their schedules? What am I in for? Wow, insane, I thought, as I imagined my three little darlings as overstimulated, overscheduled teens.

The rest of the day I buzzed through family obligations with confidence and joy. I told my husband the latest update after I got the kids to bed, and he laughed hysterically at the thought of me at a climbing gym. He thought, however, that my plan was "innovative" and his love encouraged me even more, and we slept.

36 Days Ago

I still had not spoken to my children about any of the mystical happenings that had been consuming my conscious and unconscious mind for the past few days. They were young and talked a lot, and I didn't want them trying to explain to others what was going on in our home. Although, now that I think about it, kids just say things so directly and honestly that I probably should have sent them out as little messengers. But I didn't. I acted as if all were normal. Any time they caught me acting weird, spacing out or tearing up, I would just say, "Oh, I'm okay, I just miss Grandpa."

Truth be told, with my unexpected visit, I really hadn't thought too much about my dad. But the few times I did remember he was gone, his living image that I'd seen in the kitchen would pop right into my head, and I would not feel grief, but an extra closeness. I also had the feeling that we would be together soon.

After a quick breakfast, I kissed each of my little darlings and got them off to the bus stop, each with plans to go home with a friend after school. My husband went to work. He winked at me as he left, shaking his head and chuckling at the thought of my new adventure.

Coming

I swirled through the kitchen and the rest of the house, cleaning, picking up shoes and left-behind notebooks and general stuff that just seems to appear day after day out of nowhere. I couldn't wait to pick up Tom. I bought some groceries and unpacked them when I got home, but I was too excited or maybe bilious to eat. I knew I would need some energy, so I forced down a peanut butter and jelly sandwich with some milk and waited until I could leave.

Tom was waiting at the north entrance of school for me, just as we had arranged. He hopped in my car and looked me over to see if I had appropriate climbing garb on. He smiled. I knew my sweatpants and flannel shirt were uncool, but I wanted to be able to move easily. Tom was wearing his climbing clothes: gym pants hanging halfway down his derriere and a long-sleeved T-shirt. He told me he kept his equipment in a locker at the gym and that he was ready if I was.

"You bet," I said with nervous enthusiasm. We arrived at the gym in no time, and when we pulled up I felt my stomach churn. It's the peanut butter. It will go down, keep breathing, I told myself.

As we walked into the climbing gym, Tommy was greeted by people from all altitudes. Some were regular customers, some worked there, but everyone knew Tom. One of the young men hanging on a climbing wall yelled, "Tom, ya got your girlfriend with ya today?" And his climbing partner laughed loudly. I didn't appreciate such robust laughter.

"So," Tom asked me, "do you want to go bouldering or climb?"

"I don't know."

36 Days Ago

"You choose," he said politely.

"I don't know what 'bouldering' is," I clarified.

"Oh, yeah," Tom said, and then he continued to explain that bouldering was climbing without ropes over lower, more rounded rocks. He told me how it was great practice for agility and strength, but without the rush of climbing vertically.

"Well," I said in response to his explanation, "I should do bouldering to get in shape, but I have to climb. I want the rush. I want to learn how to use the ropes...how to go up and down."

"Up and down it is," Tom said with a sweet smile. Since he was such an experienced climber and so familiar at the gym, the manager agreed to let him work with me rather than have me go through the mandatory training for new visitors, after I agreed on paper that I would not sue the gym, should I fall to my death.

My stomach again began to flip about as we pulled the ropes and carabineers out of the locker. Tom reassured me that it was a safe sport, as long as everyone is paying attention and double-checking their ropes. I really did want to believe him.

Tom's friend Jack agreed to help us with the climb, so that Tom could go beside me and give me pointers. Both boys were fabulous. My first time up was very slow, and I felt a little dizziness. But with practice, things went more smoothly. We climbed all afternoon, until my arms would not stop shaking. They had taken all the abuse two arms could take for a day, and I knew I was not improving. I was just wasting Tom's time. He read my mind.

"Should we call it a day?" he asked, suspended halfway up the artificial rock.

"I think so. I'm going to hurt someone with my arms shaking so uncontrollably. I might knock myself out. Or worse, knock you out. Then I'd be stuck up here by myself," I said, only half joking.

Tom chuckled. "Don't feel weak, everyone's arms do that. Climbing is a great workout."

"Thanks, Tom, you're sweet, but I think I need a little more practice. Could you help me again tomorrow?"

"Sure, I guess so, but what's the rush? You might want to rest your muscles for a day or two before we get back out here."

"No, I'll be okay, I need to come tomorrow," I said, and I knew that I would have to explain my plan. It had become painfully obvious that I would need Tom to be in on the great building ascent. This climbing stuff was complicated. And dangerous. And I had no business trying it on my own.

"Tom, let's head down, and let me buy you a Coke. We need to talk," I said.

We descended Kilimanjaro, which was scarier to me than going up. It was quicker, but it also took strength. The peanut butter was still stuck in my stomach. Why won't that stuff digest, I wondered. I found my mind drifting through more acceptable, easily digestible foods that I could eat before we climbed again and next thing I knew, I was standing on solid ground. I followed Tom's instructions for winding up the ropes in their ready-to-store configurations, packed everything up neatly and put it back into his locker. Tom suggested that we head to McDonald's to get a snack. After all, we had just

36 Days Ago

burned a lot of calories. The peanut butter disagreed with the idea, but I was able to keep it quiet. Maybe a Sprite would help it disappear. I was starting to hate peanut butter.

We got in the car and, as I pulled onto the street, Tom pointed out the McDonald's just a half block away.

I laughed out loud. "We should have walked over here," I said, glancing over at Tom.

"Why?" he asked sincerely.

I realized that "because we can" was not a good answer in teenager world, so I just shrugged it off and said, "No, this is fine. I'm tired anyway."

Tommy ordered two double cheeseburgers and a large fry with a medium strawberry shake. I got a Sprite. He was totally unfazed by the disproportionate servings. He dived into his burger as if just released from prison camp.

"Tom, I've got a weird story to tell you. You have to hear the whole thing before you freak out. I mean, I freaked out when it happened to me, but just let me explain because you're the first person I've told. I want to see how it goes."

"Cool," he said, nodding and chewing.

And I proceeded to tell him the story of Jesus' unexpected visit, leaving out the naked shower scene, and ending with my plan to hang a sign on a building.

"Cool," he said, still nodding and chewing. "That is wild. I wouldn't believe it from anyone else. But why would you make that up, and then tell me? I mean, if you were flipping out and hallucinating or something, you'd probably go get coffee with your friends, and tell them, rather than going through this elaborate climbing plan with your nephew. That is *so* weird," he said thoughtfully. Then he added, "It's going to take a while to sink in."

"That's the problem, Tom. I don't think we have a while. I don't really know how much time we have, but I got the impression it wouldn't be long. I sensed urgency in Jesus' voice. I need you to help. Originally, I thought maybe I could hang the sign by myself. I don't know what I was thinking. I was being ridiculous. After today, I realize I need help."

"How about a couple of my climbing buddies, too? We could do several signs, several buildings, all synchronized," Tom suggested, totally getting into it.

"That's a great idea, but would they do it? Would they laugh or think I'm a Jesus freak or something?" I asked, my vulnerabilities showing.

"No. Climbers will climb for any reason. And a mission from God would be a great incentive," Tom winked as he spoke. "They'd have fun with it whether they believe you or not. I guess we'll all know if you're crazy soon enough, right?"

"Right," I admitted. "I'm not sure I would believe me either if I were you."

Tom suggested that he call some of his buddies and that we should meet the next day and make a plan. He told me to make three signs and leave the climbing to him. I threw my arms around him with that suggestion.

"I know…I'll pay you each with whatever you want to eat after the climb. Then if you get caught, you can explain that this lady paid you to do it. That would take you out of the limelight, and let me start doing my job. Which makes me think…maybe you had better be sure

36 Days Ago

all of your friends are minors. That way if they get caught, they'll be in less trouble and can claim to be under the influence of an adult."

"Good idea. Sounds like a deal to me," said Tom innocently.

"Then it's a plan. Should we say we'll meet here tomorrow at five?"

"Again, a good plan," Tom acknowledged. "You wanna pick me up again? I'll make the phone calls and see how many guys I can get. We ought to plan to do the climb the next day. The more time that passes, someone's likely to blurt something out at school, and we'll all get busted."

"OK, you're the boss," I agreed.

"Oh no, *you're* the boss. The prophet," corrected Tom.

We both laughed and the peanut butter went down.

35 Days Ago

The night before, after climbing, after dinner, after helping the kids with homework, I had made three signs out of bed sheets. I had to run to the department store to get some nice white sheets since all of ours were patterned. I had a few old sheets that were a pale blue, but I didn't want any stains or rips, just in case people looked closely at the signs. My husband had told me I was being ridiculous, but these are things women think about.

I hadn't slept so well since the night after Jesus visited me in the kitchen. My body was so exhausted. I had tried to stay awake in bed for a little while to think through my plan some more. But as soon as my head had hit the pillow, my eyes clamped shut, and I could hear my tongue closing off the back of my throat as my breathing took on a strange whining sound. My husband had poked me and had told me I was snoring. I had rolled over, muttering "Sorry" until my passageway opened up, and I sank deeply into nothingness.

~

When I woke, my husband was already getting ready for work. He stood in front of the steamy bathroom mirror, shaving.

35 Days Ago

"I dreamed that there was this cat, and it wouldn't quit meowing, and then a train went right through the front yard, and for some reason Mary served us this really good Mexican dinner," I yelled from my bed, checking to see if that was *the dream*.

In mid-shave my husband walked to the bedroom threshold, looked at me and chuckled. "Fortunately, I did not have that dream. Fortunately, that is not THE dream. What the heck would that mean to anyone?"

"Well, do you remember what you dreamed?" I asked cynically.

"No. Well, wait a minute...I dreamed that James from work kept asking me why I didn't wear heels anymore."

"I didn't know you ever wore heels to work," I said, still a little sleepy.

"Honey, it's a dream," he reminded me.

"Oh yeah," I said and smiled at the thought of my husband in his tie and business socks with my silver-buckled black heels on his huge feet.

Having established that this was not the dream day, I got dressed and got the kids out the door for school and proceeded with Plan A. Actually, Plan B. In Plan A, I was going to climb a building by myself and attach a huge sign somehow with all four corners secured and climb to safety. In Plan B, I would be on the ground at one location. I would be supervising minor climbers, and once things seemed to be progressing well, I would drive to the next location and check on the progress there. I would continue safely driving through town until all three buildings were scaled and the mission was accomplished. I loved Plan B.

Coming

I opened up all of the signs I had made to make sure they were spelled correctly and didn't look like they had been written by a moron. I decided to add a little flourish to the bottom of one. I don't know why. I guess I thought the sign looked cold, and I wanted people to feel warm and reassured, not afraid, when they read them. Oh, those were some big assumptions...that anyone would read a sign on a building and think anything other than an apocalyptic nutcase was at it again. But hope is a good thing. Hope is what puts one foot in front of the other and keeps us from freezing in fear.

My flourish was a small doodad, looking something like this: ಈ. It really meant nothing to me. I just felt it added a little softness to the big, hard, block-lettered sign. I neatly folded two of the signs, but left the other sheet partially open so that the paint of the newly added flourish could dry. The letters were painted in black. I thought that would be easiest to read. But the flourish was in pink. I'd always loved pink, and I thought it added a touch of feminine to the masculine block letters. Am I over-thinking this, I wondered.

Just as I put the paint away and washed my brush, the doorbell rang. It was my mom coming by to borrow a jacket. She was attending a luncheon with some girlfriends who were attempting to cheer her up. Poor thing. The whole idea of going out as a widow had her completely undone. She had fretted so much about what to wear, I reassured her with an outfit idea that required my nice black jacket with green trim. Not too mournful, yet not too colorful. I ran up to my room to get the jacket, but she unexpectedly followed me, talking all the way up the stairs. I quickly wadded up the sign, hoping

35 Days Ago

that the paint had dried. I knew not much damage could be done by a premature folding of the sheet. More damage would be done if I had to explain the whole story to my mother. Her time would come, but not today. It could put me in a position of defending my climb and maybe ruining the whole thing. No, she couldn't see the sign yet, and she didn't.

As lunchtime neared, I decided that it might be a good time to pray. I asked for God to be with me. I asked God to stop me if this was a bad idea. I told God that I was so glad that I believed and so happy that God truly did exist. Of course I'd heard the "crutch" theory of religion all my life, and in the back of my mind I always thought, what if? What if there is no God? What if this really is all there is...that everything is simply one big cosmic happenstance? Those thoughts freaked me out a bit so I always clung to the idea that there was a God. A God who cared. A God who was alive in each and every person, offering hope to humanity. I believed that if we only let God lead, all of this nasty suffering in the world would end. I asked God to stay with me so I could feel God's presence to give me strength. Then I ate some cottage cheese with peaches and some Hershey's kisses.

I worked all afternoon, preparing dinner so that my husband could feed the kids if I didn't get back from my climbing pow-wow in time. I ran my son to tutoring and my older daughter to her ballet class and returned at five minutes to five. When I saw the clock, my heart just about pounded out of my chest. I dropped the kids in the driveway and yelled for them to start working on their homework; that their dad would fix them dinner when

Coming

he got home very shortly. I explained that I had to go see their cousin Tommy.

"Can we come?" they asked, showing their affection for their older cousin.

"Not this time," I said. "We just need to talk something over. You'd be bored. I'll try to be home before dinner, but if not, Dad has things under control."

I reversed out the driveway, and I could tell by the look on my oldest daughter's face that her mother was being rather uncharacteristic and a bit vague. I really didn't even wish I could explain. That would be too difficult. I was just happy to leave and get on with the planning. As I was slightly speeding away from the house, I realized that I would have to explain things to the whole family soon. There would be a pretty good chance that I would be caught, maybe arrested, possibly (hopefully) on the news, and the kids would have to be ready to defend me at school. I started to get that churning feeling again and found myself muttering, "God help me." I immediately popped a CD in the car stereo and began singing one of my favorite tunes. The churning subsided, and I smiled. I wondered, the way it can settle the heart, if music were a dimension of God.

I picked up Tommy, Tom, apologizing right and left for being ten minutes late.

"No problem," he insisted.

Still, I felt like I was giving the impression that this was not important. I didn't want him to think this was just fun. This was possibly the most important thing he could ever do. Being late was unacceptable. We talked on the way to McDonald's and Tom told me he had six "for sure," maybe eight, for our expedition.

35 Days Ago

As we pulled into McDonald's, I expected to see a group of teens looking impatiently at their watches as we walked in. Apparently, I didn't know teens. Tom yelled to a skinny young man sitting alone at a booth, and we walked over to join him. Tom looked not a bit flustered that the rest of his crew was a no-show. We were starting fifteen minutes late. Well, I guess this is my sign that this is a bad idea, I thought to myself. I realized I could not climb a building with such limited experience, and the skinny kid in front of me looked to be more of a moral support than a climber. I told the boys to order whatever they wanted, but they said they would wait for the others.

"The others? You think anyone else will show?" I asked.

"Sure," said Tom. "Give 'em a couple more minutes."

True enough, two, then four others came through the door, shuffling over to our booth. To my surprise, there was one girl. She was a beauty. Strong and lean, wearing tight jeans, her protruding hip bones showing. The guys all wore large T-shirts and baggy pants that sagged low on the hips. Everyone's tennis shoes were untied. I was amused at the discrepancy in the amount of fabric it took to make clothing for teenage boys versus teenage girls.

I was pulled back to the task at hand as Tom introduced me to his friends. I recognized Jack from the climbing gym. The others ranged from polite to barely outside the cave with their acknowledgment of me. I told them all to get something to eat, that it was on me, and that I would explain everything while we ate.

Coming

    Wow. Those boys could eat. Whoever thought two double cheeseburgers or a chicken sandwich *and* a huge burger could be consumed at one sitting? I had barely enough money to cover their dinners, so I just ordered a small Coke.

    As we piled into a booth and two nearby tables, we cleared trays and paper wrappings out of the way. I began my story. Since the tables and chairs were bolted to the floor, I asked them to lean in so that I wouldn't have to talk loudly. I had decided to tell them the whole story in order to garnish a strong commitment, but also in fairness to them, in case they didn't want to be a part of a 'religious' event. I started at the beginning, with my dad dying, the funeral, the strange visitor, the apparition of my dad, the role I was asked to carry out and finally, how they fit into the plan. All eight kids sat in silence as they listened to my story. Upon its conclusion, there was at first silence, then a burst of "no way" and "cool" and "freaky."

    When all of the exclamatory phrases concluded, I said, "Well, what do you think? Can you do it? Do you want to do it?"

    "I'm in," said Tommy. (God love him!)

    "Yeah! Me, too," said the girl.

    "I'm in," said the skinny kid, and the others voiced one form or another of solidarity with the plan. One boy, the preppiest of the bunch, said nothing.

    "What about you?" I asked. "It's okay if you don't want to do this. I know how weird it is. I don't want you to get in trouble with your parents or do something you're not comfortable doing."

35 Days Ago

"I feel bad," he said with a surfer's tone. "I mean, I want to help you and all, but the Bible says Jesus will come again in a cloud of glory, not in an orange Vee-Dub. I'm not saying I don't believe you, but it's just a little too weird for me. I think my parents would ground me for life for getting hooked up with something like this."

I was impressed with the boy's familiarity with the Bible and also with his devotion to his parents and their beliefs. I found myself quickly hoping that my own kids would have that kind of respect for me. But I realized that the future was too uncertain to even consider for the shortest of moments.

"That's fine. I'm fine with that, sweetie," I said to him. "Anyone else? Really, I need your full commitment. We're doing this tomorrow night, and I need everyone to show. If you know you have a paper due or a test the next day and you have to study... ."

All eight teens burst into laughter.

"Climbing first, studying later," said one particularly large boy.

"Or not at all," another chimed in. They all laughed again.

The preppie boy thanked me for dinner. He apologized for not being able to cooperate and excused himself from the rest of the meeting.

As he left, I squeezed my way around the booth to give him a big hug. "Thanks for your honesty," I said. "And thank you for your strong faith. I appreciate both!" I watched as he sat outside until the meeting ended, since his ride was still in on the plan.

Coming

The rest of the meeting was basically led by Tom, since I didn't have a clue what they were really about to do. They all knew of three buildings that were climbable, common knowledge among climbers. The buildings ranged in height from seven to eighteen stories, so plans were hatched as to which face of which building and which story would be the top edge of the sign. I was given the assignment of procuring some contact glue from the office supply store. Two climbers each would climb to the seventh and ninth story of two buildings. Three climbers would be used to scale up to the twelfth story of the tallest building. We would meet at the McDonald's lot at ten the next night and divide up signs, glue, ropes and anything else that would be necessary. I felt my heart racing as I listened to the excitement in the teens' voices. Occasionally, the volume would start to rise, and then someone would call them all back to the center of the table. Leaning in, they would continue in muffled voices until the enthusiasm overtook them again.

When everyone was satisfied that the plan was a good one and that everyone knew their assignments, each was sworn to secrecy until the mission was complete. We went our separate ways. As we walked towards the car, the girl ran over to me and gave me a big hug and said, "Don't worry, we got your back!" And we both laughed. I really needed that hug just then as my knees were beginning to get a little wobbly, either from fear or lack of nutrition. Probably both.

As my car cruised towards Tom's house, we talked excitedly about the plan. When I dropped him off, I think I thanked him about forty-seven times for his help.

35 Days Ago

He assured me about forty-eight times that it was his pleasure, and we parted with the desire to get the show on the road while the energy was high. But we knew that careful planning was always a good thing - a necessary thing - when climbing. I wouldn't be able to bear anyone's getting hurt.

On the way back to my house, I swung by the park and just stopped by the small lake and watched the ducks through the darkness. I wondered about their future and mine and the world's, and tears trickled unexpectedly from my eyes. Uncertainty is awful. Living with mystery is not easy or fun, I decided, even though it looked like we were having fun back at McDonald's. Maybe it is fun for young people, but when you get older, mystery and unfamiliarity become scary. We get more rigid. We like the patterns we lay down. How great it is to flow through life's moments like a duck, never anticipating danger, so fully enjoying each moment!

I tried to let thoughts of the future roll off my back as I drove home.

34 Days Ago

I woke up exhausted. I hadn't slept at all. I had tossed and turned all night and finally got up and went to the couch so I wouldn't disturb my husband. The couch was comfortable for about an hour, but after that, it was nothing more than an upholstered torture chamber. I listened as the sun rose and waited to wake the kids for school.

Then I remembered it was Saturday. I sat up with a crick in my neck that prevented me from looking more than about twenty-five degrees to the left. I massaged my neck, rolling my head around and around, but there was no loosening of muscles going on. My neck was frozen. Every time I looked to the left, I would have to turn my entire body, north of the waist. Forgetting my disability caused shooting pain from head to shoulder. Bad timing, I thought. I wanted to be in tip-top shape for my impending mission.

When everyone finally got up, I decided to make pancakes for breakfast and keep some sense of normalcy within the family. I still was not hungry, but I knew I had to eat. I had a low level of anxiety just below my surface. As long as everyone moved quietly through their motions, I knew I would be okay. But when a half-

34 Days Ago

filled glass of orange juice toppled at the table, I lost it. I yelled at the perpetrator, wiped up the mess, and threw the dishcloth into the sink as if I were a relief pitcher trying to strike out the faucet. That killed my neck, and I began to cry. The children looked at me with fear on their sweet faces, and I knew I had blown it.

I quickly hugged them and apologized, and again, said I was just sad over Grandpa, which was slightly true. I had thought of my dad often throughout the night, wondering if he could see me. I wondered if he were proud of me for being picked for this mission. I wondered if he had his doubts about my ability to be effective. He had been a very successful man, and I could have used him at that moment. I wanted to feel one of his big bear hugs and hear the "don't worry, that which does not kill you makes you stronger" Nietzsche quote that he liked so much. Why was I afraid I was about to die? Were we all about to die?

The stress of being a prophet was definitely getting to me. I decided that after the whole sign-hanging thing was over and I could stop being secretive, I would feel better. I never liked secrets, but I felt like I had to keep things quiet until the signs were hung. Then I would spill everything I knew to anyone who asked and let them think what they would. I wouldn't have to be persuasive (which I was not, particularly). I would just have to be honest. Truthful. Full of truth.

After the spectacular appearance of my dead father, I had questioned what exactly "truth" meant. What I thought was true—that my dad was dead—seemed now to be untrue. So I decided that I would tell my story and let each person filter it through their set of beliefs and

Coming

values and decide their own truths. Soon enough we would all know that the solution is always love. And that was the only thing that I now believed to be true.

The kids bounced back from my dramatic little scene quickly and ran out of the kitchen to watch cartoons. My husband just held me, and shaking his head, walked out the door to go to the hardware store. His plan for the day was to take down an old antenna on the roof that kept looking worse with every wind storm. He also was going to buy a pane of glass to replace one in a living room window that had a small crack in the corner...a crack that had been there for four years since I had bumped the window with the vacuum handle.

I had asked him to do something normal, from the days before my dad died, when things were simple. No matter how dumb or meaningless, I wanted simplicity. Had I been selfish all these years? Should I have been working for justice in the world instead of gardening and hanging with friends and decorating my house? I began to feel guilty, then told myself that God probably wants us to enjoy life. And that's what I had done my whole life...I had truly enjoyed life. But the thought crept back into my brain...was my enjoyment of life selfish? I wrestled with this question all morning, alternating between patting myself on the back for a life well lived, and kicking myself in the pants for a life wasted on inane pleasures.

As my husband returned from the hardware store and set to work re-glazing the broken window, I wondered what in the world he was thinking. Surely he had fears about this whole thing, but he never really let me know he was afraid of anything and took all things in

34 Days Ago

stride. He was a master at perseverance and could push through obstacles as if they were revolving doors. His attitude inspired me, even though we did not talk much about the past couple days or the future. He was content to be in the moment. I needed that from him. But I also needed someone to talk to. An adult, to sort things out. I thought that maybe I ought to come clean to my parish priest and see what he thought of this whole thing.

Just as quickly, I decided not to.

Then the idea came back into my head. Speak to the priest. Get things off my chest. Allay my fears.

No, I couldn't do it until after the sign hanging. If anyone knew, it could jeopardize the whole mission, and the kids could get in trouble with the law. We were taking a gamble as it was. No. No one must know.

But if I talked to the priest, I would feel less nervous, more confident, more powerful.

No.

Then I remembered Jesus telling me that when I got a nagging feeling to do something, that was him nudging me, and I was to follow his lead. As my husband began to head for the roof to remove the antenna, I told him that I was thinking about talking things over with Father Michael. He thought it was a great idea. He probably was thrilled to have someone else assess my psycho-story.

I called the church office to make an appointment with Father Michael. He could see me at two-thirty. So for the next couple hours I straightened up the kitchen, bought glue at the office supply store, and checked and rechecked that my signs were in the closet.

Coming

At two-twenty I was sitting in my car at the rectory driveway, again second-guessing the whole "come clean" idea. I dropped my head back and closed my eyes, exhaling all of my stress. Just as I decided that I probably should not go in, a tap on the car window made me jump out of my skin. I swung to the left, again straining my neck, shooting pains all the way from my scalp to my left shoulder blade. There, smiling, no, definitely laughing, was Father Michael. He knew he had scared me. But even more frightening, I was stuck. No turning back. We walked into his office as I massaged my neck with one hand and beat him on the arm with my purse for his juvenile trick.

Once inside, I felt peace slip over me like a satin sheet.

"Father, what if the world were to end?" I asked.

"Whoa, having a few small spiritual issues, are we?" he joked.

"No, I mean, how bad would it be, really?"

"Well, how you die I think depends on how you live. If you live connected to God through others, loving yourself, serving others, that is all God asks of us. You will die in peace knowing that your purpose here on earth was fulfilled and that it's time to go home. On the other hand, if you are self-centered, thinking your own life is more important than any other, what awaits you can be a fearful thing. Why do you ask?"

"Oh, I don't know," I lied. "I just feel like there is so much horror in the world, the world is such a mess. And sure, I see beauty too, but so many atrocities...not just people being mean...people being pure evil. What will happen to us?"

34 Days Ago

"As you know, people have been predicting end times since the beginning of time. It's natural to wonder what kind of crescendo we're creating…what the big cymbal crash will be. But you know, if you live that Great Commandment, it just doesn't matter. Whether this world ends or not, you've got a place with God, and that's a good place to be."

I had to think for a minute about the Great Commandment. I recalled, "Love God with all your heart and soul and mind and strength, and love your neighbor as yourself." Nice, I thought, but it sounded too simple to be profound.

"But do you think the end will be scary?"

"For some," Father Michael proposed.

"For you?" I asked.

"No, not at all for me. I've looked forward to seeing God face to face for as long as I can remember. And just ask anyone who has been through immense suffering…there are worse things than dying. Dying to this world and rising to the next is the promise of the Resurrection. It gives us hope…not a crutch to lean on, but true hope."

"Do you believe in hell?" I asked, nervously.

"Oh, I can't say for sure. But I do believe that God is love. I think that maybe when we are faced at the moment of crossing over with that Supreme Ultimate Love, some people could be faced with the shame of how they have lived this life. If they were cruel and evil, I believe it will feel as if they are burning in fire, as if demons are ripping their flesh. Their desire for a "do-over" will be so great that it will indeed be hell. They will be separated from the peace of God. Conversely, heaven…that place where all those who 'get it' hang out and live together in justice and compassion...I imagine there's nothing more beautiful."

I sat, trying to imagine Father Michael's heaven and hell, when he spoke again.

"What brings this to your mind today?"

I focused on his eyes now, debating frantically in my head how to answer. "I think it's coming," I said.

"Really?" he asked, smiling slightly. "Why do you think so?"

Fixing my eyes again directly on his, I answered, "I don't *think* so, I actually *know* so. Let's just leave it at that, okay?"

No longer smiling, he quizzed me with a serious tone, "Just leave it? Are you sure? That's a pretty big feeling you're having there," he said.

"More than a feeling," I corrected him. "You've helped immensely, and I cannot thank you enough. Can I have a hug?"

I don't know where that came from, but somehow I felt that one hug for the road would somehow pass some of Father Michael's faith and strength into me.

He stood and opened his arms. I tentatively walked to him and carefully wrapped my arms around his waist and held back tears as I felt power surging through me. The power of love, I thought. The power of compassion. Wow, it was so intense. I stepped back, taking a deep breath. I thanked Father Michael again for his wisdom and patience with me and got back in my car with a new feeling of resolve.

As I pulled away from the rectory, I saw Father Michael staring at me out of his office window. He was a

34 Days Ago

sweet and rather shy man, and I hadn't meant to upset him. Poor guy, I thought. What did I just dump on him? Oh well, we're all about to be dumped on...he just got a little heads-up. He'll come out fine in the wash, no doubt, I thought.

When I got home my stomach kept flip-flopping. I tried to do some laundry and keep busy. I just couldn't. Finally, I took some ibuprofen for my neck, and I lay down on the living room couch and closed my eyes and began to pray. I'm not sure if I was praying or sleeping, but somewhere along the line I got some good rest and sat up feeling refreshed and calm.

Gradually, I got an uneasy feeling. Something was wrong. What time was it? It was too dark. It was only five at night; it shouldn't be dark yet. My heart began to pound. This is it! He's coming now...the world is cast into darkness. I'm too late. I didn't do anything to prepare the world. God, I am so sorry I screwed up. I'm so sorry, I cried. Then I said aloud, "I told you I was not a good person for this job!"

A thunderclap that seemed to be yelling back at me made me jump. I waited.

Rain? Just rain? I hadn't thought about rain. I smiled at my panicked reaction to darkness and apologized loudly, as if in a shouting match with God. God's voice was thunder. God's message was rain. Rain. Now what, I wondered. What about my plan? I couldn't send those kids up buildings in the rain. That would be irresponsibly dangerous. I was barely okay with the dangerous part anyway. The phone rang, and again I jumped, grabbed my heart, and ran to pick up the phone.

Coming

It was Tom. He and the others had talked and agreed that they shouldn't climb in the rain. He was obviously feeling embarrassed to tell me. Maybe he was afraid that I would want the show to go on regardless. But I quickly assured him that I would not have let them climb even if they had wanted to. His voice relaxed, and we talked about a rain date. He told me that all of the others but one could do it the next night. One had to work, and would get fired if he didn't show up since he had missed a few too many shifts in the past. We talked about how one building had had three climbers, so that we would be all right if a climber dropped out. Two climbers per building would be acceptable. A bare minimum. Tom said he would call each of his climbing buddies to set the new plan for the next night. I thanked him profusely for his help and apologized for the rain. He laughed and told me that he knew I had a direct line to God, but that he doubted that I had ordered the rain. I conceded, hung up the phone, and cursed the rain.

33 Days Ago

I awoke to the sun piercing my eye and I jumped out of bed shouting, "Yes!"

My husband, who had already showered, smiled and told me that he thought I might be happy to see the sun. He had checked the forecast, and it was supposed to be a beautiful day…and night. I threw my arms around him and gave him a big hug, the left side of my neck still a little sore, but loosening up. I was so appreciative of his quiet support. I knew all of this was weird for him. Maybe he didn't totally believe it, but he was willing to take the ride with me, letting me drive. I told him how lucky I was, and I gave him a kiss. He told me that he loved me.

The whole family got ready for church and went to the usual Mass. I waited all through Mass for Father Michael to say he had a special announcement. I thought he would tell the congregation about our meeting the day before and that the end of the world was coming. He would get the ball rolling for me. When he said, "The Mass is ended, go in peace," my jaw dropped open in disbelief. "A little help!" I wanted to yell from my pew, but remembered that I had a plan, and it was a good one. Just as quickly, I second-guessed myself. Maybe it was a bad plan. Maybe that was why God sent the rain. Was it a message to me? Or was it a coincidence? Jesus, God can be so confusing...so mysterious! I wished God would just speak to us and let us know if we were on the right track. Following the last song, we left our pew chatting with friends and acquaintances, but I knew I was being a bit short with all of them. It was not my fault. I was totally preoccupied with the dilemma of whether rain was a sign or a naturally occurring event that happens every so often in this world.

I whispered to my husband to take the children out, that I would join him in a minute. As the church emptied, I went over to a side chapel where others had stayed to pray their rosaries or to light a candle. I knelt down and pictured Jesus' face as I now knew him. I spoke frankly with him. Jesus, I prayed silently, you know time is short. If my climbing idea is a bad one, please let it rain tonight. If it rains tonight, I'll give it up and go back to the drawing board. If it doesn't rain, I'm taking that as a sign that you are in collusion with us. Okay? I don't hear you. Okay? I waited, but no voice, no vision. Just the silent answer of a listening God.

I met my family at the car, with children whining that I had taken too long, and we headed home. We decided to spend the afternoon together at the zoo. I still hadn't told the children anything about my special visitor or given them any hint that their future was going to be a little bizarre. We just enjoyed the frosty day, laughing at the animals, eating funnel cake and drinking hot chocolate until we were so tired we could drop. We stopped by Burger Wizard on the way home to top off a perfect day in the eye of a child. I was happy to give

33 Days Ago

them this great day. We had so much fun together; I knew it might be the last time we were able to play together as a family for a while.

At home, the children climbed into bed, and I read them a story about animals. They could never get enough of animals! But they were asleep before I closed the book.

"Wow, that was a fun day," I told my husband as I flopped on the couch exhausted, but just as quickly, my adrenal glands sprang into action with the thought of meeting the climbers in two hours. I was fired up and wide awake. There was no rain. Only stars in the sky. Was this my sign or an area of high pressure? I had to stop obsessing over that. I got the sheets that I had made into signs, glue and snacks that I had bought for the teenagers. I knew they were always hungry. I walked around the house and up and down stairs about seventeen times, making sure I had everything. I opened up the signs to be sure they looked all right. Shoot, I thought, as part of one sheet was stuck to itself as I tried to open it up. The little flourish I had made was apparently not completely dry when I hastily folded it up, and now it just looked like scribble. Not having enough imagination to turn this damaged squiggle into something recognizable, I refolded the sign and decided that no one would be paying attention anyway…the words would be the grabber. I loaded my supplies and signs into my minivan and gave my husband a big kiss.

"Be careful, honey," he said as he held me tight.

"You know I'm not climbing," I told him.

Coming

"I know, but you can still get hurt or in trouble. Give me a call if you need me," he said kindly as I rubbed his head for good luck and headed to the van.

My hands were shaking as I pushed the key in the ignition. I began frantically trying to start the van, but it just wouldn't start, which made me more nervous. I realized that I needed to calm down. I closed my eyes for a minute, took three deep breaths, then opened my eyes again. I was calmer. I started the car with ease and pulled out of the driveway with my husband grinning and waving from the door.

Back at our McDonald's parking lot meeting place, the smell of fast-food burgers was beginning to get to me. Of course, I was the first one there. I was proud of myself for not letting their tardiness upset me this time. Actually, they were not even tardy. I was early. I just continued to breathe and practiced relaxing my muscles, letting my thoughts float out into the atmosphere and my tension release. I felt great, breathing, relaxing, until loud honking brought me back to reality.

They were there. All six of them in one car. They piled out of their Honda Civic with the enthusiasm only young people can exude, high fiving and totally fired up for the climb. They all heaped into my minivan, and we went over details. Since one of the kids had to work, we now had only two kids per building. They already knew which pairs were climbing which buildings, impressing me with their organizational skills. They told me that they didn't take risks…that they knew that safety is the number one rule in climbing, but that fun was the number two rule. They divided up the ropes that Tom had already arranged into bags with the names of the build-

33 Days Ago

ings to be climbed scribbled on them. We decided to all go in my van, hitting each building together so that we could all help each other. Also, we could discuss things together, if any changes came up. We drove extremely lawfully to the first building.

It was an office building seven stories high. We got out of the car and stared up at the building in silence. My neck hurt to look up that high, but my pain became nothing worse than a pebble in the road, and I kicked it aside. The two assigned climbers spoke first. "Let's do it!" they cried in unison. They opened their bag of ropes and carabineers, and I handed them the folded sign and the contact glue. They strategized on how to hang the sign once they were at the seventh floor. I kept my mouth shut since this was definitely not my area of expertise. My dinner started to rise into my throat as the climbers went to the base of the building with all of their equipment. I covered my mouth with my hand to keep the food in. The others quietly shuffled around, helping them set up.

"Remember," I said, "be careful and don't worry. If we get caught, I will take all the heat."

"No problem" was their only reply as they began shimmying up the face of the office building, climbing about ten feet apart from each other. With ropes in place and both climbers working their way up, I stood in amazement at their strength and athletic ability. At the top, one climber took the folded sign, which he had stuffed into the back of his pants, and opened it up. The sheet opened, but it was difficult to tell which way was up as the boy held onto one corner. He moved the sheet through his hands over and over again, with those of us

Coming

on the ground yelling as quietly as we could when he should stop and glue that corner to the building. It went on and on, as he passed the corners through his hands. Then he would backtrack, with those on the ground disagreeing. Finally, after what seemed like a half-hour, he had the correct corner in his hand and was using contact cement to glue it to the building.

After holding the sheet onto the glue to let it set, he slid his hands along the top edge of the sheet, grabbing the other top corner. Suddenly, he started swinging on his rope to meet his partner who was hanging ten feet away from him. He latched onto a window frame and handed the correct corner to his buddy, along with the glue, and swung back to his side of the sign, pressing his hand back down on the corner. The other climber held up his corner and after those of us on the ground told him to raise his side, then lower, then raise it again, he slapped the corner of the sheet against the glue and held it in place. It was crooked, but it was done and they rappelled down the building in no time. Again, the kids' enthusiasm swelled as they congratulated the climbers. As they gathered up the equipment and put it back into the bags, we gazed up at the sign.

In bold black letters it said: **EVERYONE WILL HAVE A DREAM. EVERYONE. SAME DREAM. PAY ATTENTION.** They looked at me for approval. "Perfect! That's it," I said, "let's go do the next one."

As we loaded into the van and drove off, I could not stop staring at the sign in the rearview mirror. We did it! They did it. It was not raining and we did it. I started to laugh, and they chattered all the way to the next building.

33 Days Ago

    The next building was an abandoned factory building. It was nine stories high, and this time it was a boy and the girl going up. They got the bag of ropes and equipment that Tom had organized. I opened up the sign and put a big #1 on the back of the corner that the first climber had to glue, and a big #2 on the back of the other top corner. This would speed things up a bit and lessen the time kids were hanging by one hand, which made me almost sick to my stomach. I refolded the sign and handed it the boy, and the other climber handed him the glue. The kids walked around the base of the building for a couple minutes before setting up and, like Spiderman, the two were working their way up the wall with ease. The excitement was swelling as they went all the way to the assigned level. With amazing agility and ease the boy grabbed the #1 corner and held it tightly to the building, with the contact cement drying in a minute. The boy swung over, meeting the girl hanging from her rope, and handed her the #2 corner. She eyed the levelness of the sign, and plastered it down without asking for a consensus, and it was as straight as a Vermeer at the Louvre. Good girl, I thought. They slid down like thieves, throwing their fists into the air in celebration of a job well done, and we moved on down the road to the final building.

    We approached the last building slowly. It was a combination of office space and condominiums, eighteen stories high. The trick was to get to the twelfth story without anyone in the top floors of condos noticing. It was now about eleven-thirty, and most people would be in bed on a Sunday night, but surely not everyone. About a third of the condo lights were still lit. As I

Coming

marked the corners of the sheet, I noticed the pink squiggles, and the messiness of it upset me. Disappointed, I tried to pick off some of the bits of paint and make it look nice again, but we were in a hurry. I let it go.

Tom and his friend, Jack, positioned themselves at the base of the building. With ropes and equipment in place, we all agreed that this one must be done in silence if the residents were not to be alerted. Tom and Jack began their ascent with confidence. They hand-motioned each other if they saw people in their windows and would stop briefly until the coast was clear. Up they went with dexterity and vigor. It truly was a thing of beauty. Tom, upon reaching the twelfth floor, grabbed the sign out of the back of his pants. He quickly found the #1 corner, but then, feeling his pockets for the glue, realized that we had forgotten to give it to him. The last climber, the girl, dropped her jaw open, and put her hand to her mouth, eyes big as moons when she realized she still had the glue in her pocket. One of the boys did a throwing motion with his arm, to let Tom know he would try to throw it to him. Tom silently overexaggerated "no" with his head. Almost immediately, Tom began rappelling back down to get the glue. The sheet, which was in his hand, floated up as he began to drop, and it caught the eye of one of the condo residents who was passing by his window. He came to the window and looked all around, but we didn't think that he saw us. Tom was already down at that point and stood as flat to the building as he could. Jack was suspended at the twelfth story.

I told Tom that he didn't have to go back up, that we had two good signs in place, but he was halfway up the

33 Days Ago

building before I realized my pleas were going unheeded. Again, at the top and panting from the double climb, Tom glued the corner to the building. Swinging across would be trickier this time, with people inside. A light had gone on in the window between Tom and Jack, and they both swung just to the sides of the window. Both boys peered into the window slowly, then quickly pulled their heads back. The light went out, and they waited a full three minutes, which seemed like an eternity. They pulled the sheet across the window and tacked it to the other side. As Jack held his corner in place, the whoop of a siren sounded out of nowhere. Pulling in slowly behind the minivan came two police cars. I ran back to meet the police, the kids looking nervously at each other as if deciding whether to run or stay.

"Can I help you, officer?" I asked with all the innocence I could muster.

With police radios squawking, the large police officer looked me up and down and asked if this were my van. I told him it was. He asked if I was with the kids on the building, and I told him that I was. Suddenly, we heard the sounds of a helicopter coming toward the building, shining a huge spotlight right on Tom and his friend. I could just barely make out in the dark that it was a Channel 6 news helicopter. Lights in the condos began to pop on, and heads came to the windows to check out the late-night disturbance. Once he turned on his light, I could see the silhouette of the man behind the sheet that had just been hung. I imagined his confusion, which tickled me.

Tom and his friend, Jack, waved to the helicopter, which sent the friends on the ground into hysterical

Coming

laughter. The light then shined down on them and they all waved and danced in the light. The spotlight went back up to Tom and Jack, who just hung halfway down the building, enjoying the attention.

"Ma'am, what's going on here?" the officer enquired, looking up at the climbers and the sign.

"Oh, it's a long story. Go ahead and take me in if you have to. We'll drop the kids at their car, if that's okay," I said.

"No ma'am, that's not okay," he said in a tone that I thought was unnecessarily snippy. "We'll have to take you all in to the station to sort this out." He made a call on his radio, saying numbers and letters, and I think requesting back-up, while the officer from the other car went to the building to coax the boys down. Residents began to come out of the building. Some were in their robes and others in boxer shorts and T-shirts, but they were asked to go back into their condos until everything was safe. As if we were dangerous!

The residents wanted to know what was going on, but the police insisted they return to their homes. I was questioned as to the purpose of this stunt, which I told them was strictly to hang the sign. I tried to assure the officer that we were not trying to break in or case the joint or any other malfeasance. Simply hanging a sign. The officer asked if I understood that defacing private property was a crime, and I told him that I didn't really see it that way. The sign was just temporary and would probably fall down in a day and there would be no destruction of anything, other than my sign which, frankly, I had worked fairly hard on.

33 Days Ago

    Once the boys were safely on the ground they collected their equipment and put it into bags. We were hauled off in seven separate police cars, all under the spotlight of Channel 6 and now also Channel 2. Spotlights were crisscrossing from the sign to the police cars and back to the building, and we pulled away with sirens blaring. I prayed for the kids, and I thanked God that they were all safe, and I prayed for their parents. I thanked God for no rain, and with a deep breath, I said aloud, "Okay, God, here I go…don't leave me now." And off to the police station we went in handcuffs, feeling a part of the biggest crime bust of the century.

~ 32 Days Ago ~

This day actually started at midnight, as do all days, but we rarely start counting then. However, this was the beginning of a very long day. At the police station, I was taken out of my handcuffs (those things hurt!) and questioned repeatedly about what I had done.

Gradually, the parents of the kids arrived looking nervous as they came into the station. I could see them entering, talking with officers, pointing in my direction, but I couldn't quite make out what they were saying. As they completed paperwork with their parents, some of the kids would look my way and smile; others would look my way, then look down shamefully, and one would not even look at me at all.

I had tried to explain to the police that it was entirely my fault for getting them into this and that I would take full responsibility. I said that they were bribed into doing it with cheeseburgers, which is as good as gold to a teenager. I pleaded to let the kids off easy and since they were all minors, I was assured that they would probably get community service and maybe a small fine, but that that would be up to the municipal courts. Unless they got good lawyers, they would have to go to court some time within the next couple months. I hoped that

32 Days Ago

by the time the court date came up, all of this would be a moot point. At any rate, I was prepared to pay all of their fines and court costs. The community service wouldn't hurt them.

Back to me. They asked me if I wanted to make a phone call, which I did to my husband, and told him that everything worked out great. I was bubbly on the phone, which drew looks of suspicion from the dispatcher nearby. I saw her eye another officer, signaling for him to come listen to me. I cut the conversation short and told my husband not to worry and to stay home with the children.

They left me in a cell for hours as they dealt with the teens one by one. I was getting quite sleepy. I could tell the sun was coming up. I thought I needed to get home to get the kids to school. "Can I make another call?" I asked.

"You had your call," an officer snarled back.

"But I have to get home and get my kids off to school," I explained.

"Shoulda thought of that last night, ma'am," he said sarcastically.

"Can I just tell my husband I won't be home in time?" I pleaded.

"I'm sure he'll figure it out, unless he's as crazy as you are," he said.

"Hey, that's unnecessary," I snapped.

"Whatever, you'll be out of here when we're finished with you," he said, not even looking at me as he shuffled papers.

A few more hours passed with me telling my story about fourteen times, starting with the visit from Jesus.

Coming

That was my beginning point. I had to start somewhere, and maybe the police were not the most sympathetic bunch with which to start, but they were a captive audience, and they kept asking me to repeat my story.

At eight-thirty in the morning I got a psychiatric evaluation which was actually rather fun. I joked with the psychologist, but he was pretty much all business. I thought I was hilarious, and I was sure he wanted to laugh. I think I was starting to get a little punchy from lack of sleep and a general feeling of indifference to what others thought about me. I knew who was in my corner, and he was all I needed.

Just before noon, I was finally released after fingerprinting and signing my name on every imaginable form, agreeing to go to court, agreeing to release the psychiatric evaluation to someone or another, acknowledging that my personal items were returned to me, agreeing to pay for my car, which was apparently impounded overnight, and on and on. I called a girlfriend to pick me up, which was pretty fun—telling her I was at the police station.

When she arrived, she told me she had just been watching the noon news when I had called. Right after she hung up with me, there I was on the news being put into a police car in handcuffs. They showed the boys on the building, waving to the camera. Then they focused on the sign, reporting that the message was quite enigmatic, and that two more signs were found on buildings by neighborhood residents. All of the signs said the same thing: **Everyone will have a dream. Everyone. Same dream. Pay attention.** Then she told me the news anchor tried to segue into the sports bit by saying, "I'll tell you what I'm dreaming about...spring training." How pathetic!

I told the whole story for the fifteenth time that day to my friend who had to pull over to the side of the road. She knew me well and knew I could not, would not, make this up. She started to shake and couldn't drive. Her eyes began to tear up, and I reassured her that everything would be okay.

I told her how calm and gentle and fun Jesus had been. I revealed that those who treat others with compassion would have nothing to worry about. I explained that we would all have one more chance to shape up...we would have a dream. Everyone in the world would have the same dream, and then we would know that it was God speaking to us and that we had better fly right. And my job was to let everyone know that Jesus was coming so that they would pay attention and know the dream was from God. People needed to talk about their dreams and compare until they found the very dream that was from God. Then everyone would know. Everyone would know how to live. God wanted us all to feel love. It hurt God so badly when we turn away from love.

Now the tears were flowing like a waterfall off my friend's nose and chin. She was sobbing in disbelief, in fear, in confusion. I leaned over and held her tightly as we sat in her car on the side of the road until she could drive again. She took me to the lot where my car had been impounded. She told me she would meet the kids at school before they got on the bus and drive them home. And I realized now was the time I should tell my children, before everyone started talking about it.

Coming

I gave my friend one more hug at the impound lot, and she drove off, somewhat witlessly, down the road to pick up my children. I hoped that she got control of herself and her car before my kids got in.

I paid for my car and the man at the lot had a small television on behind the counter. He was big, bald, dusty and as open as a bar's first night. It was instantly obvious he had seen the news. I didn't have to wait to see if he recognized me. He did.

"Hey, I saw you on the TV," he exclaimed, emphasizing the "T." "Ever once in a while we do, nature of da binness, ya know. That was somepin'. Hey, whatta those signs mean? You got da ESP or somepin'? Whassup with dat?"

I blurted out most of the story, number sixteen for the day, and was getting good at just highlighting the main points. Then something unexpected happened. The big man with the dirty shirt came around the counter and dropped to his knees and began to call out, "Praise Jesus!" over and over. He grabbed my arm and begged me to have mercy on him. I tried to pull my arm away and tell him that I was not one to be granting mercy to anyone...I was simply the messenger.

"Please don't hurt the messenger," I begged. "I have to spread the word." Then I had an idea.

"Sir," I half yelled over his blubbering. "Sir," I tried again. He looked up. "Sir, I need help. I need *your* help. Will you please be a messenger, too? I need to tell the whole world. I can't do it alone. I need to spread the word and have those who heard it from me spread the word some more. Can you do that for me? Can you get out there and tell everyone you know or see? Tell them

32 Days Ago

my story. They probably won't believe it, but that's not your problem. Just tell them the story. Tell them to pay attention to their dreams. Then they'll know. And you'll be a messenger, too. You're my first recruit. Are you in?"

The man stopped crying and pulling on me. Slowly rising off the dusty floor, he threw his arms around me. He held me so tightly I could scarcely catch my breath. My nose was smashed onto a button on his chest but I couldn't turn my head. Wow, that was an interesting expression of love, I thought, as I almost fell to the ground upon his release of me.

"Count me in," he said, smiling broadly. "Onward Christian soldiers!" he exclaimed, saluting me and whistling the old hymn, wiping his nose on his sleeve. I always hated that hymn. I'd never liked comparing a Christian to a soldier. Don't get me wrong, it's not that soldiers can't be Christian. I just didn't care for the implied violence of the war metaphor. But I smiled at his enthusiasm and told him to "keep the faith" as I got my keys and drove off.

I went straight home and found three news vans outside my house. As I pulled into my driveway, the paparazzi jumped out of their cars and came running at me, cameras rolling. I told them to relax and come in the house and offered them some tea. I really wanted a beer, but I thought that might give me a bit of a credibility problem in mid-afternoon, so I just got some water. The camera people discussed the best place for me to sit with the lighting in the home and we began a civilized interview. I told them that they had to take turns with questions, but that they could ask me anything, and I would answer honestly.

In the middle of the first question, my three sweet little darlings came pouring into the house, my friend having dropped them off from school. Each of my kids had a friend along since I had promised that they could have a play day after school. I had forgotten all about this agreement during the long night at the police station, but there they were, with plenty of questions of their own.

"Mom, what are you doing?"
"Why are all these people here?"
"Can I have a snack?"
"We brought the class hamster home; do you want to see it?"
"My tooth hurts."
"Were you on the news?"
"Nick's mom said that you are in big trouble."
"Can we get out the finger paints?"

I rattled off answers to each question as best I could, and after petting the hamster, microwaving popcorn, and laying finger paints out on newspaper at the kitchen table nearly simultaneously, I apologized to the reporters and refocused on what had apparently become the secondary interview of the afternoon.

The first question from the reporter was a doozey.

"Why did you think it was okay to hang signs from buildings?" one reporter asked.

I was expecting questions about the meaning of the signs, not my ethics.

"Well, I needed to get the attention of a lot of people and this was the only thing I could think of. I didn't

32 Days Ago

think it would really offend anyone or hurt any property."

Next question. "But I heard you made six teenagers do your dirty work. Did you use your influence over them as an adult to lead them into mischief?"

Whoa, I thought, they were excited to do it. But I answered apologetically, "Yes, that was probably wrong, but I knew I didn't have the strength or expertise to get up those buildings by myself."

The third reporter finally asked the question I was waiting for. "What do those signs mean?"

Yes! I thought, here we go. Repeat of story, number seventeen. And I gave the account of a visit from Jesus who was coming back in a short time and wanted all people to know God and love others and, in order to give people one more chance to believe in love, all people in the whole world would have the same dream on the same night.

"Mom, can we have a soda?" a small voice yelled from the kitchen.

"Split one with Nick, honey," I bellowed. "Sorry, go on."

Back to the first reporter. "And you think that people will believe you?" she asked cynically.

"It doesn't really matter to me. I guess it matters to God, but not to me. I'm just the messenger. And I didn't go looking for this assignment, by the way. I was happy with my life when this whole thing fell into my lap, and now my life has changed forever. But I'm sure it can only be for the good, no matter how weird it gets." My fatigue enabled me lay it out honestly.

Coming

I fielded a couple more questions, and, when everyone seemed to be satisfied, the reporters left so that I could check on the hamster. It had been finger-painted with bright primary colors and then decorated with popcorn, and was walking slowly on the kitchen table like a living, embarrassed popcorn ball. On a good day, I would have been upset with the mess, but on a bad day, it was the most beautiful sight I had ever seen. I started to laugh and could not stop. I was hysterical. I was delirious. I was exhausted.

The kids saw an opening and took it. They began to fling finger paints at each other, and that was the end of all frivolity. I put my foot down and yelled at them to stop. My bipolar response had them baffled, and, after an hour of cleaning up, I drove their friends home, regaining my equilibrium.

When we got home, I sat my children down in the family room and told them the whole story. Number eighteen for the day. But this time I did not spare any words. I explained everything to them, their eyes widening with every new detail. I had to remind them to blink once in a while. They were so precious, so accepting. They were too young to question my motives. They just ate up the story with complete faith in me and in God. No wonder Jesus loved children, I thought. They are such an easy audience. No judgment, no over-thinking, full of play, full of love. Just the way we're supposed to be.

My husband came home from work early just to make sure everyone was all right, even though I had spoken to him earlier in the day and let him know that I was home. I told him that everything went great, but that

32 Days Ago

the police paperwork had been a tad tedious. We all sat down together to watch the local evening news. Wow, slow news day, I thought—the signs were the top story. We clicked around the channels, and every channel had shots of the signs or Tom and his friend waving from the face of the building, or my interview.

"Oh God, I look obese," I said disappointedly, as I saw myself on television. My kids assured me that I didn't. But jeez, is that really what I look like, I wondered with disgust, totally distracted from the crux of the mission.

When the story was over on each channel, the children jumped up and down and clapped for their superstar mom. I tried to convince them that it wasn't about me. My husband walked over to the silent phone and hovered his hand over it, waiting.

It took five seconds. He handed the phone to me and the phone rang, and rang, and rang again, each time I hung up. I promised everyone I'd tell them the whole story later, but asked them to try to believe me even though it was the weirdest thing they had ever heard. I could tell some would try, but some wouldn't.

About a dozen or so calls in, I got a call from Tom. He told me that one of his friends had called him, the guy who couldn't do the climb because he had to work on Sunday. Tom told me how the guy's dad, upon hearing the story of the kids climbing the building, said that he would have kicked his son out of the house for a stunt like that. The dad thought that the teens had brought shame to their family names and should all be kicked out. Tom's friend was so relieved he hadn't gone. The rain was his salvation.

Coming

The rain, I thought. The rain. I had hated the rain. I thought it had ruined my plan, but it hadn't. And now, well, now I wasn't sure what to think about the rain.

Tom laughed at the goofy shots of himself hanging from the building and said he didn't know what had gotten into him. The pressure was off him, however, after shots of the others waving and dancing stole the show. Tom asked if I was okay and if I got in a lot of trouble. I assured him that everything would be just great. I told him that I could never repay the favor he and his friends did for me, and, before we hung up, I asked that he sleep well and not be afraid to dream. He was a good guy, and he would be okay through whatever was coming our way. He thanked me for the adventure and wished me luck, and I didn't know if I'd talk to him again before the end. I told him I loved him.

The calls continued to come in all night until I lost track of the number of times I told the story. We got the kids in bed and told them they didn't have to go to school the next day, but they were excited to go. Great, I thought, more messengers. I just hoped that they didn't get teased or hurt. I whispered a little prayer for their protection as I tucked them in and kissed them goodnight. I told them how proud I was of them and reminded them to always believe and be strong, no matter what people said. I suggested that if someone said mean things to them, they could say a little prayer for that person who obviously needed a little help. They each gave me goodnight hugs.

When I came out of my daughter's bedroom, my husband told me I had three more messages: one from a

32 Days Ago

cousin, one from my best friend, and one from Father Michael. "What did Father Michael say?" I asked.

"He just said he'd pray for you," my husband answered with a shrug.

"That's it? Is that good or bad?"

My husband said it could never be bad, and I had to agree. We lay down on the couch together and waited for more calls. I had that beer that I had wanted so badly, but it turned warm by the time I finished it with all my lengthy conversations. The calls finally stopped at about eleven-thirty and we went to bed totally exhausted. It was definitely the longest day of my life. Except the one time I stayed up almost two days straight when my oldest daughter had appendicitis. And then there was the time in college when I stayed up for almost three days straight after going to a music fest the day before finals and ended up drinking so much coffee that I twitched the whole fourth day while trying to sleep. Anyway, this was way up there on the list of long days, and it was definitely the most bizarre.

31 Days Ago

Breakfast was the liveliest it had ever been in our household on a school day. The children, who usually were not talkative at all in the morning, were bursting with laughter and teasing and incessant ramblings. They flew out of the house with the speed of a tropical depression, building to a hurricane. My husband, not so eager to go to work and face his peers, decided that working would be the best thing to do. He had to believe me. Although I wasn't sure exactly what he was telling people at the office, I thought he probably handled it all diplomatically like he always did, not passing judgment, just speaking from his knowledge base.

As I was loading the dishwasher with breakfast dishes, the telephone started up again. Oh, God, I thought. Give me strength...here we go again! As I answered, I was quite surprised to hear that it was a producer of the national morning show, AMerica (pronounced A-M-America), who had seen our local coverage and was intrigued by the whole situation. Through my stutters and blunderings, I agreed to have them fly me to New York to tell my story on the next show. It would be a short segment; I just needed to tell my story. They were interested in what would drive a suburban mother to a stunt

31 Days Ago

like this, and they wondered about the hidden message of the signs. I tried to tell him that there was no "hidden" message, that the message was clear and direct, but he cut me short and told me that I would receive further information on my travel plans.

I hung up with my heart pounding so hard that I could hear it in my ears. National television! Do I have to do this? Is this part of the job description? I can't go to New York City by myself! I sat down on the kitchen floor and nearly hyperventilated. I tried to slow my breathing and my pounding heart. As I calmed, I clearly realized that my speaking on a national news show was exactly what I had to do. I had to warn people. It was my *whole* job description. And if I made a fool of myself, if I looked fat, if I spit when I talked, so what? It would not matter to anyone in a few days.

Then I had a sinking feeling. I thought of the Bible, where throughout the New Testament there was talk of Jesus returning, as if it would be any day. It had been over two thousand years and still nothing. Maybe I was jumping to conclusions, thinking Jesus would come in a few short days or weeks. Maybe I was duped like the believers of the olden days. Maybe he would not come back for another couple thousand years. Maybe he was trying to trick me into getting the world shaped up, with false hopes. Maybe everyone would talk about the fanatical fat lady on the national morning show. Maybe they would talk about it for years. Maybe when I died, they would remember only this dark side of my life.

"Jesus!" I called out. "Is the time now? Are you coming *now*? Should I really tell the world to be ready now? Please don't make me look like a fool. I am not that brave."

I waited for Jesus to appear and reassure me. The phone rang. I ignored it and waited for the blessed appearance. "C'mon, Jesus," I whispered softly, as a gambler whispers into his dice before rolling.

I waited.

I waited through three more phone calls, and on the fourth, I realized that God was not coming to my aid. I answered the phone. It was my husband. He had been calling to tell me that he had to be in New York the next day for a meeting and was just checking to make sure I would be okay with that.

A smile of consolation crept across my face as I realized that God *was* with me. God was sending me to New York *with* my husband to ease my fears. I told my husband about the AMerica offer, and he told me to call them back and let them know that we would need two seats, but that his company would pay for his. We figured his mom and dad could watch the kids for one day, and he would make that call. His parents were the most detached, unemotional people I knew, and I thought that they might lend some composure to our manic children.

After speaking again with people at AMerica regarding travel plans, I began to tear through my closet looking for the perfect outfit, alternating thoughts of "who cares" with "I have to look my best." I packed lightly and laid out clothes and pajamas for the kids in order to make my in-laws' job as easy as possible. As it turned out, we would be leaving that evening and returning the next afternoon. AMerica was taped live, and I would have to be there early in the morning. My husband's

31 Days Ago

meeting would also be over by two in the afternoon, so we could fly home together. Things fell into place so easily. Interesting, I thought.

I had accomplished all of that, and it was still not even lunchtime. I skipped lunch in order to be interviewed on my front porch by another local news station. I got a call from three lawyers, offering to represent me in my civil disobedience case. I refused. I hoped I wouldn't need one.

Another local station managed to squeeze in another interview before the kids came home from school, and I survived retelling my story countless times on the phone. A quick early dinner and my in-laws arrived to spend the night as my husband and I took a taxi to the airport.

The taxi driver, upon telling us he was a Nepali immigrant and that he listens to his car radio all day, immediately addressed me with a strongly accented voice. "Hey, you're the crazy lady with the signs on the buildings."

"Yes, that's me," I admitted with dubious pride.

"Is it true? You saw Jesus? He said he's coming? He said we're all going to have the same dream? He wants us all to be loving and kind? You are supposed to warn the whole world?"

"Wow, you really got the details, sir," I said.

"I gotta admit it's a little scary. I almost didn't go to work today, but then I thought, you know, what if this lady is a kook. No offense, but I do have to pay the bills unless my landlord is Jesus Christ himself," the cab driver said with a grin.

Coming

"No, you're right. You should work. Work is good. It is good to contribute. Look how you are helping my husband and me right now. What you are doing is a good thing. We all have to help each other. Our work is our way of building our community. Keep working, sir. Keep working," I told him.

My husband looked at me as if he wondered what happened to his wife. I looked like his wife, but I didn't sound like her. I had never been particularly philosophical and definitely had never given out advice like that before.

We continued the ride to the airport in basic silence, and I wasn't sure what our driver was thinking. Or my husband. When we arrived, the driver opened the taxi door for me and, pushing a tattered copy of the Bhagavad-Gita towards me, asked me to autograph it for him. He apologized that he didn't have a Bible, but explained that he was a Hindu and I let him know that a good Hindu was a good person, and a good person, in any religion, is all God wants us to be. I declined autographing his sacred book, urging him to have 'The Real Deal' sign it when he came. He bowed and thanked me and offered his hand to help me out of the car.

I could not help but give this kind man a hug. As I tried to release, he continued to hold me tight. So I regained my grip on him until my husband called my name gently. The taxi driver jumped and let me go, bowing and thanking me some more, sprinkling 'namaste' liberally between his kind words.

I bowed back and thanked him for the ride and told him not to be afraid. My husband grabbed my hand and

31 Days Ago

started trotting with our carry-ons towards the long check-in line.

The airport was a stressful place, as it had become ever since all of the terrorist activity in the air, and I was never quite at ease with flying until I reached my destination. The flight was uneventful, but still I felt a low level of uneasiness throughout the flight. As we landed, I could feel a release of the deep tension that I had been holding, my shoulders dropping back into their resting place several inches below my ears.

Another taxi took us to our hotel in Manhattan. My body was exhausted. My eyes were dry and my face had that travel glaze upon it. It was nearly midnight, and I had to catch some sleep before getting up early for the morning show. Their driver was picking me up at six-fifteen, and I got another wave of panic as I thought about what I was really doing in New York City. Don't think, don't think, let the time pass and the worry will pass with it. This was a trick I had used for many years now. I just pushed something I dreaded out of my mind and let time march on, and the next thing I knew, I was in the middle of the dreaded affair. And dreaded affairs, I found, were never as bad as I imagined they would be. We all seem to have resources deep within us that allow us to deal with anything. Don't think, don't think, don't think, I told myself as I laid in my bed and closed my eyes and breathed in stagnant hotel air until I drifted off.

✦ 30 Days Ago ✦

With the rising sun came my new friend, nausea. The "don't think" trick was not working at all. My husband had gone to the lobby to grab some coffee and a bagel before his meeting, and I showered and dressed with such shaky hands I don't know how I got my dress zipped at all. Hair dried, make-up on, shoes on, ready and waiting by six. I was wide awake and apoplectic and hardly able to remember my own name.

My husband came back in the room just as the front desk rang our phone and told me that my driver was in the lobby. My dear husband hugged me and whispered in my ear to imagine all of the people at the television station having a pumpkin for a head and their faces carved out of the pumpkin. I laughed and gave him a hug and trembled all the way to the lobby until I saw the driver. His eyes looked to me to be triangular; his grin was wide with a smattering of teeth. His complexion was orange, and I smiled at him and knew I could have some fun with the morning. After all, it would be over before I knew it.

At the station, I was greeted by a whole crop of pumpkin heads, offering me water and coffee. They fussed over my hair and make-up and ran my mike and

30 Days Ago

checked the sound. They went over the instructions of where I would sit and how I would get settled during a commercial break. The whole interview, they said, would probably last about four minutes or so. Four minutes! No sweat, I tried to convince myself. One sweet pumpkin head with long blonde hair told me she was an intern and how nervous she had been on the first day but that now it was just a job like any other. She commented that I seemed pretty calm for a first-timer to national television, and I thanked her and complimented her beautiful smile.

I met the young man who would be interviewing me. I had always thought he was handsome on television, but up close he looked plastic and unreal. Men with make-up and hairspray have never really been a turn-on for me, and I felt sorry for him having to play this game every day. Just as quickly I thought of the salary he was making for playing this game every day and my sympathy subsided.

He was kind and reassuring during the commercial break and briefed me on the questions he would be asking me. The commercials seemed to take forever. It was even longer on the program side than it is on the living room side of the television. I settled into my place on the couch next to him. He gave me a reassuring wink. Finally, the countdown and we were on the air. After introducing me as a suburban wife and mother who had gone to illegal lengths to hang peculiar signs in my community, the first question came:

"Tell us what the signs said."

My throat was tense and trembling, so I took a huge inhale and spoke as I exhaled, looking out at the pumpkin behind the camera. "I hung three signs, and they all said the same thing. They said: 'Everyone will have a dream. Everyone. Same dream. Pay attention.'"

The second question: "And what did you mean by this?"

"Well, as it says, everyone in the world will have the same dream someday, and we are to pay attention to that dream," I said, disturbed that I could not control the shakiness in my voice.

Third question: "Do you know what the dream will be or when we will have it?"

"No, I don't know the answer to either of those questions. But I have no doubt that it will happen, and I do believe it will get everyone's attention."

The fourth question...the zinger: "How do you know this will happen?"

Deep breath. Shoulders down. Smile. "Well, this is where my story gets really weird, I do admit. My dad died two weeks ago."

"Oh, I am sorry," the host interjected.

"Thank you. He died quite suddenly, and it was a shock to the family. The day after his funeral, a man came to my door. I thought he was probably someone who knew my dad or someone with a flower delivery, but as he spoke, he told me that he was Jesus and that he was coming. As in the Second Coming. Of course, I thought he was a creepy kook and was about to hit him over the head with a plate of pastries, but then he made my father appear right in front of me, and I almost fainted."

Fifth question: "You're saying your deceased father was standing in front of you?"

30 Days Ago

Now I felt myself loosening up. My dad was with me at that moment. I could feel him.

"Yes, I know it sounds like I'm hallucinating or needing major grief therapy or something, but he was right there. Jesus would not let me touch him. And then dad just disappeared."

"And what else did this man who claimed to be Jesus say to you?"

"Well, this is when he told me that he would be coming and that he wanted everyone to be filled with the joy and love that happens when they know God. He said that he was tired of the pain and horrendous suffering that we are inflicting on each other, and that basically, it's just time. He asked me to spread the word, you know, kind of like John the Baptist did before Jesus came the first time, so people could prepare their hearts and turn to love."

"Well, that is quite a story. Why do you think 'Jesus' picked you?" the host asked in a tone I didn't really appreciate.

"That is the question of the hour," I said. "I have no idea. I'm not really holy, although I do believe in God and try to live a good life. But I'm not that great, and I'm not well connected and I don't have a whole lot of confidence. I hate to say it, but I wondered if God made a mistake. I know God typically does not make mistakes, but this time I really wonder. Maybe he got the wrong address or something. It's a mystery to me."

The host chuckled. "Well, you *are* on national television telling anyone who has tuned in, so I guess you're more capable than you think you are!"

"True, true. I never would have expected things to go this far," I admitted.

One final question: "You had some teenagers scale those buildings to hang the signs. I understand there were arrests for trespassing and defacing property and possibly other charges. How do you feel about that?"

"Oh, I never wanted the kids to get in trouble, but I knew I could not climb a building by myself. So I made sure they were minors and under my persuasion, and I have a feeling by the time this whole case goes to court, the point will be moot. If not, and if I've misunderstood and Jesus really is *not* coming soon, then I'll pay my fines and do my community service with my tail between my legs. And I'll tell my family they have the option of getting a new mom if they want. But I don't think that will be necessary. The message was clear to me."

"Well, that is some story. I guess we'll all know soon enough if the dream comes. I want to thank you for being our guest today on AMerica, and I hope all goes well."

"It's up to us now. If things go well, it's because we tried. If things don't go well, I assume it will be because we just didn't love. Thanks for having me on," I said with sincere gratitude, extending my hand to shake the hand of my host.

"Our pleasure. And coming up next...a new discovery in the reptile world that will turn some heads...and I am warning you, if you don't like snakes, you may want to cover your eyes. Coming up, right after these messages." Cut to commercials.

The host thanked me again, and told me I was a pleasure, to which I may have blushed a bit, and all of

30 Days Ago

the pumpkins disappeared from the heads of the people behind the scenes. I saw them for the first time. Some stared at me, shaking their heads. Others laughed together and I wondered if they were laughing at me. I was ushered back to the guest waiting room for a drink or snacks before the driver would return me to the hotel.

Back in the guest waiting room, people entered one by one, asking me more questions until the room was full and people were pushing and arguing. I found myself up on a chair, telling anyone who would listen that they did not need to be afraid and that all they needed to do was love God, love themselves and love others. They didn't need to run to church or fast or flagellate themselves. They just needed to love and feel the peace.

A station manager began pulling people out of the room and telling them to get back to work and apologized to me for their behavior. I told him that it was no problem, that I was glad they were curious.

He scoffed and helped me off my chair, and I got the feeling that he thought I was a phony. Whatever. Not my problem. Or was it, I wondered. Should I work on him or let him go? I decided to give it a try once, then let it go. I looked at the station manager as he walked me down the hall to meet my driver, and I said to him, "Your mother is fine, she's healthy and happy."

He swung around, frowning, angrily grabbing my arm and asked, "What did you say?"

"I just said your mom is fine. I don't know why I said it...it just came out," I said with a shrug.

"Do you know my mother?"

"No."

"Do you know anything about my mother?"

"Nothing."

"My mother was severely depressed and committed suicide when I was fourteen, and I've hated God ever since. Everyone always says God doesn't give you more than you can bear, but apparently God overestimated. I've despised God for heaping too much on her. It just wasn't fair."

He searched intently into my eyes, his blue eyes swimming in a pool of tears.

"I'm so sorry. I had no idea. I shouldn't have said anything. I'm sorry," I said, pulling away and running towards the driver.

As the driver and I went through the revolving door to the street, I glanced back and saw the station manager, his forehead lowered to the palm of his left hand, his right hand against his thigh bracing himself. The darling blonde intern was running to him to make sure he was all right as I turned to get in the car and go back to my hotel.

Good one, Jesus! I snapped in my thoughts. I lectured Jesus silently the whole way back to the hotel, and I asked him not to pull that on me anymore. It was too intense. Jesus never did.

Back at the hotel I flopped on the bed and kicked my shoes across the room, and I called home to talk to my in-laws. I asked if it looked like the camera added five pounds or if I sounded like a loony person, and they just kept telling me that it went great and that the kids were doing fine. They suggested that I enjoy the rest of the morning in New York.

I thought maybe I should sleep, but then decided maybe I should stay awake. Time is short, I thought,

30 Days Ago

why sleep any more? Stay up, take it in! I changed into jeans and a sweater and my sneakers and decided to check out New York. My husband and I were scheduled to leave on a five-twenty-four plane, so I had a few hours to explore. I seemed to be in a safe part of town, so when in New York....I walked. I walked for blocks and blocks. I stopped for lunch at a tiny café, and ate like I was starving.

The city was amazing. I had never seen so many people at one time. People everywhere. I imagined it would look like an anthill from above, little humans streaming in lines through the city. I thought about ants, hard workers, those little guys, and I wondered what would happen to them when Jesus came.

I didn't get back to the hotel until nearly two-forty-five and I met my husband coming through the glass doors. His meeting was over and it had been a good one until after lunch, when an office assistant mentioned that he had seen me on AMerica. He had asked if I was related to my husband, which sent the rest of the meeting off course, until they adjourned with a "good-enough" attitude for the day. My husband admitted he was slightly embarrassed about the whole thing, but only because it was his hang-up, not mine. I appreciated the humility. When we got back to the room, the message light was blinking on the phone.

It was an urgent message from the producers of the *Here's Hope Show*, asking me to return their call as soon as possible. The *Here's Hope Show* was an extremely popular daytime talk show that had been airing for many years. The host, Hope Winfield, was a self-made woman who brought important issues to the public, particularly issues that interested women, but also other ethical and moral issues that concerned humankind. She interviewed guests without bias, always ending her program with the words, "That's all for today, but remember, there's always Hope for tomorrow," which was both self-promoting and reassuring. She knew how to appeal to both the intellect and the emotions. She was the queen of daytime television.

I dialed the number they left, and the person on the other end asked if they could put me on a plane to Chicago so that I could be a guest on the *Here's Hope Show* the next day. This is getting out of hand, I thought. This is not me. I really don't want to keep doing this. I did my part, now I just want to go home and wait.

But my husband reminded me of the enormous impact that the *Here's Hope Show* had, not only on our own country, but around the world, and that maybe it was my duty. I knew he was right. I just didn't know if I could do the pumpkin thing again.

My husband called home, checked on his parents, and told me all was well on the home front. He said that he would go with me to Chicago, and it would all be over by tomorrow at this time. That didn't sound so terrible, so I called the producer back and they arranged for a flight from LaGuardia to O'Hare, leaving at five after five. We threw our things into the suitcases, hailed a taxi, and the driver, probably from some African nation, drove us back to the airport, speaking of dreams, faith, and hope the whole way. Déjà vu swept over me.

29 Days Ago

The *Here's Hope Show* is taped in front of a live audience, but at least there was the possibility of editing since the show was prerecorded. I didn't have to worry about having powdered donut on my face or a coughing spell. These things could be edited and the show would appear smooth as glass. The problem was that I knew Hope Winfield's guests were typically on for more than the four minutes that I had been on AMerica, and often there was only one guest for the whole hour. This was a frightening thought that hadn't occurred to me earlier, and I started to do the nausea wave again.

Chicago was a nice city, but the traffic was intolerable to me. I liked, as in New York, the scenes of people out walking. Dressed for the weather and walking. These cities were alive and had a hip feel to them. I imagined living in downtown Chicago and how my life would be different. There would be more crime and locking of possessions. More suspicion of neighbors. But I would walk to stores and we would go as a family to more parks and art shows and concerts, which are so accessible in downtown Chicago. There would be more diversity in the schools and in the neighborhoods. We would take public transportation, which was practically nonexistent back home in the suburbs. We would be a more cultured, more current family of the new millennium, but we also would not have the trees out our windows and the patio overlooking the swing set in our own yard where the neighborhood kids come and play together. I spent some time debating internally which lifestyle would be most appealing, should it turn out that reincarnation is an option.

We arrived at the studio in the morning. This time my husband accompanied me to the studio and was with me as I was prepped. Having him around was definitely helpful. I could not have been alone for a second, leaving me with my mind to do those terrible things that it does to me. My husband, knowing me well, would start talking about something random like why coffee stirrers have a seam in the middle, and I was able to delay the dread with inane banter.

I found out that I was not the only guest for the day. I was sharing the show with a man who had written a book on apocalyptic thinking and trends. I was worried that he would be critical of my story, since end-of-the-world scares have come and gone for as long as I could remember. But I met the author, and he was intelligent and approached the subject from a factual point of view. He did not cast judgment on any groups. He just explained how people arrived at their conclusions and where those people are now. Some of his examples were of cults that had suicide pacts to "get out" together, only to find out the rest of us didn't go anywhere. Other examples were individuals who had been able to be fairly influential in the public domain, but what happened to them when the date in question had passed made me feel

29 Days Ago

sick. They were criticized mercilessly, before being completely forgotten.

He spoke with me in the guest waiting room for a long time about my "vision," and I never felt like he thought I was hallucinating or out of my mind. He took a few notes as we spoke. I wondered if he would want to be headlining his next book with my story, but I knew there would not be a next book. I was relieved to find that no famed psychologists would be on the show. I really didn't want a public psychiatric evaluation.

Showtime. I had packed a flask of Kahlua in my purse and took a small shot before walking out onto the stage. Kahlua, I suspected, would take that shaky edge off, and I was hoping to smell more of coffee than liquor.

Hope Winfield was beautiful and gracious and glowing. It was weird to have an audience clap for me as I was introduced. Most of them had never heard of me, since this whole issue had just developed over the past few days, but they were swept up in the tone of the show, and they applauded. Or maybe there were "applause" signs that they obediently followed. At any rate, I was not used to a celebrity welcome, and I felt unworthy.

The interview went along as most had, and I soon found myself at ease and in the familiar position of being quizzed about the whole experience. I explained everything again from the point of my father's death, to the visit from the stranger in the orange Volkswagen, to his unusual revelation and outrageous request from me. I described the signs that I had made and the climbing of the buildings, at which time a large screen appeared be-

Coming

hind us, and a video from the news helicopters showed the boys rappelling down the building, waving by the signs they had hung slightly crookedly. I told the audience of my reluctance to be the one with this mission. I said that I had just come up with this crazy plan on my own, that I had used the climbers as pawns, but that it seemed to be getting the word out. I admitted that I did not know anything about this global dream event, and that I did get feelings of panic that the whole thing was too crazy to really happen. We broke for commercial after commercial, and as the show went on, the commercials came at breakneck speed.

My husband, who had been given a front-row seat, was asked by Hope how he felt about the whole thing. He visibly squirmed in his seat, smiled, cleared his throat, then calmly said that he had known me for a long, long time, and that anything I say, I mean, and that anything I do, I do well, and he would always support me. The women of the audience exploded with a collective sigh of admiration and applauded furiously.

Hope asked me about the non-Christians of the world. She wondered what they would think of Jesus' coming. I told her that Jesus had never mentioned religion to me. He only spoke of love. He seemed to me to be love incarnate. I told her that I had the impression that he connects with anyone, no matter which religion, as long as they lived with the light in their soul shining. Commercial.

As it turned out, the other guest only had about eight minutes to talk about his book and the show concluded with me and about five minutes of my summation. Hope

29 Days Ago

asked me, "So, if you've heard from Jesus himself, what is the solution for our troubled world?"

I pondered briefly, then replied with confidence, "The only thing I know for sure is that the solution is always *love*."

"Very nice...beautiful," Hope agreed.

I really wanted to take credit for that line, but I just smiled.

"So what do you think we are all supposed to be doing right now?" she asked, perplexed.

I spoke with authority, without hesitation, asking individuals to be honest in all things and compassionate. I asked them to believe in their own beauty and to look for the beauty in others. I said that anyone who could harm or take the life of another would have a difficult time justifying it in the end. Then, building up a head of steam, I lashed out at our government. I said that unless it was able to be moral, protecting life, protecting workers, supporting families, strengthening our communities, and healing the environment, politicians were culpable of severe mishandling of our human and natural resources. I ranted that the wealthy needed to stop using their money to influence governments for their own interests, and should instead use their money to help those who are so desperately poor. The government did not need to be everything to everyone...we certainly could help each other on our own without being legislated to do so.

I chastised foreign governments for hoarding charitable donations and letting their own people suffer, saying they would have to answer for this. I ended with the guarantee that it was not too late...that today people

Coming

could do a one-eighty and change their lives and begin living in The Way of peace. I said that if most of us turned together, the world could turn upside down, and the evil could shake right out.

The room burst into applause, and I could feel my face heating up and prayed that it would not be bright red. I lowered my head and breathed deeply, trying to hide from the camera. As the program ended, Hope gave me a hug, and I told her how impressed I was with her generosity and ability to bring important issues to the public's attention. She told me that she was always learning and trying to do her best, and I guaranteed her that that is all God expects of any of us.

We left Chicago as quickly as we could. I had had enough of interviews and fame and just wanted to be back home with my family. A flight attendant on the airplane recognized me from the AMerica interview and really did not have too much comment. After the acknowledgment that I was 'that lady,' the subject did not come up again for the rest of the flight, and I was treated as anyone else. I thought I had wanted to be left alone, but I also wanted my news to explode within people. This reaction of indifference was too similar to the reaction to everything going on in this world. I wanted to see passion. Relief and disappointment vied for my attention all the way home.

Our reunion with the children was filled with great joy. You would think we had been gone a month, and I felt as though we had crammed a month into two days. After reviewing the trip with the in-laws, they, too, seemed anxious to go home. When they left, we ordered Chinese carry-out for dinner, and we promised not to

29 Days Ago

answer the phone or the door for the rest of the evening. This time was ours. We were going to try to be normal.

The children had seen a recording of AMerica, so we talked about that and New York and what it would be like to live in a big city. The kids told me how school was going, and I asked if friends were talking about me and how they could handle certain situations and comments. Then we played board games and laughed and ate popcorn.

My youngest daughter bit a hard kernel, and her first baby tooth came out, bloody spittle seeping from her mouth. She was ecstatic! Her first tooth. She ran to the desk and got an envelope and, after washing the tooth as clean as it could get, she slipped it into the envelope and sealed it and ran upstairs to put it under her pillow for the Tooth Fairy. That, we decided, was a good time for us all to go to bed, and I kissed each of my sweet children goodnight. My baby's face was gleaming with joy at her newfound maturity. It was glorious to be home and to be a mom.

~ 28 Days Ago ~

I felt like I had a normal life for a few hours. My family went about their business of school and work, and the phone was silent. Unusually silent. Deafeningly silent. I had gotten used to the constant ringing and had such pat answers ready that I was no longer intimidated by calls from friends, acquaintances, media…you name it, I was ready for them.

But the silence was weird. I was not ready for that at all. I began to think that everyone had heard enough. The novelty had worn off. Business as usual for everyone. After all, it was that way for my family, why would I expect everyone else to stop their lives and flock to me? That's all it took. A hint of self-doubt. A pinch of self-loathing. The floodgates were open.

All morning I questioned what I had been saying to the press and to my friends. Would I lose everyone I had ever loved over this crazy mess? Would people stand by me? Maybe I really was losing it. I really didn't know much about intense and sudden grief. Maybe I did have some sort of hallucination. Oh, God. Did I make this whole thing up? Panic swept through me. I could actually feel the tingling of terror. My body began to ache. I curled my knees up to my chest and cradled them with

28 Days Ago

my arms and, dropping my head, I began to cry. Sitting on a window seat in the kitchen I began to rock and ask myself, what have I done? What am I doing? What have I been saying? Who am I, thinking I am some sort of modern-day prophet. Oh my God, how have I embarrassed my family? I have to get counseling.

"Jesus!" I cried out. "Jesus, I need you now. Come on, show your face to me. I need to know you're real. I'm dying here. Please, come hold me." I waited and sobbed. "If you come now, I will know that you are real. I will totally believe and never doubt. If you don't come, I'm afraid I am not who you thought I was. I cannot do this. I'm the wrong choice. Pick someone else."

The kitchen door blew open several inches and then stopped. I swung my head around to see Jesus walk through. I waited. I breathed so hard it hurt my lungs. Tears were still streaking down my cheeks. I waited.

Damn it, was that just the wind?

"Jesus, where are you?" I yelled as I closed the door. I didn't care if the neighbors heard me. They obviously thought I was crazy already. "Please don't leave me here with my fears. I can't do it. I don't want to do it anymore. Please, I'm done. Find someone else. I'm sorry!" I said aloud to Jesus as if he were there. But he wasn't. The kitchen was quiet. The whole house was quiet. The neighborhood was quiet. The entire, absurd world was quiet and I was about to lose my mind with the power of a nuclear explosion.

I took a deep breath again and fell back into a kitchen chair. I closed my eyes and breathed, and when I opened them, I noticed it was noon. I could not eat lunch. I felt like I was about to have diarrhea. But I did

Coming

slowly get up and make myself a cup of tea in the microwave. Totally drained, I walked like a zombie into the family room and turned on the noon news.

Oh no, I sighed as I heard the lead story, regret pulsing through my veins. The news was showing a video that someone had constructed and apparently posted on the Internet. I caught most of the video, which started with a clip of me speaking of Jesus' coming from the AMerica interview. Then it cut away to the kids hanging the signs on the buildings and dancing on the ground for the cameras. But with some grunge song about the devil playing as a soundtrack, it looked as if the kids were performing some sort of satanic ritual. Then, when it cut back to an interview with me from a local news station, small knobby horns grew from the image of my head as I spoke. My face gradually reddened and then morphed into a hideous demonic countenance, just as I was saying something about how I wasn't sure that hell was a *place* so much as physical and emotional separation from God. My voice was lowered into an unnatural timbre, as is done digitally with victims who don't want to be identified on television. Then my head filled the screen, and a digitally manipulated evil laugh that would have made the devil himself inflate with pride spewed out of me. Finally, the following words scrolled across my distorted face in bold letters: **Only the Antichrist would try to make you believe there is no hell. Beware of false prophets!** The screaming distorted soundtrack that closed out the video must be the theme song in hell, I thought, if hell did indeed exist.

The newscaster reported that this was among the top-viewed videos on social networking sites and had

28 Days Ago

hundreds of thousands of hits already. It was sponsored by the extreme Christian fundamentalist group "Glory To God," or "G2G" as they were more popularly known.

I was familiar with G2G. They were an enormous Bible-based enterprise with television programming, radio programming and huge praise conventions. I went to a praise convention once out of curiosity. They seemed to be focused on being saved for the afterlife, but not so much guidance was given on how to reach out and save each other from despair and domination in this life. And they portrayed a God who was judgmental, whereas I hoped for a God who was quick to forgive. So I never paid much more attention to their activities or their evangelizing. I figured that there were many paths to God, and I had chosen a different one from them. Did they have to soil my path?

With an enthusiastic tone and overly eager smile, the newscaster commented on the wonders of Internet tools that could manipulate just about any image until it was difficult to discern whether it was real or not, and acted as if the video was otherwise unimportant.

Unimportant! That was the worst news possible. I was already feeling vulnerable, but now I felt as if I were being totally manipulated. What had I done? I had spent nearly two weeks investing all my energy into promoting the coming of Jesus, only to find myself touted as the Antichrist. What went wrong? I began to tremble and nearly vomited. I changed the channel as if that would delete what I had just seen.

A noted theologian was being interviewed on Channel 6, also regarding the claims I had made nationally on AMerica. I held my breath. The interview was already in progress, and I grabbed the remote and clicked up the volume about twelve times. I listened as I walked over to the family room door, then watched the television with one foot pointed toward the bathroom.

"Of course, people over the centuries have proclaimed visions of Jesus, while others have made proclamations of end times," the theologian was saying. He continued, "What makes this situation different, is that this woman claims to have seen Jesus, to have seen her deceased father, and that the message from Jesus is that the end times are coming, but she does not give us a date. Most self-proclaimed prophets give a date. The so-called dream that she claims Jesus said each of us will have will be the telling part. If that does indeed happen, there will be no denying the dream is from God. Something that unusual could not happen without supernatural power. Time will tell. Although I will say that it is not unusual for God to speak to us in our dreams. In the Old Testament, it was common for people to attribute the wisdom of dreams to God. The Bible tells the story in Genesis of Jacob wrestling with an angel, as in a dream. And in the New Testament, angels delivered important information through dreams. However, dreams can be enigmatic, as are parables of the New Testament. God apparently does not like to just feed us answers. God likes us to wrestle with them and discover solutions for ourselves. Then we tend to remember the lesson better."

"So you believe that this could, indeed, be the end times?" the commentator asked.

"I think," said the theologian, "that we are called to live as if it is always the end times. Why cram for a final exam, when you can learn all along the way? Jesus told us to be ready, that we do not know the hour when he will return. So whether the hour is now or in five thousand years, we must be ready, and make life matter."

"On that note, Reverend, thank you for joining us this afternoon. And coming up, a peek at what the weekend weather has in store for us."

I pressed the remote, the television blackened, and I moved back to the couch and sat silently, staring at the blank screen. His words were soothing to my soul. I noticed I was no longer trembling, my brow no longer furrowed.

Okay, I thought, I'm not crazy. Maybe someone thinks I am evil, but I'm not crazy. Some people are taking this seriously. People are thinking. If that's all I do - make people think - then that's probably a good start. People have to think. Think about how they're living. Think about how they're degrading, devouring, destroying each other and all of creation.

I went to my stereo and put on Aretha Franklin's "Think." Immediately, I felt fantastic. I sang at the top of my lungs as I danced around my family room. I laughed, and I danced myself into a squat, then jumped up again, arms waving in the air as I sang out about freedom. You know, crazy has its benefits. I felt crazy and free.

When the song ended I collapsed onto the couch, out of breath and out of fear and, again, content to see where the whole adventure would take me. I no longer thought I was insane. I knew my visions were real and I felt strength like Aretha's voice in my veins. Jesus was with me. I knew he was. I could almost feel him looking at me. I could almost hear him laughing at my song-and-

Coming

dance routine. Jesus lived in a strong black woman named Aretha. I loved him and knew I didn't have to try to hide anything from him. Freedom.

The rest of the day continued as would be expected. The phone began ringing and I was back in my element. I talked on the phone all afternoon to my cousin, then my neighbor's mother, then a guy I used to work with ten years ago, then my mom, then a receptionist at the dentist's office (confirming my check-up appointment). When the kids came home from school, I unplugged the phone while I found out about their day. There is nothing like undivided attention. Real listening. True love. It was fantastic.

After dinner my husband told me he had had a rough day at work trying to answer questions that should have been directed to me. Poor guy. He was not properly armed. He didn't see Jesus, feel him, hear him. He had only heard my version, which lost a bit of punch in the translation, I'm sure. It is easy to trip someone up who is not one hundred percent positive.

We came up with a single phrase that he could use the next time anyone asked him anything about the antics of his wife. We decided he would simply reply, "You said it!" which is a wonderful expression when wanting to confirm and deny something at the same time. We laughed as we imagined the scenarios.

"Was that your wife with the kids on the buildings?"
"You said it!"
"Did your wife really see Jesus?"
"You said it!"
"Your wife is crazy."
"You said it!"

28 Days Ago

He felt better and we watched news programs and talk shows all evening, critiquing the comments, laughing at the jokes about me on late night TV and finally heading to bed. Strange day. Crazy life.

27 Days Ago

Saturday. Doesn't everyone love Saturday? It was a beautiful, sunny day. The temperature could barely be felt against my skin as I walked outside to get the morning paper. Only when a light breeze blew, did I feel the soft touch of air. It was unusually warm for February and a welcome break from the cold winter days. I felt humidity in the air. Spring, it seemed, was right around the corner. I decided to read the paper on my patio and enjoy my coffee with my husband while the children slept in. I did change from my pajamas to some sweatpants and a lightweight, long-sleeved shirt, just in case some visitors started early. We got our coffee and a bowl of strawberries and headed out to the patio.

There, to my surprise, on the front page, was a photograph of the sign that I had made, hanging from the tallest building. I thought the local media hoopla had blown over. The photo was a close-up shot, so much so that I almost didn't recognize it as my sign. The focus was on the little pink flourish I had added to soften the picture, that pretty little doodad that now looked like random squiggles. The doodad now looked more like this: กรุณา. The headline read,

"KARUNA: Is Jesus Buddhist?"

27 Days Ago

That got my attention. When I was little, I assumed Jesus was Christian. As I got older, I realized Christians were people who followed Jesus, but Jesus himself was Jewish. But Buddhist? I never considered Buddhist. I wasn't really sure what Buddhists believed. I'd never heard of the word *karuna*. I could not read fast enough. I read aloud as my husband listened intently.

Apparently, Thai Buddhists from around the country and the world noticed the word *karuna* on my sign. It was written in Thai and means "compassion." My heart pounded as I recalled my first conversations with Jesus when he had defined love as compassion. He had used that word *compassion* often. The article continued. Karuna is a universal concept in all Buddhist sects and there was a controversy as to how this Thai word got onto the signs made by a Christian woman in a non-Buddhist community. In fact, there were no Thai Buddhist temples anywhere in the area, as far as I knew, and my husband and I discussed if we knew anyone at all who was a practicing Buddhist. I read on swiftly.

"Karuna," the article stated, "means compassionate action. It is the diminishing of suffering of others and is the complement to wisdom. With enlightenment comes the understanding that we are all one, and therefore, with wisdom, we alleviate the suffering of all indiscriminately, Buddhists believe." Again, I recalled Jesus speaking of the connectedness in heaven and feeling God's energy throughout. Is this what the Buddhists are trying to accomplish? Was this the same thing, I wondered.

The fact that the Thai word for compassion was on the sign hanging on the building that got most of the publicity, the one where the climbers got caught in the act, raised some eyebrows in the Buddhist community. Why was this word on this sign? Did Jesus direct this woman to paint *karuna* on the sign? The sign said "Everyone will have a dream. Everyone. Same dream. Pay attention." Then there was the word *karuna*. Was that a sign? Would that be the dream? Would that be the message of God? The Buddhists agreed that karuna is central to restorative human interaction. The article had comments by Buddhist priests and lay believers of many traditions. Consultations and speculations. It knocked my socks off.

I recalled a favorite quote from my college American Lit class. It was from a poem by Emily Dickinson that stated, "The truth must dazzle gradually or every man be blind." I sat in wonder of universal truths that I had been ignorant of all my life, now gradually enlightening me.

My husband asked me about my little flourish and I assured him that I just meant to put a little flair at the bottom of the sign because the big block letters looked so hard. He called me "a girl."

I read on in a related article about auras. The article explained that an aura is the energy field that is believed to radiate from all living things. Auras are sometimes seen with the naked eye, although scientific testing has yet to provide reproducible results. Apparently the pink karuna had cast a pink light over the sign as the helicopters circled and shined their spotlights. An aura, the article explained, is the result of all of the chakrik colors combining in and around a person. "Chakra" is the Sanskrit word for wheel or circle. In Hinduism it is believed that there are seven chakras in the human body and they

27 Days Ago

line up from the top of the head to the base of the torso. The chakras are believed to be the source of our vital energy, linking the energy of the cosmos with organs and emotions and colors as they spin. Pink, the article said, is the aural color for compassion. I looked up from the newspaper at my husband and gave him a "Who knew?" look. Pink auras emit feelings of love, compassion and purity. Pink can also reflect times of new vision or new love, we learned from the newspaper.

Compassion. New vision. New love. Energy. I put the paper down. "Are people reading too much into this?" I asked my husband. We continued to discuss whether it had been an accident or some sort of divine meddling. If God wanted to orchestrate that, what else has God orchestrated in our lives that we thought were little coincidences? We bantered back and forth between the whole divine-plan versus random-living argument. We were both more confused than ever with the presence of the word karuna and the aura. It made us laugh and scream at the unobtrusive ways of God. Why does God have to be so mysterious, I wondered. Wouldn't life have been much easier if God didn't talk to us in dreams and parables…just lay it on the line and stop the guesswork. It was exhausting.

Apparently everyone in my town was on basically the same schedule, because within ten minutes my neighbor leaned over the fence and, upon seeing us reading the paper, asked my interpretation of karuna. As I spoke, the phone rang in the kitchen, and my dear husband got up to get it, shaking his head in disappointment with the interruptions of an otherwise beautiful morning. The phone was for me. Big surprise.

Coming

As I talked on the phone with the fourth person of the morning, my husband got breakfast for the kids and decided to take them for a hike since it was such a beautiful day. I placed my hand over the receiver, and I asked him to take them to the zoo again instead, so that I could meet up with them when I got finished with all the calls. We discussed our meeting time and place, and as I returned to my conversation on the phone with apologies, my husband and I both knew that I would never get off the phone and join the family.

Sure enough, I talked all day, either on the phone or with people at the door. At one point, there were fourteen miscellaneous people in my living room, getting into a heated discussion about dreams, Buddhism, auras, baseball and politics. I heard only snippets of several different conversations as I floated through the room from door to phone to guest and back again. Who needs to go to the zoo? I had my own zoo right in my own house.

As I was speaking to a rabbi about finding strength in common ground, a crash of glass shattered the peaceful gathering. One woman screamed, more from being startled, but a small piece of glass had grazed her arm, drawing blood. Shards of glass scattered across the living room carpet, and people instinctively backed away. The culprit was a rock wrapped in paper, held tightly by a rubber band. We all just stared for a few moments at the rock, as if waiting for it to read the message to us by itself. Finally, a young man of twenty or so leaned down and picked up the paper with his winter gloves still on. Smart, I thought. We had all seen enough crime shows to know that you never disturb the evidence. The young

27 Days Ago

man pulled a pencil out of his pocket and gently pulled the rubber band away, releasing it without ripping the paper. He must have been a professional crime-show watcher. He opened the paper as the crowd in the room held their collective breath.

He quickly read it to himself, then, looking around the room, made eye contact with me and held it out for me to read. I didn't have gloves on. I didn't want to touch it. I was stuck between the perverse desire to hear bad news and the rational desire to throw the rock back out the window so that it would not ruin the peaceful gathering in my house. The perverse desire won, as it nearly always does, and I asked the rabbi to read the letter aloud.

He slowly pulled some reading glasses from his breast pocket and, leaning in toward the letter that the young man was still holding, read, "*Only the Bible contains the truth. The book of Revelation holds the Good News. Anything else is false. We will stop you as swiftly as we pray for you.*"

"Call the police," the rabbi calmly said and cell phones flipped open all around me.

"I already got 'em on the line," one take-charge woman said.

The police were in front of the house literally within seconds, and I could see some sort of scuffle going on out the window. Avoiding the glass on the floor, people in the house rushed to the front door to find the police interviewing a few people in the yard. As a second, then third police car arrived, four or five men tried making a run down the block but were chased down by the police and wrestled to the ground. Some bystanders were gathering in small bunches for protection. Others were trying to help in the chase, but were called off by the police.

The whole thing was unsettling. I hated violence, and I had never in my life seen it in my own yard. I thought about the words, "We will stop you" and I worried about what exactly was meant by that. Did I need to fear for my life? Or would they just prevent me from going on the news again until the whole thing blew over. People who employ nonviolent tactics typically do not throw rocks, I realized, and I decided that maybe I should fear for my life.

I couldn't believe this was happening. I doubted that the fundamentalist G2G group was behind this. As far as I knew they never promoted violence. But exclusionary teachings can be appealing to unstable individuals who seem to embrace extremes.

Trembling, I went to the broom closet and grabbed the vacuum to clean up the broken glass. A few other women came over and helped me, while the rest of my uninvited guests spilled out into the yard to join the spectacle. I threw away the larger pieces of glass and smiled as I vacuumed up the small splinters, realizing as my vacuum handle neared the window that the broken pane was the same one that my husband had finally fixed the other day.

The police were aware of my new celebrity status, and I'm sure they had seen the Internet video. They confiscated the rock, the rubber band, and the note from the young man, slipped it into a plastic bag and said that they believed that they had the perpetrators, and we had nothing else to worry about. I truly tried not to worry.

27 Days Ago

But trying not to worry was as successful as trying not to remember my own name.

People slowly filtered back into the house, and we resumed our conversation, now with a bit more tension in the air. The volume in the room was higher, the phone continued to ring, and the crowd swelled both in the yard and in the house. But I insisted on keeping the focus of conversation on the coming of Jesus and not the violence of man. Someone was kind enough to duct tape a piece of cardboard over the broken window pane.

When my family returned, it did not occur to people to give us some space. People from as far away as one hundred twenty miles showed up at my door, hearing that I was a prophet and wanting me to impart my wisdom to them. I had a group of twenty or so in the front yard now saying the rosary together in hushed tones, respecting our privacy and being careful not to block others from coming or going. My kids went down to the basement to play, after trying to fill me in on their 'super-fun' day. I resented not being with them and did not particularly like the sacrifice. I was a rotten prophet.

My husband saw the broken window and looked at me across the room with a face of disbelief. I was in the middle of a conversation with two people, but when I saw his expression I covered my mouth with my hands to hide my smile. Fear for my own safety vanished with such an unfortunate twist of fate for the window. I started laughing and could not stop. I mouthed the word 'sorry' to him and blew him a kiss across the room. He went to the closet and put his coat back on and I knew he was heading back to the hardware store. Although I wouldn't blame him if he walked out the door and never

Coming

came back. Things had gotten out of control in our happy little home.

At dinnertime, more people arrived with hams and food, well-meaning neighbors who had just gone through the meal-making motions for me when my dad died. And here they were at my service again. They didn't ask if I needed help. They knew. They were amazing people, extremely generous. Compassionate. Karuna, I thought.

I laid the food out on the table, and people grazed as they mingled, and my house swelled to capacity; some people praying aloud, some arguing, most questioning. What? When? How? Why? Who? I had few answers, really, but I had all the same questions. The only difference was that I was not afraid, as I could tell most of them were. They weren't panicking. They just had an undercurrent of the fear of the unknown.

The kids sneaked dinner down to the basement, which was usually forbidden, and I could tell by the looks on their faces they were trying to get away with something. I had neither the energy nor the desire to reprimand them about something so trivial. I became lost in my thoughts, wondering what other trivial things I had distorted to a level of supreme importance with the children. Had I taught them what is most critical in life? Or maybe the main lesson they had learned was to keep their rooms clean. I felt an overwhelming sense of dread as I thought of my dear children totally off the track, cruising through fields of pettiness. I excused myself from a conversation and slipped into the basement.

The kids saw me coming down the steps and I could hear them hiding plates of chicken wings and cans of

27 Days Ago

soda. "Don't worry about it, guys," I said. "I really don't care today about food in the basement. Come sit with me and tell me more about your super fun day." They talked, and I listened, and they talked some more. We turned on a video and began watching together as we sat in a pile on the couch until we all fell asleep.

Dreaming of people grabbing me and pulling me, I tried to pull loose, reclaiming my own arm, now being tugged upon. The jolt awakened me to my husband shaking my arm in an effort to arouse me. He was dressed, with his coat on. I had no idea what time it was. The kids that had piled around me were gone.

"Honey, I'm taking the kids to my parents' house," he said calmly.

"You're what?" I asked, pushing my hair back out of my face, yawning.

"I'm leaving."

"What time is it?" I queried.

"About eleven."

I really didn't know if it was morning or evening, and being in a dark basement gave me no frame of reference.

"Where are the kids?" I asked, still trying to buy a clue as to what was going on.

"The kids are fine, they're in the car. Things are just getting a little too crazy around here."

Finally I realized what was happening. It was nighttime, and he had made a clandestine plan to sneak out before I was awake enough to protest.

"No, don't go. We'll be okay. Jesus will watch over us and protect us, and we'll be safe," I said with total faith in my vision.

Coming

"It's been two weeks since all this started. Our life has been turned upside down. You've spent the night in jail. Our home is no longer our own. There are death threats and vandalism against us. And still you hang on to your story. Good for you, but I just can't. There's been no dream. I don't have any encouragement from anyone but you that this whole thing is real. People at work think you're a head case."

"They think I'm a head case?" I protested, knowing that his speech was making perfect sense and yet, I was not crazy. I had a vision. I could not back down from my mission.

"Sorry, I shouldn't have said that," he spoke calmly, "but I can't get any work done. I'm embarrassed to even show up."

I had feared that he couldn't hang on too long to my tenuous story, but I never *really* thought he would leave. He had always been a good sport. He even said on national television that he supported me. He couldn't leave me now. How would anyone believe me if my own family abandoned me? I couldn't go on without his support.

Ah, that was the problem, I realized. I had taken him and his loving support for granted. I wrapped my arms around him to tell him how much I loved him. He peeled my arms off, and, ducking under my embrace, he stood up and said, "Good-bye." Just like that.

"No, honey, we can work it out," I started to beg.

"Not me. I think the kids and I need to give you some space to work out your own stuff. When you're ready to let go of this little project you have, give me a call," he said, now with a tone that was more biting.

27 Days Ago

"Come on, you know I didn't make this stuff up. Why would I do that?"

"Maybe your life was getting a little dull. Kids in school all day. Nothing but time to conjure up a little excitement."

"How dare you! I work my tail off all day long while you are at work, and the kids are at school, and I don't get any performance evaluation, which would be stellar, if I do say so myself. But no, that doesn't happen. But do I complain? No, I think my job as mother is the most important job in the world, so I just do it," I said, getting indignant.

"That's what I'm talking about. Maybe you snapped. Hard work, no pay. I respect what you do all day, I really do. But I think you must need something else in your life. I feel like you just didn't get enough recognition, so here we are. A total circus. With you in the center ring, all spotlights on you."

"Okay," I said with resignation. "I see what you're thinking. I'm sure everyone is thinking the same, and I have to admit, I've questioned myself over and over to make sure I wasn't hallucinating. Just go. You'll see, and then you'll be sorry for abandoning me just when I need you the most! Go ahead. Take the kids and go. You'll be sorry!" I screamed through tears and threw the couch pillow at him as he turned to leave. And the worst part…he didn't even turn the slightest bit as the pillow hit the back of his head, as if he were accustomed to being assaulted by me. This was a disaster. Totally uncharacteristic. We had the perfect marriage.

I heard the front door close, and my reality made a complete shift. My husband had left me. My family was

Coming

falling apart. If this whole thing was a hallucination, I would definitely end up divorced, and it would be impossible for me to get custody of my children. I began to shake like a leaf. I couldn't catch my breath. I screamed at the top of my lungs for God to save me. Nothing.

~ 26 Days Ago ~

I rolled over and shook my hand furiously, trying to restore blood flow, and realized it was the only part of me that had slept soundly. Still in the basement, I had tossed and turned and sobbed and kicked and prayed and cried some more. I think I had finally slept for about an hour and a half when my buzzing arm woke me. I dragged myself upstairs. I called to my husband. No answer.

He must have cleaned up the mess in the house and shut the door on the last visitor while the kids and I were asleep in the basement. Before he smuggled them out, the jerk. I called each of the kids. Nothing. He really took them, I thought. Unbelievable. Now what am I supposed to do? I can't face the public anymore. How embarrassing that I can't even keep my own family together.

I checked the time and realized it was time for church. Church. I didn't want to go to church. We always went as a family. Talk about having a spotlight on me. Everyone would know my very personal agony before the priest reached the altar.

I sat down and cried some more. I could stay home and pray. After all, church is not the only place you find

God. God would understand. I would spend a full hour, just like church, in private prayer, I rationalized. I took a deep breath and leaned back in my chair to pray. I cleared my head as Jesus had taught me so that I could catch the thoughts of God. I realized I had done plenty of talking to God in the last eight hours. Time for me to be still and listen. Prayer was, after all, supposed to be a conversation.

Within a minute of being still, I felt as though I should get up and go to church. But I'm praying here, I argued with my own consciousness. Go, would pop back into my head. No, I'm safer and better off here today, I argued with what I thought was my own ego.

Go.

Suddenly, I realized that nudge of which Jesus had spoken. And this was stronger than a nudge. It was completely disrupting my contemplation. It was a direct order, and I was overwhelmingly frustrated that God could not cooperate with me on my own plan. All right, you win, I thought, and I got up to go to church.

Now it was getting late, and I had to hustle to get to church on time. For some reason my wardrobe took on inflated importance, and I tossed clothes around my room, dressing and redressing as if I were in a Macy's fitting room. Finally I emerged, dressed, hair combed, teeth brushed, huge bags still hanging under my eyes from crying, with hunger building. I frantically looked for the keys to the van in the key basket, but couldn't find them. Then I realized my husband had taken the van the night before, the jerk. Taking a big breath to push the tears aside, I grabbed the keys to his car and flew to church.

26 Days Ago

I slipped into a pew in the back of church. Suddenly I had to go to the bathroom and slipped right back out and went to the restroom. Sitting on the toilet I discovered that my shoes did not match. They were both brown slip-ons, but a mismatched pair, and I considered going right back home. Instead, however, I sulked back to my seat and tucked my feet under the kneeler.

Throughout the Mass, several heads turned my way and smiled and nodded, and I wondered what they were thinking. I'm sure they were full of questions: "Where's her family?" "Why did Jesus pick her?" "What's with the bags under the eyes?" "Does she know her tag's sticking out in the back?" I reached to the back of my neck to check the tag of my dress. I tried to pay attention, I really did. But I was so preoccupied. My full attention was being given to what I would say to people about the absence of my family or about the presence of Jesus.

I really didn't want to get into any of those conversations. I had given up my whole day previously, and I wanted to spend this day with my family. I recalled Jesus telling me that we must get what we need, but also make sure everyone else has what they need. Love was a delicate balance, he had said. I spent the majority of Mass trying to decide how to get what I needed, which was time with my family to re-energize and feel normal, and how to give others what they needed, which was the information that Jesus had passed on to me.

I weighed each option and the scales would tip from one side to another and back. I was confused and I decided to leave right after Communion. I almost never did that, but I really wanted to sneak out without being barraged with questions or caught with my ridiculous shoe situation. I was truly an awful prophet.

I drove off as people came streaming out of church. "Yes!" I said exuberantly, having avoided the flock. I called my husband on the cell phone as I drove, hoping he would be ready to come home or that at least we could all spend the day together hiking and acting like everything was normal. He didn't pick up, the jerk. I left a message and headed home to change clothes.

As I grabbed some breakfast, I called his parents' house. No answer. I called him again about thirteen times. Voice-mail. Okay, I get it, I thought. He's not ready to reconcile. It hasn't even been twelve hours since he left. I'll give him some space. I can go on a hike by myself, I thought. I'm a big girl.

I felt a little more confident about giving myself what I needed. Then I thought of all of those people in church, like lost sheep, bleating, wandering without direction. But I realized that most of them were probably on their way home to eat and go about their day, cleaning, shopping, napping, or watching basketball. As a whole, we are not lost sheep. We are people of routine who do not wander. We follow our patterns without straying one iota. If we are lost, we are lost together.

I drove about forty-five minutes out of town to a nice trail along the river. I had to clear my mind and just enjoy the beautiful February day. Just feel it and smell it and touch it. I missed my family, but I knew all was in God's hands and that we surely would be together again soon. They needed a break and I really couldn't blame them. I knew my husband was not a jerk. He was a good man caught in the middle of an absurd situation.

26 Days Ago

Despite being alone, or maybe because of it, I had a rich day. I returned at about five in the afternoon only to find, once again, a crowd outside my door. There were more news vans, more rosary-sayers, more gawkers, more hams, and more brownies on the doorstep.

But unbelievably, our family van was pulling up in front of the house. Beaming, I drove up behind it, honking vigorously. People on the lawn probably assumed I was hoping to get their attention. But the only attention I wanted was that of my own family.

I felt great. I was ready to do what I had to do. It was as if I had met God in the bare trees, the rippling creeks, the wild ginger, and the sweet trill of the American goldfinch. I felt empowered. I ran over to the van and jumped in to kiss my husband, and the van was swarmed.

The kids were not in the car. My husband spoke up somewhat sheepishly, "I just stopped to get the kids' backpacks. I thought maybe we'd drive over and see your mom. The kids miss her."

"Sure," I said, trying to hide my disappointment. "Why don't you have dinner with her? She could use the company. Just pizza or something…keep it simple." My disappointment turned to a deep understanding for his position as I looked at the insanity around our van and house.

"I'll go in and get their backpacks," I said. "Wait here."

I was barely able to open my car door. People were grabbing at my jacket and touching my head and messing up my hair. I stepped up onto the floorboard of the

Coming

car so that I might rise above the crowd. I didn't, as I'm rather short, but it somehow emboldened my voice.

"Hi everyone," I said, as if greeting my cousins on Thanksgiving. The crowd quieted. I continued, "I'll be happy to talk to you tonight, but my kids have homework. I'm going to run in and get their backpacks so they can go to Grandma's to do their work in peace. I'll be right out. After my husband leaves, I'll be happy to answer any questions you have, and you're welcome to come in the house. It's getting a little chilly out here. Please, just make a path for me to get to the front door, and I'll be right back."

Just like in the Old Testament, the sea parted, and I was able to jog into the house and quickly look around for everyone's backpack. I made a quick phone call to my mom and asked her if my husband and kids could come by to do homework. I told her they could order carry-out pizza, and she was thrilled to have the company, even though I knew it threw her into a bit of a tizzy. She typically did not do things on the spur of the moment, but since my dad had died, everything had changed for her. Everything. All of her routines, all of her conversations, everything. It was good for her to have the company.

I realized our kitchen was a little messy, but I quickly put things into perspective and ran out to the van with three backpacks and some money for pizza from our "Treat Me" jar. I gave my husband a kiss on the cheek and asked him to give the kids a big kiss and hug for me. He promised me he would, and I knew that I would have to be content with him as my surrogate. As the van

26 Days Ago

pulled away, the nice path in the sea of people closed in, and I was smothered.

People tugged and pulled and yelled and pushed microphones in my face. My hair! Stop messing my hair, I thought angrily. "Stop, wait, hold on, just a minute, give me a second, give me some space." I begged for mercy, but was not heard. I felt a quick adrenaline rush as I thought that someone in the crowd could hurt me, stop me from spreading the word. And I was getting so claustrophobic I had to get some space, no matter what the cost.

Finally, I let out a howl like a coyote. The crowd fell silent. I howled again. The sea parted, and I walked, howling all the way up to my front porch. The crowd stared, waiting to see what the canine prophet would do next. What I did next was laugh.

The crowd, realizing their pack mentality, laughed too. "Okay," I said, "let's be civilized. If you could line up, I'll prop the door open, and one by one, I'll give you each a few minutes to ask me anything you want. I will sit in a chair in my living room and put another chair next to me. When you have the chair, it is your turn, and I will give you my undivided attention. We have some food, and I will make some coffee. I will sit until you have all been seen and are satisfied. I want to thank you for coming and being respectful of me."

I smoothed my hair as I spoke, and people began lining up. I asked a couple of strangers to help me set up the food on the dining room table and the chairs in the living room. I pointed to the coffee maker, and they found coffee in the refrigerator. The crowd seemed to arrange themselves in an orderly fashion. I noticed two

Coming

police cars that had pulled up in front, and saw the officers speaking to some women in the rosary group. Within a few minutes one car pulled away, but another parked, and the two police officers flanked my front door, screening visitors as they entered, which was comforting to me. When all was set up, the two helpful strangers announced that I was ready, and people began buzzing with excitement.

I took my seat in a wingback chair in the living room and through the window I could see people lined up down the block. I could not see the end of the line, but it didn't matter. I was committed. I had gotten what I needed for the day, and I was ready to help others. As it turned out, most of them needed reassurances that the following days would not be scary, but beautiful.

The first to sit beside me was, to my surprise, Father Michael. I hadn't seen him in the crowd outside, but then I had kept my head down most of the time. He just wanted to say a prayer with me, a blessing and a prayer of thanksgiving for my courage. I could strongly feel Jesus' presence moving though him with his loving words. My eyes filled with tears at his compassion for me, and I thanked him. Instinctively, I stood and hugged him and told him he was welcome to sit with me if he wanted. He asked me if I wanted him to keep order, but I told him that I thought the crowd was under control, and he politely nodded to me, grabbed a ham sandwich, and left though the back door.

The next person was visibly shaken, not as composed as Father Michael. Scared to death, really. I had never seen her before and she told me she lived only about fifteen minutes away. She was older than me,

26 Days Ago

maybe in her late fifties, and divorced with grown kids. I could tell she was frightened at the thought of being alone when Jesus came, but I assured her that it would not be a frightening event if she was a good and compassionate person. She feared retribution for her mistakes, and I suggested she apologize to God today for those mistakes and return to love. She was humble and didn't want to take too much of my time, although I could see she wanted to stay longer. We both rose and I hugged her. I didn't really think about it, I just did it. She seemed to need it. Surely we all need it. I held her tightly for half a minute, and I could feel her tension release. I kissed her on the cheek, brushed a tear from her eye with the pad of my thumb, and she left with a sweet smile on her face. I watched her walk towards the back door, and when I turned, there was another man, a reporter, already in the chair next to me. His cameraman knelt alongside.

He was from a small neighborhood paper and had questions regarding the foreign word, *karuna*, and the aura that was reported on in the weekend paper. He wanted my reaction to the Buddhist coverage. He wanted to know if I had intentionally put the Thai word there, or if it was coincidence or some sort of divine intervention. I had given this question much thought and told him that I believed the word for karuna was "of God." He asked me what I meant by that.

I told him that I thought that sometimes people think of God, sitting in some celestial palace, in front of six billion television monitors, each tracking our every move. When God desires, they believe God presses a button and intervenes in our lives. I told the reporter that, instead, I believe God is inside each of us. I believe that God is life-giving and loving and unifying, and that any actions that have these effects on creation are "of God," whether we do them in a prayerful, well-intentioned way, or just haphazardly.

The reporter listened, scribbling notes without looking at me. The camera was focused on me, and the cameraman's light was blinding. I blinked and squinted. The reporter asked a few more questions that had already been covered in all of the papers and interviews. Yet I answered them again, and when he was satisfied, he flipped his notebook closed. He stood and extended his arms to me for a hug, which I happily obliged. As he pulled away, the cameraman turned off his light and camera. He set the camera down and gave me a hug, although I could barely adjust my vision to see him. I nearly got my eye poked out with the toothpick he was twirling in his mouth.

Each person in turn asked me questions of heaven, Jesus, atheism, the Torah, poverty, subtle energy, hell, HIV-AIDS, evangelism, jihad, social justice, adultery, Revelation—you name it, we talked about it. And amazingly, I had a calm answer for every question. It turned out the solution was always "love." I smiled upon remembering Jesus telling me the solution was always "love" and how that had frustrated me. He always means what he says, I recalled.

Each person rose, and we embraced as if drawn together with magnetic force. Each person left seemingly content. I never tired of the conversation. Rather, with each question I felt challenged, and with each answer, I felt more and more assured of God's presence in the

26 Days Ago

room, in the community, in the world. I was on fire, and there was no stopping me.

If the phone rang, I would just ask the person in line nearest the kitchen to grab it and take a message. At one point, the person yelled to me that it was my husband. Suddenly, I was a bit torn. I was fully into serving the needy in my home, but did my husband really need me or did he just want to undermine me? I told the message taker to ask him what he wanted. I could hear the messenger explaining to my husband who she was and what was going on in his house. I smiled at the randomness of the situation. Everyone was so calm and helpful.

"He says the kids want to say 'Good-night'," she yelled above the crowd.

The older woman with whom I was speaking at the time told me to go ahead and get the phone. I nodded to her gratefully, and then I bolted to the phone. I spoke to each of the kids briefly and told them that I loved them and to sleep tight and that they could come home soon. I choked on those words a little bit, but knew inside of me that it must be true. I returned to the woman patiently waiting for my wisdom. She seemed to be able to tell that I was a bit shaken and rather than me continuing with my abounding wisdom, she whispered in my ear, "Hang in there, dear, it will all be just fine." *She* hugged *me* and smiled, and I absolutely knew she was right.

Who was she? What did she know? Who planted her in the house at this moment, I wondered suspiciously. More of Jesus' shenanigans, I figured, and thanked him silently.

I welcomed guests until well past midnight. I think the line grew as people found out what was going on. In

Coming

general, people hate to miss something big. The last person in line closed the front door and stepped inside to wait his turn to get into the living room to speak to me. I called the police officers inside and thanked them for being so attentive all night at the door. They helped themselves to a cup of hot coffee and a few small sandwiches and bade me goodnight. Luckily, it had not been too cold for a February night. Still, leaving the front door propped open all evening had the furnace working overtime. People had entered the house chilled, but left warmed.

Finally, I rose for the last hug and closed the back door behind the last visitor. There were about four slices of ham left and a couple buns. There were also a couple brownies left. The coffee pot had enough for three or four more cups, yet I never made more coffee and I had seen many people in the kitchen drinking and eating before they left.

I was reminded of the loaves and the fishes, and wondered if another miracle had taken place in my house. It was one-forty-five in the morning before I had the kitchen cleaned up and fell into bed. I was still full of energy. I should have collapsed after so little sleep the night before, but I lay down on my back, jiggling my left foot. I rewound the tape in my head of the evening, recalling certain visitors that made an impression on me and certain questions that broke my heart and certain answers that surprised me as they came out of my mouth. I longed to hold my husband and kiss my children goodnight. I probably lay in my bed for an hour, until sleep finally dropped its curtain on my hyperactive mind.

25 Days Ago

I awoke at three-thirty-three a.m., knowing that I had had the Dream. The big one. I knew it. I wanted desperately to call my husband, but I didn't want to wake him and rob him of the opportunity in case his Dream hadn't come yet. So I slipped out of bed and went downstairs. The Dream was not obviously "of God." It was not about love. It was not about judgment or the end of the world. It was just a simple Dream. But somehow, instinctively, I knew this had to be it. I stumbled through the darkness of the family room and turned on the television, frantically pressing buttons to quickly quiet the volume, before realizing there was no one home to wake. I fumbled over buttons on the remote until I found the channel button and switched to the news. I had my answer within seconds.

A report was coming from the BBC. The reporter was on location in Auckland, New Zealand, where apparently the city had been in quiet chaos much of the day. People had spent the whole day slowly coming to the discovery that something mystical had happened during the night. It was humorous hearing accounts from family members and friends in New Zealand about how they came to the realization that they had all had the same Dream. The talk of the American woman's vision also slowly spread through the country, until people were disoriented. Some had rushed to church. Others kept their children home from school and closed businesses for the day. In some areas, people had crowded into the streets to share their experiences. In other areas, it was eerily quiet. It was about ten-thirty at night in New Zealand, a day ahead of where I was. People had had their Dream in the early morning, at about three-thirty. They had awakened and began talking about it, and it took a few hours for the realization of the uniqueness of the situation to take hold. As night crept across the globe, others also had the Dream around three-thirty in the morning in their local time. Some devil's advocates who had heard about the Dream had planned to stay up all night to see what would happen if they didn't dream. Many of these fate-tempters reported a vivid daydream that, lasting only a few seconds, coincided with those of the others dreaming in their sleep.

One by one reporters asked individuals to recall their Dream from the night before. One by one, the same answer flowed. It was exactly like mine. It was freaky. It made everything so real. My stomach sank and I felt like I might throw up. This is it, I thought. This whole crazy Jesus thing was really real. I had emotionally thrown myself into the evangelizing stuff and sort of forgot about the primary mission—that Jesus was coming. End times. Now it was real. Now I had to believe and so did everyone else. I could not stop listening as people, now in New Delhi where it was the middle of the afternoon, were describing their Dream that came to them in the early morning.

25 Days Ago

A nicely dressed professional woman recalled her Dream in a British accent. "There was a field. It was bright yellow and I was looking at it from very far away. I thought, how beautiful. But as I came closer, I realized it was a field of dandelions. Millions of them. Most in full flower, but some had already gone to seed and the air was filled with small, soft, drifting parachute-like seedlings. I felt dismay at the distribution of this weed, and my Dream turned from one of beauty to one of trepidation as I saw this dandelion weed spreading. I woke with a strange feeling of panic over this silly weed."

"How did you know this Dream was special?" the reporter asked.

"I had no idea. In fact, for all intents and purposes, I had completely forgotten it until I turned on the radio while I had my morning tea. I heard others describing their Dream and suddenly the memory of my Dream was vivid in color and emotion. I had had the exact same Dream!" she said incredulously. "Then I heard on the radio of the American woman who had appeared on the *Here's Hope Show* and her signs that she hung on buildings, and suddenly this Dream has become important indeed. But I am not sure what it means," the woman admitted. The camera cut to a picture of my sign hanging on the side of a building.

The reporter concluded with a few statements about how I had claimed to have a visit from Jesus himself, and that Jesus told me everyone would have the same Dream. In order to spread the word I had hung signs on buildings telling people to pay attention to the Dream. "Apparently," he continued, "*everyone* is paying attention. Back to you, Niles."

Coming

And with that, the reporter tossed back to London, where the anchor reported an "explosion of interest" in the Dream. Experts of all sorts were called in. Each gave theories and interpretations that could not have been more different. One dream analyst remarked that *what* you dream about is not as important as how you *feel* about the dream; what your impressions are as you awake. Another said that dreaming of dandelions portends misfortune, while yet a different dream expert commented that dreaming of dandelions means a long, happy future for you and your mate.

A slew of theologians each had theories about the dandelion. One suggested that the omnipresence of the dandelion, its existence in practically all parts of the world, correlated with the omnipresence of God. I thought of a cute little saying my friend Sally once told me: "There is not a spot where God is not." Good job, Sally, I thought.

Another theologian commented that the field of dandelions was extreme in its brightness, symbolizing the pureness of Christ, similar to the transfiguration of Jesus written about in scripture. Another commented on the dandelion's appeal to children and that we must all be more childlike in enjoying the simplicity of life, that Jesus had advised us to be like little children.

I was glued to the television all morning. Hours went by as I watched one program after another. At about seven-thirty my family showed up in the driveway. As anxious as I had been to see them, I could not even meet them at the door. I couldn't tear myself away from the story on TV. The children were sleepy and came in and curled up by me on the couch, after each getting an

25 Days Ago

enormous hug and kiss. My husband's face was pale. He seemed to be a bit dazed. I knew he had had the Dream. He looked at me. I just offered a nod of affirmation and acceptance. Affirmation of what was happening in the world. Acceptance of his unspoken apology. We couldn't speak. He sat down next to me and put my hand in his, and we watched the news as it cut from scenes around the world of people packing into churches, mosques, and temples in prayer, to deserted streets, to crowded cafés in Europe. Opinions flew like machine-gun spray. No one could be found who had not had the Dream. No one.

We sat like zombies, watching and listening, until well after eight when I realized the kids were late for school. Forget school, I thought. We're shutting down today. No school, no interviews, no dentist appointment, nothing. We're hunkering down and waiting. My husband called into work and was told not to bother coming in. Nothing was running. The New York headquarters of his business was shut down. There was trouble with banks and businesses overseas that were in various levels of operation, but many were just incommunicado. He was told to check his e-mail and wait for further instruction. This was to be considered a paid vacation day for all employees.

I changed the message on my answering machine. When people called, they now got the following message: "Hello. Yes, we had the Dream here, too. I know nothing more than you do. I, too, am watching the news. I am not giving any interviews today. I need to spend the day in prayer. Thank you for understanding."

Coming

The kids were more excited about a day off school than a global phenomenon, so I let them rejoice in their innocence. It was wonderful not answering the phone or talking to people. We kept curtains and indoor shutters and blinds closed so the media could not spy on us. There were no cars on the street outside except for a few media hounds in front of my house. The smattering of people who had been keeping vigil on my front lawn swelled in number, but they prayed in stillness and silence. It felt as though the atmosphere were heavy, pushing down on the whole city, keeping us from moving around.

It was cold and gray. My family spent the whole day indoors, grazing occasionally on anything that was easy to prepare in the kitchen, often gathering together to pray for courage and wisdom to do the right thing.

"I'm sorry," my husband finally said to me quietly as we sat in front of the television.

"Stop," was all I could say. Some of his words had hurt, but I totally understood his predicament and we didn't need to go back to that conversation.

"I mean, I should have believed you," he said ashamedly.

"No, no. I don't blame you. A little doubt is a good thing. It keeps us from blindly following dictators or terrorists or others who divide in the name of truth. Besides, this whole thing is unbelievable. We'll be fine. You did what you had to do. It's okay."

"But I shouldn't have—"

"Stop, it's over. It's okay. We're okay. No, we're great. You're great. Thanks for coming home. This is where we'll begin, alright?" I asked.

25 Days Ago

He lowered his head and nodded affirmative, but I could tell that guilt had a grip on his heart.

I jumped on his lap and pulled him to me and gave him a big kiss. "We're moving on," I said. He smiled and kissed me back, and, as news programs began repeating themselves, we took a break from television and I showed my husband how Jesus had taught me to sit and breathe deeply and relax and let God's love move through him. The kids wanted to try it too, so I talked them through it, although they were a little squirmier than I wanted them to be.

The world waited. We had our sign. But what did it mean? As I listened all day to the experts, even through the inconsistencies in their theories, the meaning of the Dream slowly became obvious to me. I melded some of the ideas together until I had it figured out. I was positive of the Dream's meaning.

I got the most valuable information not from a theologian or a dream expert, but from the plant taxonomy expert from the University of Missouri at Columbia. "The dandelion, or *Taraxacum* as it is botanically known," he explained, "is one of the most adaptable plant species, now living in virtually every climate in the world. It can put up with harsh conditions that many of its competitors cannot. The dandelion is very difficult to get rid of," he said. "If you go to war with them, they will fight back fiercely. If you try to pick them or trample them, the familiar fluffy seedlings will scatter and reproduce quickly. If you try to dig them up, the cut roots double and the dandelion will come back with a vengeance. Putting harsh chemicals on your lawn can be just as dangerous to you as to the dandelion." Half jokingly, he added "The best thing to do with dandelions is to learn to love them."

Then he continued, "In many parts of the world, the dandelion is not considered a weed at all. It is beneficial. Most people are not aware of the dandelion's medicinal value. The milky sap is good for skin irritations. Dandelions are a diuretic and a tonic for the liver. Also, dandelions are delicious and more nutritious than spinach or broccoli. They are rich in vitamins A and C and are a good source of iron and calcium. The leaves have often been used in salads and soups, tasting something like greens. Roasted dandelions are used as a coffee substitute in many countries. Dandelion wine is also a favorite in some areas. The best advice I have when it comes to dandelions is to work with them rather than against them."

Eureka! Love is the solution. Again.

The field of dandelions in the Dream looked beautiful to everyone at first. If dandelions represent people of the world, there is a big beautiful world of humanity. Upon seeing the seedlings flying, people got an uneasy feeling, a feeling of encroachment, of not being able to keep the dandelions at bay. We all feel this way about others. Strangers are fine, as long as they don't get into my personal space, my neighborhood, my country. And as soon as we go to war with others, we only make more enemies. The enemy doubles, triples, the war escalates. We have seen it throughout history again and again. The answer, as the professor pointed out, is to look at what the enemy has to offer and cooperate and cultivate, rather than eliminate. All of humanity is filled with potential, and, upon being given conditions where they can

25 Days Ago

thrive (which might even be a bare minimum, as in the case of the dandelion), the offering of each is wonderful. I realized that so many people in the world do not even have the bare minimum in which to grow. Their social environment is too harsh, even for the toughest of species. Humans can treat others so pathetically, I realized with shame.

All afternoon we gathered in front of the television, marveling at what was going on around the world. I could hardly believe it was really happening. "This is really it," I found myself repeating over and over. I peeked out the window off and on all day, looking to the sky to see if there were any unusual cloud formations or celestial wonders. Finally, by dinnertime, I realized that Jesus would not be coming on this day because people needed a chance to change, to turn, and coming too soon would be against Jesus' desire for all to find love. We just got the message, the real deal, not a prophet's ranting, but a true mystical phenomenon. People needed to absorb the Dream, to have a chance to see the beauty rather than the threat in others. There was so much that needed to change. I hoped it wouldn't take hundreds or thousands of years. I had to believe that Jesus would be back soon. I had to for my own sanity and with that realization, I went to bed right after the children, believing that there was no time to waste. Tomorrow I would have to contact the media with my understanding of the Dream. I would need to be strong of mind and body. Unfortunately, sleep did not come.

~ 18 Days Ago ~

A whole week had passed since the global Dream. The good news was that all charges related to the climbing stunt were dropped. And the bad news was, well, there really wasn't any bad news. The week was a fog. I met with many in the media and explained the meaning of the Dream, as I interpreted it. I took a whirlwind tour from Washington, D.C., to San Diego, to Boston, before retuning home. I was called to meet with politicians to consult with them on how they might best use the insights of the Dream to make policy decisions. Me. A policy maker! If they only knew. I met with influential business leaders who wanted my advice on how best to proceed with trade and economic decisions. Me. A business consultant. Who would believe! I met with some of the country's top theologians at a conference in Boston, to reiterate everything that had happened to me and advise them on how to lead their congregations. Me. A theological shepherd! What's up with *that*?

Police and special security had escorted me practically everywhere I went. Somehow the word had spread that I could be in danger or maybe that is how important people are always treated. Or maybe, I realized, important people are always in danger, which was a thought

18 Days Ago

that dismayed me. But the week went on without incident, for which I was grateful. I figured that those who were originally threatened by me reconsidered their platform after experiencing the Dream and found their aggressive efforts counterintuitive.

I had invitations to Australia, England, Germany, Sweden, Jordan, Singapore, and Nigeria, but granted each phone interviews since it was impossible to fit everything in. I got comfortable with flying and public speaking. My mother, spooked by the whole thing, had moved in with us, and, being newly widowed, was totally overwhelmed. She and my husband held down the fort at home. All schools and most businesses had closed indefinitely. The world was watching the sky. And me.

I did not feel the pressure of the world, however. I felt that goose-bump energy running through me with each meeting. Everywhere I went I felt the energy flowing through the room, through each person in the room, and it was exhilarating. There was a palpable compassion driving each meeting as people came together with a common purpose, a dandelion application to life. No one was taking the Dream lightly. It was clear that something extraordinary had happened. Even those who did not believe in God believed in the power of compassion and cooperation and took the Dream seriously.

Many businesses continued with a skeleton crew, giving employees the option of coming in or taking some time off. Everyone seemed to understand the gravity of the situation. No one was forced to work. Airlines pared down flights to just a few daily from any given destination. In general, people were not traveling. Some were going home to be with their families. A few were

Coming

going to destinations they had always wanted to see. But mostly, cities were ghost towns. People tuned in to the television and online news twenty-four/seven. The only place where you could find life, for sure, was at places of worship. Any time of day or night, churches, temples and mosques were filled to capacity. Some people were camping out, sleeping on the floors. People talked in normal tones to each other, even through prayer and song. It was deafening and cacophonous. Food and trash littered the aisles. People fainted. People chanted. But no matter what happened, people got along. I was invited to speak at many churches during the week, but could only get to four that were in my immediate area. At one church, I did not speak until one in the morning, but the church was full and everyone was attentive. People sang hymns at church like I had never heard them sing. The world, it seemed, was on fire. Love of life, it seemed, was back.

There had been no crime since the Dream. Nothing horrific, anyway. Some underage drinking (kids never take anything seriously). Minor traffic infractions like failure to use a turn signal. Some twelve-year-old tried to buy cigarettes. There was not a murder, not a rape, not an armed robbery, nada. The police, who were required to show up for duty, patrolled the streets, but could have been back at the station playing "Go Fish." The world seemed orderly and tranquil. When the shot did ring out, it rivaled the "shot that was heard around the world."

~

18 Days Ago

I was driving down the street to get some gas in the car, and my youngest child wanted to go along. She was in a booster seat in the back seat of the car, even though she was six, since she was a skinny, little thing. It was cold and grey, with clouds threatening snow. I was driving slowly, enjoying our talk of the bare trees against the ominous sky. We talked about snow and sledding, and I rolled all the windows down to see if we could smell the snow coming. We both took a deep breath. I heard what sounded like a firecracker, just one, maybe a backfire, and my mind thought how unusual that was. Then my baby said, "Mommy, I think I better go to the hospital." Confused, I turned around and saw blood emptying from her little chest.

"Baby, what happened!?" I screamed.

"I don't know, mommy," she said weakly, her face paling by the second.

I began to tremble so badly that I could barely drive. I had to force my foot onto the accelerator and push hard because my whole leg was shaking so that it could no longer be trusted. I turned right at the first light and began to calculate how long it would take to get to the hospital...ten, maybe twelve minutes, I guessed. I argued with myself over whether I should pull over and call 911, try to call 911 on the fly or just keep driving. I didn't want to slow for a second, so I kept driving. I reached back and tried to press my hand to Baby's chest to stop the bleeding, but I couldn't reach her. I felt for her hand and held it tightly.

The streets were desolate, and I ran right through stop signs and even stoplights. I glanced back at my daughter and she seemed to have drifted off to sleep. I

Coming

frantically shook her hand and called her name to wake her up. The amount of blood spilling from her was disgusting, but I could tell she was not dead because the blood was still pulsing out of her.

"Wake up, honey. We're almost there. We'll get you fixed up. Wake up, Baby." Baby's eyes fluttered a bit, and I floored it, the adrenalin rush in full swing. I released my grip on Baby. My mind cleared, and I whipped open my cell phone as I drove. I dialed 911 with bloodied fingers and told a dispatcher that I was just a mile from the hospital and that I had a daughter that had been injured, maybe shot, and she needed help right away. I told them my location and within seconds, a police car pulled in front of me with lights on and escorted me the rest of the way to the hospital. My eyes were sharp, my muscles tensed, my heart pounding so loud that I could barely hear the siren that pierced the quiet streets. We made a sharp turn into the emergency room entrance, and I pulled up right under the overhang at the double doors. As the car stopped, I heard a terrible, sickening sound coming from Baby. A gurgling sound. The death rattle. Baby, and a part of me, died in the parking lot of the hospital.

Emergency crews met us immediately and pulled her onto a gurney, but I could tell by their frantic actions that it was a desperate situation. Once in a treatment room, they began using paddles to restart her heart, and I felt as if my heart disintegrated. I spoke with the intake receptionist, who called my husband immediately. Only after about fifteen minutes did it begin to dawn on hospital staff who I was. Slowly, the buzz of their latest patient's fame spread through the ER and I could see

18 Days Ago

people staring at me with confusion. I stayed in the room with Baby as the doctors and nurses worked on her, opening her chest and clamping and shocking and injecting until I thought I might pass out.

When my husband and my brother ran frantically through the doors together, I burst into tears and ran to them and we embraced. I heard the doctor call the time of death and my knees buckled. My husband caught me and pulled me over to a chair. The look on his face was more than I could bear. It was worse than seeing Baby, open and lifeless. His face was furrowed into a shape that I had never seen on him, a shape that screamed of panic and horror. A nurse gave me a sip of water and I could hear them cleaning up and covering our bloodied child.

The rest of the day was a blur. I remember the hospital staff telling me that a bullet had pierced her aorta and there was nothing anyone could do. It was a jagged shot, and she had lost blood too quickly. I remember talking to police. They had asked me if I had any enemies, and I mentioned the G2G Internet video and the rock that had been thrown through my living room window, but somehow I had never really felt them to be life threatening, just bullying. The police asked about where the shooting had happened, and my recollection was clear on that. I remembered how we had looked at the clouds, and I could see, like a photograph, the Meat Market sign below the clouds. I remembered little else. Somehow, we made arrangements for 'the body' which was so difficult to say. Somehow we told the other children. Somehow we told my mother the news, which was unbearable because she not only felt the loss of her

Coming

baby grandchild, but the insufferable pain of her daughter. I remember getting home late and crying all night.

17 Days Ago

I must have dozed off near morning, because when I awoke I did not want my life anymore. I wanted to retreat. To forget. To withdraw from life. I began to shake uncontrollably as I awoke and every muscle in my body ached. My head was pounding with tension. "How could this happen to us?" I cried to my husband. "Why would God pick me and not protect me? How can I do God's work if I'm destroyed?"

My other two children climbed in bed with me and sobbed. They wanted Baby back. Baby. My sweet Baby. My second child was really only a baby himself when I had gotten pregnant for the third time. All through my pregnancy we spoke of the baby, letting him kiss my belly and talk to his developing sister. Finally, when the baby had come, my son simply called her "Baby" and so did the rest of us, thereby solidifying the birth order. I thought she might become embarrassed when she entered elementary school and demand to be called by her legal given name. But on the first day, when roll was called, she indignantly stated to her kindergarten teacher that her family called her Baby, and so others learned to call her that too.

Coming

How could God take my Baby? I wept all day. My mother tried to busy herself by fixing me some tea and holding me tightly as I cried. But I could tell grief had smothered her, and she barely had anything left to give. My only consolation was that Baby was with my dad, somewhere. What if my dad had not died? Who would be taking care of my little darling? Surely Jesus does not have time to hold all of the children who need him. She was with my dad, and that gave me a moment of peace. All day we shuffled around the house and made the surreal arrangements for our daughter's funeral.

As dusk settled over the house, the doorbell rang. Police officers at the door informed us that they had their suspect. It turned out that a shell casing found at the Meat Market matched the bullet that pierced my dear Baby's chest and the owner was apprehended at his home. The police told us that the guy had even given a confession after initially trying to deny any wrongdoing. He said that he used his hunting rifle which he kept at the store for protection. Just in case, he had said. He had said that he was a lousy hunter and that he had aimed for me, but the car was going faster than he calculated and the bullet hit the backseat instead of the front.

He had wanted me dead. I had ruined his business. He had mounting debts to pay, and, with all of the recent talk of dreams and doomsday, no one was buying his meat. Business had already been slowing, thanks to the big discount stores that were beginning to sell meat, as well as online bulk purchasing. But this latest series of events completely shut down sales. He was desperate. He irrationally thought that if he killed me, killed the messenger, people would get back to work and school

17 Days Ago

and he could have his life back. He could pay his bills. He showed no regret, the police said, other than killing the wrong target.

We talked about the formalities of pressing charges and how the criminal justice system operated and what other details to expect. But I really didn't listen. Why, I wondered. Why even arrest this cruel idiot? He was pathetic and selfish and soon he would be tortured by the hellish pangs of his actions. My husband, on the other hand, was following all police advice and taking notes and asking questions while I just sat, withdrawing into myself.

As my husband walked the police officers to the door, we found people, thirty, no probably more like fifty, walking our way, holding candles and standing quietly in our yard. One officer's radio broke the silence with a report of an angry mob at the city jail. Hundreds of people, the radio announced, were shouting, wanting the "meat market maniac" to be released to the crowd. All officers were being called in to don riot gear and prepare for the worst.

The officers left quickly, and I collapsed back into my chair in a heap of despair. Things had been going so well. Life was good. Life was easy. How can life change so quickly? Now we were back to death and violence. What happened to love? Love is the solution, I wanted to scream. But there would be no screaming. I was heartbroken and disgusted. I wanted to throw in the towel at this whole hopeless mess. Is this the way God feels every day, every moment, I wondered.

With every ounce of energy I had, I pulled myself out of my chair. "I have to get to the police station," I

Coming

said to my husband. "This is wrong. People need to settle down and listen to their hearts. We need to get back to peace."

My mother urged me not to go, but she knew in her heart that I was the only one who could calm the situation. She knelt down and put her arms around my two (I could no longer say three) children and began to pray an ancient prayer, The Memorare. My husband and I grabbed our coats and gloves and scarves and headed out into the quiet sea of candlelight in the front yard. I thanked everyone on the lawn for their show of support and told them that our family really appreciated their prayers and that we were uplifted by them. I asked them to say a prayer for the people downtown at the station who were getting angry. I told them that we all wanted justice, but that justice is deep, and difficult, and most of all, must be born of love. I told them that they were welcome to stay or go, but to please stay away from the already unruly crowd at the station.

My husband and I carefully backed out of the driveway and headed downtown. People were streaming down the sidewalks towards our house, presumably to hold vigil. It was amazing. Strangers. Complete strangers lifting us up in prayer, standing in the cold to show their love. Suffering in love. That's it, I thought. That's the kind of love we need. Unselfish love. Quiet, unassuming love that lifts and heals. Not riotous revenge, which divides and instills fear. I told my husband that it reminded me of the verse in the book of Matthew where Jesus talked about dividing the sheep from the goats. The gentle sheep were in my yard. The destructive and misguided goats, even though their intentions were

17 Days Ago

good, were at the police station…one goat on the inside and a mob of goats on the outside.

"Or is it a gaggle of goats?" My husband joked and I smiled for the first time since my Baby and I looked for the snow.

"I need a bullhorn," I told my husband. He suggested that I call the police and have an officer meet us at the coffee shop two blocks from the station. Then we could drive carefully into the crowd, and let me announce, from the safety of the police car, that justice will be handled and that their goat-like behavior must end.

I made the call on my cell phone and the police were willing to send an officer. Four cars actually, with officers fully suited in riot gear, insisting that my husband and I put on the helmets and chest protectors. I had asked them to bring a Bible, and I searched as quickly as I could for the verse about sheep and goats. Of course, whenever I looked for a verse, I could never find it. I was the queen of quasi-quoting the Bible. I always figured it was more important to spend time reflecting on the gist rather than memorizing verbatim. But with this crowd, I thought that I had better be specific. I finally found the verse and curled my finger in as a bookmark.

The police let my husband get in the car with me, after some persuading. They had wanted him to follow in another car, but I told them that we were a team and that I couldn't do this without him. We got into the second car in the procession, and cautiously, with sirens giving up slow whoops, inched into the crowd of angry sympathizers. With one car ahead and two behind, we pulled in front of the station where a police officer was at the front door with a bullhorn, trying to persuade people to

Coming

go home. When he saw us stop in front, he receded into the station and locked the door. It's all me, I thought.

I slowly opened the car door and stepped out. People were yelling and screaming and it took a few seconds for anyone to recognize me. I was bundled up in my winter coat and riot gear, after all, and probably had mascara smeared all over my puffy eyelids from crying. I must look like a monster, I thought. But I truly didn't care. Both my husband and a police officer tried, to no avail, to grab my arm as I moved into the crowd, Bible in hand, up to the top of the steps to the police station door. I turned on the bullhorn with the shrill shriek of a bullhorn novice.

"Hi," was what came out. I smiled at my own lack of power and charisma. "Hi," I repeated, waiting for the crowd to quiet, and slowly they did. When I could hear nothing but a dog barking in the distance, I continued. "I know that the murder of my daughter is an outrage. I've never known anything so absolutely horrifying. I know you have come here out of support, looking for justice. I know that you believe what you are doing is right. But please, remember the Dream. The dandelions. This man, I don't even know his name, has had troubles in business. He had no right to take a life, but he was a desperate, misguided man. He has blocked the love in his heart with his overwhelming despair and has consumed himself with his own problems. All he needed was dialogue, but maybe no one listened. Maybe he tried to defend his business, but no one cared. Remember the dandelions. We have to look at what others have to offer, instead of trying to get rid of them. Maybe our community is suffering by losing small businesses.

17 Days Ago

Maybe we should have listened to him. Maybe it is not too late to listen to others."

"But we want justice. Put him to death! He is a killer!" someone in the crowd yelled, and the whole mob began to bubble up again.

Again, I let the bullhorn squeal and they quieted down.

"He will get justice. We have a system for that. But whenever anyone suffers, we all suffer. Yes, today, my family suffers, and I see that the community does also. But if we hurt this man, again, our whole community will suffer. Harm to anyone or anything is harm to all," I said, remembering Jesus' words. "Harm, to the good or to the bad, is harm. I am urging you to reach out in love. See what our community can do to heal. Let the courts take care of criminal justice, but it is up to you to take care of community justice. We have to look out for each other and make sure others are not suffering. Go home and check on your neighbors. See what they need. See what you can do to help. Spend your efforts in peaceful dialogue, not aggressive action.

Then I opened my Bible to the Book of Matthew, chapter 25 and read: "When the Son of Man comes in his glory, all the angels with him, he will sit upon his glorious throne, and all the nations will be assembled before him. And he will separate them one from another, as a shepherd separates the sheep from the goats. He will place the sheep on his right and the goats on his left. Then the king will say to those on his right, 'Come, you who are blessed by my Father. Inherit the kingdom prepared for you from the foundation of the world.'" I closed my Bible and implored, "Go home. Be alert. Be a sheep. Don't be a goat. Go home. Say a prayer for my baby, for me and my family, and then reach out and make sure your neighbors are okay. Feed the hungry, welcome the stranger, clothe the naked."

I waited as no one moved. Finally, after what seemed like an eternity, a young man in the front of the crowd turned and started working his way out through the others. "Thank you," I said to him. "Love is the solution. Always. The solution is always love." And more people began to turn to head home and I quietly and humbly thanked them and told them that everything would be all right. A few pockets of people lingered. But as the police got out of their cars with riot gear on and slowly removed the gear in front of the protesters, they got the message of peaceful resignation and they, too, went home.

The police thanked me and told me that the man who killed my baby was asking to speak to me inside in the jail. Maybe I'm a prophet, but I'm not a saint, I thought. I'm not ready.

"I can't see him face to face now," I told the officer. I could barely believe that I had just spoken in support of a man who had hurt us more deeply than ever imaginable. I heard myself talking, but I was numb inside. My husband and I slowly walked back to the coffee shop to get in our van and head home. As we drove home in silence, I thought I heard my Baby say, "Good job, Mommy," but my head was swimming with such strange visions that I could not swear to it.

☙ *16 Days Ago* ☙

I never ate meat again. No one asked me why. I don't think anyone noticed. Something about hunting, about stalking, about killing, sickened me to the point of vegetarianism.

All morning we busied ourselves with finding the right clothes to wear for the visitation and the funeral. The phone was strangely quiet. People seemed to respect our need for privacy. My brother and his family came over for lunch, as did a couple of our good friends. It was the first time I had seen Tom since the climb and he sobbed as I met him at the door. His heart was broken at the loss of his silly, admiring cousin.

We served ham, of course, and turkey and some mostaccioli and green salad and pasta salad and fruit baskets and brownies and cookies and Black Forest cake. "Enough to feed the Chinese army," my friend said. Surely, my neighbors are going to tire of feeding us, I thought. It was a semi-solemn day, with some tears, but also some laughs as only good friends and family can get away with on such an occasion.

We had a visitation for my daughter that evening. The largest church in the area, a huge stone Methodist church, graciously opened her doors to us, even though

Coming

we were not members, since our small parish could not handle the crowd. The small casket at the front of the long aisle looked wrong. Caskets shouldn't be small, I thought. My family stood, or at times sat, near the casket, which was kept closed. One by one, friends, relatives and strangers hugged us, many stopping at the casket to say a prayer. One woman came all the way from Oregon. Another family drove over from Kentucky. Priests and ministers and rabbis showed up from who-knows-where to show their respect. It should have been exhausting, yet somehow I couldn't wait to greet each visitor. Each hug nourished me as if gruel for the starving. I never cried. I couldn't, even though almost everyone who met me sobbed as they hugged me. I found myself comforting *them*, just as their hug lifted me. Hours went by, and my husband, my mother, my brother and his family, and my kids were all held up with the power of love. I never would have believed that I could do it. And I know that alone, I could not have.

15 Days Ago

We buried Baby.

14 Days Ago

I now knew what it was like to suffer, to want something so badly that every fiber of my being ached. If I could just hold my baby again. Just for a minute. I would trade anything to have her back again. It was easy to think of nothing else. Only Baby, all the time. No matter how I tried to engage in life, my mind throbbed for my little girl. It felt as though the fire that used to be in my heart was smothered. My eyes constantly seeped tears. I spent time alone in my room, begging for Jesus to hold me, but he was a no-show. Forsaken.

My mother begged me to come into the family room and watch television. I ignored her pleas. She called out several times, finally sending my daughter to cajole me into coming out of my room. It is so difficult to resist a child. I shuffled into the family room just to keep peace, to let my family think that I was trying, even if I wasn't. I sat, staring blankly at the television. My mind wandered, thinking of how Baby used to draw peace signs on the front sidewalk with chalk. Always peace signs.

The word "miracle" caught my attention.

My mind drifted from my front sidewalk to the television in front of me, and what I saw shocked me. For many, many years there had been unrest in the Middle

14 Days Ago

East. The Arab states hated Israel, and Israel, with the backing of the United States and other western countries, held firm in their desire for their claim of what they believed to be their God-given land. Tensions between the west, Israel, and the Arab states had simmered to the brink of catastrophe. I had followed developments in the Middle East as best as I could for several years, but things got more and more complicated. I learned that not only was there Israeli/Palestinian trouble, but there was discord amongst various sects of Islam and branches of Judaism and Christianity. The whole region had been the centerpiece for world troubles for years. Much of the infrastructure of the region had already been destroyed in conflict. But much worse, thousands of lives had been taken or displaced in the name of entitlement, revenge or jihad.

The anchor on CNN was reading a statement from an influential Middle East Muslim cleric. I didn't catch his name. Enormous reconciliation and cooperation had been achieved in an unprecedented meeting that he and other imams had attended for the last two days. What unprecedented meeting? I didn't hear about that. Then my mind drifted to the funeral of Baby and my heart cracked. I took a deep breath and refocused on the television.

Apparently, the imams had gathered in a secure place in Doha, the capital city of the small country of Qatar. For four days and nights they discussed Islam, Islamic states, Islamic differences, the future of the Middle East, the Dandelion Dream and their own dreams for the region. The cleric reported that amazingly, tempers were kept cool and all discussions were diplomatic in nature, with swift consensus. The imams were calling for the immediate dismantling of all terrorist organizations which "only taught recruits how to die, not how to live." Those encouraging or harboring terrorists would be severely dealt with by a newly established Middle East Peace Court.

The random division of Arab states drawn after World War I was determined to be counterproductive. Therefore, geographic boundary adjustments in the region that allowed strength as well as healthy competition within the various cultures were recommended.

Economic experts were organizing a rebuilding campaign of the area, with a plan to more equitably distribute oil monies to give jobs to regional contractors. Western countries were compensated with a promissory note to be paid with oil barrels for training local unskilled workers.

A call for all occupying nations to retreat within their own borders was demanded so that Muslims could begin the business of organizing their own Islamic governments, "giving praise and glory to the one true Allah." An Islamic government, they reported, meant that all government offices, businesses and schools would follow and respect Islamic rituals and holy days, but that Jews, Christians and others would be welcomed in the region and allowed to practice their own faiths, with understanding and respect for the common scriptures that the faiths shared.

The results of the meeting were called "a miracle." Similar treaties had been tried for decades, usually without consensus of participating parties, bringing only

14 Days Ago

fleeting peace. But this time, the agreements were accepted by all of the Middle Eastern countries.

Even more amazing, Israel, the Arabs agreed, had a right to exist. The national boundaries of Israel were to remain intact, including the disputed occupied territories. But an agreement had been drawn up leasing a contiguous portion of Israeli land to the Palestinians for the next one thousand years at a price of only one dollar per year. The Palestinians had rights to organize their own sovereign state and peaceful affairs without interference. A just and equitable water sharing resolution was being negotiated. The Prime Minister of Israel somewhat begrudgingly agreed with this land lease arrangement, knowing that some constituents would be unhappy with the situation, but voiced pride in the fact that Jews were keeping their land and generously sharing it with others, particularly a state that had been considered an enemy. The Israeli Prime Minister also conceded to a joint custody agreement with Jewish, Muslim, and Christian authorities for the precious, disputed holy city of Jerusalem. Jerusalem would be the new world model for peaceful cohabitation of all cultures and faiths, the brightest spot on the globe.

With the atrocities of the past seared into the collective memory, it was emphasized that any acts of terrorism against the Israelis would draw harsh punishment from the Middle East Peace Court, which was to include Israeli members. The spirit of cooperation was high, as the fatigue of fear and retaliation had finally crested.

My mother, my husband, and I all dropped our jaws and looked at each other in disbelief. Then my mother said, "It just goes to show, you cannot shake hands with a clenched fist!"

"Nice one, Mom," I said.

"Indira Gandhi, honey," she replied, returning her focus to the television.

A nuclear war starting in the Middle East had become so imminent that most Americans had gathered supplies and food in emergency boxes. It was not to the extent of the Cold War of the 1950s, where air raid drills drove students from their desks to kneel on the floor and cover their heads with their arms. (As if our skinny little arms would protect anything from a nuclear blast!) But the U.S. Office of Homeland Security was continually raising and lowering alarm levels for the American public. It had become routine, with hardly any attention paid by the average person. Yet I believed the threat of war etched fear deep into the mind of humanity. We were becoming suspicious of everyone and everything. We distrusted strangers and many loathed life on a subconscious level. The weariness of fear had taken its toll.

The Dandelion Dream, the challenge to look at another and see what they have to offer rather than what they are trying to take, was changing the world. A part of me wanted to take a little credit for the collective change of hearts in the Middle East, but I knew that without the Dream, I would be just a crazy woman hanging signs on a building. I tried to encourage myself, thinking that if I hadn't hung the signs, people would not have been alerted to their dreams and maybe the global dream event would have been missed. But I didn't really believe that six billion people would have the same dream on the same night and nobody would notice.

14 Days Ago

Thoughts of Baby drifted into the room. This time, they came to my mother, who said to me, "Baby would be so proud of you now! She was so excited about the whole dream idea, wasn't she?"

I couldn't answer. My husband left the room. I think he was crying. The other kids looked at me with trepidation to get my reaction to the mention of Baby's name, which they knew usually sent me into hysteria. But this time I smiled and they ran over and jumped in my lap and I kissed them both over and over.

∽ 13 Days Ago ∾

As I walked out my front door, people in the yard seemed to sense that I needed my space. They were silent as I gingerly waded through what seemed like hundreds of bouquets and teddy bears and letters that had been placed on our front lawn since Baby was killed. I couldn't believe her death touched so many others. Every action truly does ripple outward.

I went for a long walk. I hoped that maybe my desperate sadness was lifting a little, but I just felt dead instead. I didn't really care if I lived or died. I didn't care if a tree fell on me and pierced my heart. I didn't care if a car jumped the curb and crushed me. Life was okay. Death was okay. It didn't matter either way.

As I became aware of my thoughts I realized that *this* is the desperation that people all over the world felt every day. They had nothing to live for. Death was not a threat. Without the experience of the joy of life, the fear of death is not a factor.

Suddenly my heart ached, for the first time not for Baby, but for strangers. I felt the pain of millions of others that I had never met. My steps slowed as I tried to go beneath my pain and search deep within my heart for the happy life that I had been so privileged to live. Memo-

13 Days Ago

ries began to drift into my mind like a vapor, vague memories of my childhood and playing in my neighborhood. I breathed deeply and smiled softly. The memories became clearer and crisper as I recalled my school years, my school friends, my road trips, my laughter, and my family. My steps quickened. Now, even the vision of Baby made me fill with amusement and delight. I found myself walking with a huge grin on my face.

Upon summoning all of these exceptional events of my life into my consciousness, I abruptly stopped walking. I stepped off the sidewalk and leaned against a grand old oak. Facing east, I closed my eyes and felt compelled to pour some of my joy into the minds of the despairing people everywhere. I tried to share my bounty, my blessings, by somehow teleporting feelings of elation to anyone whose mind was open enough to accept the gift. I hoped that maybe, even if only a fleeting feeling of the joy I held in my heart would enter the hearts of the desperate, it would be enough to sustain them a little longer. Maybe it would give them enough hope to keep trying.

I had never done anything like that before, but I thought that maybe it was prayer. Maybe prayer was really compassionate, unselfish intention. For the first time I realized how much I really did have to share. I felt alive again, more than ever before. It seemed as though everything I saw became crisper, everything I heard became sharper, everything I smelled became sweeter. I felt a deep connection to everyone and everything.

I am an instrument in a huge orchestra, I thought, remembering the words of Jesus, and I could finally feel his presence, which I had craved for so many days. He was with me, and I knew it. Tears welled up in my eyes as I felt the love of God wrap around me and fill me with every breath.

Leaning against the rough bark, I dropped my head back and gazed into the pale blue sky, streaked with wispy clouds. I thought about how I had known tremendous joy in life, and now, after Baby's death, I could say I knew tremendous suffering. But the suffering somehow united me with others. I realized I had been hoarding my comforts, unaware of, or unconcerned about others. I had tried so hard to insulate myself from the discomforts of life, I had contributed to the systemic oppression of others. My lifestyle was selfish. I had always wanted my family to have the best of everything: a beautiful home, good meals, nice clothes, a great education, plenty of opportunities for learning and growing. These things consumed my days.

These are all good things to have, but I didn't work to make sure others were comfortable, too. Oh, I had done some charity work when it was convenient for me. But charity now seemed like giving a dog a bone, then sending it back out in the rain. I had to change my life. I had to change how I lived. I had to invite the dog in, invite humanity into my everyday consciousness. We had to learn to live together, even if it meant giving up some of my family's comforts.

I sucked up the chilly air around me, and with a spring in my step, I began walking back home, my walk turning to a run as I could not contain my newfound joy of solidarity. Being united in suffering also unites us in joy. This life is truly a contradiction, I thought. No won-

13 Days Ago

der people don't get it. "Yin and Yang" the Taoists called it...the dance of opposites, leading to harmony.

I trotted up my front walk and threw open the front door, calling out with urgency to my family. They all came running to me, afraid of what they might find. But when they saw me beaming with joy, they smiled and my kids jumped into my arms. My husband, a little confused with my new mood, looked at me sideways. I walked over to him and, placing my cold hands on his warm cheeks, planted a big kiss on his lips. He didn't kiss back at first, until the kiss endured, and then he apparently threw his confusion out the window and we kissed passionately right in front of my mother. She was never one for the public display of affection.

"Oh for God's sake! I think I prefer the numb, grief-stricken parents," she said with playful disgust, as she turned to the kitchen to prepare some lunch for us all. My husband and I, holding hands, went to the couch in the family room, where of course the television was droning on. I sat on his lap and he just stared at me, bewildered, brushing the hair from my face.

As Mother brought a platter of sandwiches cut into little triangles into the room, along with a basket of chips, the news caught our attention once again. We all dived into the casual cuisine, piled as close to each other as we possibly could on the couch, and grazed as we listened.

It was being reported that Latin America was deeply touched by the collective Dream and the rumor of Jesus' Second Coming. Drug cartels in the countries of Mexico, Bolivia, Peru, Venezuela, and Colombia were switching their illegal coca and cannabis crops over to

Coming

solar wind farms, to the amazement of the both the U.S. and local governments. Illegal farming was no longer seen as an ethical choice, and it was calculated that solar wind farms could reap more profits in the alternative energy trade.

Paramilitary groups who had protected the crops were no longer needed and were given the opportunity to invest in solar wind farming. Plans were underway to build storage and transport for the energy collected in the sometimes sunny, often windy, mountainous countryside. A new technology had produced smaller, less obtrusive wind turbines with compact solar heads, so that if it was stormy and windy, energy would be collected as easily as if it were calm and sunny. It was a peaceful and hopeful resolution.

Weapons collected from drug runners were being taken to collection stations at the local Catholic churches where they were to be dismantled and melted down to make parts for the windmills. Swords into plowshares, I mused. And then I remembered how Jesus told me to look at the bounty the earth has to offer and to take from her with gratitude. These people were capturing the sun and the wind and using it for the benefit of others, just as Jesus had said we should. Good for them…they're on the right track, I thought with excitement.

I steered my attention back to the report to learn that drug lords, unable to quell their competitive spirit, tried to outdo each other with generous job offers to peasants to assist in the vast overhaul of the industry. Peasants were shown lining up for jobs to destroy illegal crops, to work in turbine assembly factories, or to help lay cables. Smiles were on the weathered faces of old men as they

13 Days Ago

spoke through an interpreter to the reporter about their "dream come true" of being able to support their families. The children, obliviously twirling and playing, added to the sense of celebration. Peasant women were throwing their hands in the air, praising Jesus. Even I could understand their Spanish at that point.

People in other countries such as Argentina, Brazil, Paraguay, and Chile, which were crucial exporters of the illegal drugs, made statements regarding their solidarity in cracking down on any illegal trade. Ships and crews would be seized and dealt with harshly. A zero-tolerance attitude was adopted by an international committee on narcotics, who promised government assistance to groups dedicated to the growth and trade of legal crops.

The U.S. State Department had a representative from the Bureau for International Narcotics and Law Enforcement Affairs claiming that alternative programs had been encouraged for years, and he couldn't believe that overnight everything was coming together. The agent sounded skeptical, but was trying to his best to trust in his adversaries' progress.

The report switched to drugs in this country. What would a drying-up of the source do to the drug use in America? Experts in law enforcement and drug rehabilitation responded. I learned that almost twenty percent of the crimes in our country were committed to obtain money for drugs. Over two-thirds of inmates in local jails, upon urine testing, were found to be under the influence when committing their crimes. Drugs and alcohol filtered out proper social inhibitions and emboldened those with an urge or a grudge to do something that they would not have done if not under the influence. The cost of drug abuse in our society, experts said, was billions of dollars in loss of productivity, law enforcement, rehabilitation, health care, and other hidden costs.

"A society without illegal drugs?" the Director of Natural High Rehabilitation Center repeated the reporter's question. "Oh man, a society without drugs would be like heaven on earth if you ask me!"

I smiled. A new heaven and a new earth. Here we go.

✎ 12 Days Ago ✎

Although it had only been six days since my Baby was taken from us, it seemed like months. So much had happened in the world. The days seemed to suddenly carry an extended load of minutes. Our lawyer called and told us that we needed to meet with him to officially press charges against the man who shot Baby. It was Sunday. Some people never stop working, I thought. The killer was being held on three-million-dollar bond in jail and an arraignment was set for Wednesday. We told the lawyer we planned on going to church. I didn't want to deal with the horrible man. I wanted to have my memories of Baby and forget the man that took her. I didn't want to look back to that day. I only wanted to look back beyond that day, or forward. I needed, for the protection of my heart, to skip over that day. But the law would not have it, so we set a meeting at our house for one o'clock.

My husband, my mother, my two children and I dressed for church. It would be the first time facing the public since the funeral. At church the priest would pray for the repose of Baby's soul, and I didn't know if I could stand to hear the words. But it was Sunday, and on Sunday we always went to church, so we lifted our chins, took deep breaths and headed to church with dread.

As we parked the car, church friends, as I call them, came over and put their arms around us. More joined in as we walked to the door of church. They talked about how beautiful Baby's funeral was, what a beautiful child Baby was, how strong our family was, how lucky I was to know Jesus. It was those last words, coming from an older woman, that rung like a bell tolling in my head. How lucky I am to know Jesus, I repeated in my head.

She was right. If I hadn't had Jesus come into my home and heart before Baby died, I didn't know where I'd be at that moment. How could I ever let Baby go? When the tragedy first struck and I called for Jesus to show up, he didn't, and I felt lost. But when I finally relaxed and let my mind drift away from my own heartbreak, there I felt him. Strong and present. Filling me with joy and peace and giving me strength for the next moment. I was so lucky to know Jesus. To know true Love. When I first met him, I didn't want to know him personally. I didn't want to tell the world about him. I wanted to quietly follow him from a distance. I didn't have the courage to blaze a trail. But here I was, able to smile and feel deep calm, even after losing my dear child. I knew only God could do that within me.

Every word of the mass resonated in my heart. I had never heard the words so clearly before. They were magnificent. They were filled with praise and hope and love for our God. I had always mumbled through responses that I had known all my life, but this time it was like hearing each word for the first time, and I shed tears

12 Days Ago

through the whole service because of the richness of the relationship I could now communicate to my God.

When I returned to my pew after receiving Communion, I knelt and closed my eyes as I always did. I had gotten in the habit of doing that a couple years earlier so that I wouldn't just watch the parade of parishioners coming back from Communion. I had realized that my mind had been too much into judgment mode and not enough into gratitude mode, so I closed my eyes until the parade was over.

But this time when I closed my eyes, instantly a bright light flashed against my eyelids as if I were experiencing the Big Bang in my head. I saw the cosmos and the view swiftly zoomed in to earth and its inhabitants. I saw faces of people of every nation and of every age. I saw the deeply wrinkled faces of old men and women staring at me. The beautiful supple faces of children...some laughing, some crying, some moaning. I saw single mothers with their children. Sick people and caregivers. Athletes. Poets. Musicians. I saw teachers teaching and writers writing and singers singing and bosses bossing. I saw men in prison. I saw women in shelters. I saw families at dinner. I saw men holding hands. And a woman nursing her baby.

I saw men in robes and suits and almost nothing at all, and headwear of all kinds. I saw women with scarves and adornments. Dark skin and light skin. Blue eyes and brown eyes and green eyes. Each was looking into my eyes. The images flashed so quickly it seemed impossible that I could really make out their features, but the detail was exquisitely sharp. Finally, I saw an infant, naked and wriggling on his blanket, cooing as if beckoning me to pick him up and love him. Then there was a loud snap, like a rubber band hitting my skin, and I jumped as if I had indeed felt the pain. Then all went black.

All of this happened within seconds and I had to sit back in the pew and regain my composure. My heart was pounding, but I wasn't sure if it was from adrenaline or extreme love for humanity. Jesus had told me that the Kingdom of God, the State of Love, was within us. But I had not realized the magnitude of God-Love until that moment. And I realized that in that love we are all intimately bound. We are one body, I thought. It was a profound experience, like nothing I had ever had. It was overwhelming.

I'm sure people thought I was playing the grieving mother and they tried to divert their eyes from my constant eye-dabbing, but they probably didn't notice the smile beneath my tears. Tears of intense love and pure joy.

After Mass, again we were surrounded by well-wishers and I stood like a mountain. But my mother announced that if we didn't get some lunch soon she would start getting fussy and the crowd dispersed and let us go. My mother was right. She was getting fussy. She criticized the tie of one man, the sniffling of another woman, the misbehavior of certain children, the smell of another man...did we think he'd been drinking so early? It was judgment of the first degree. We hurried home and got her some lunch.

At one o'clock our lawyer promptly arrived in a business suit and tie. I pushed extraneous items out of our living room into other rooms, trying to look like I

12 Days Ago

kept a clean house, but I'm sure I didn't fool him. As I looked into the dining room, there were seven different piles of papers. In the family room were clothes, shoes, newspapers and a sewing basket. In the kitchen, food and dishes. The living room was a small oasis of cleanliness, but clutter was closing in fast. I cared. The lawyer didn't.

We reviewed papers and signed and dated and signed and dated. We discussed charges and I asked what would happen to the man if he were found guilty of murder in the first degree. The lawyer explained that the perpetrator would at least get life in prison. Or there was a good chance he would get the death penalty. The lawyer lit up at the possibility of having this man pay with his life. "Depending on the judge," he explained, "you can almost guarantee this guy will give an eye for an eye." He seemed sure that this would bring us comfort.

It sickened me. "I don't want the death penalty," I said.

"Well, it is not really up to you," the lawyer explained. If he is found guilty of murder, which seems to be a slam-dunk, the judge or jury will decide his fate. You will have a chance to make a statement, but it is ultimately up to the judge."

"Maybe I don't want to press charges, then. I can't live with the death penalty. I don't care if he killed someone. I cannot take a life. I cannot let our government do exactly what he is in jail for doing, what our society says is wrong. If a man steals from me, the law does not say that I get to steal from him, and all is even. If someone assaults me, the law does not say that he should now be tortured. No, in fact the law is very clear

Coming

that authorities may not lay a hand on someone in custody. Why, if someone takes a life, does the government think that taking a life will make everything even? We'll never be even. You can never measure one life against another," I said with passion.

My husband looked at me with puzzlement. "Honey, we have to press charges. He has to be held accountable for what he did. We can't let him walk free."

"But I do not want to be accountable for taking *his* life," I insisted.

The lawyer, adjusting his tie and shifting in his chair, changed his demeanor as he realized that putting a man to death was not the justice we were seeking. "You know," he said, "it *is* the judge's job to apply a sentence with consideration to the family of the victim. The judges *do* listen carefully to their wishes." Wow, he changed his tune. I didn't fully trust the justice system.

"I would like to see the man," I announced.

"Honey, I don't think that's a good idea," my husband said quietly.

"Your husband's right," the lawyer interjected. "For the sake of the trial, we cannot let you speak to each other."

"I will not speak about details of the crime to him. I want to speak to him *about* him. I want to know how he thinks," I explained.

"I'm afraid that cannot be allowed. It will affect the trial," the lawyer reiterated.

"But I don't know how to press charges if I don't know what his intentions were. What if he just freaked out and is so sorry? What if he could never do anything like this again? How could I have him sit in jail, with no

12 Days Ago

possibility of enjoying life again? I need to talk to him," I demanded.

"With all due respect, ma'am, I appreciate your sensitivity. But this man has had six days to think of nothing else but reasons why he shouldn't be found guilty. What one does, one is responsible for, no matter why or how or when one does it. One must give back to society in accordance with the severity of their crime," the lawyer said calmly.

"Okay, that makes sense," I admitted, "but I still want to look into his heart. Off the record. I will go ahead and press charges, but I want to talk to him. And I heard a few days ago that he was asking for me."

"Yes, he's been asking to speak to you every day," the lawyer said.

"Then take me there, will you? We'll sign these papers and then you can take me there. You can listen the whole time. You can record it. Or not. Whatever you guys do. Please, just let me talk to him. You know this is a special situation," I said, throwing down my "special status" card for the first time.

My husband reached his hand over to me, but I stopped him. "I'm okay, I just need to do this. You don't have to come," I told my husband.

"I don't think I can look at that man. I just want to move forward," my husband explained.

"Fine, I understand. You shouldn't have to ever look at him. It's just something that I want to do. That I need to do for myself," I said.

We signed umpteen papers and the lawyer gathered them up, tapping them on end on the coffee table and inserted them into his briefcase. He made a call on his

Coming

cell phone, mentioning six or seven names and legal terms until I could no longer follow at all. Into the phone he said, "Right, right, right, all right. Right," then told me we had the "go-ahead."

I got my coat and kissed my husband and told him I would be back in a few minutes. What a change in attitude from the morning, I thought. Earlier in the day, I could barely go to church for fear of facing the sadness of Baby's death. Then I felt uplifted and cherished during Mass. And now, I felt compelled to go see her murderer. I wanted to look deeply at him. See his vulnerability. See his capacity for contribution to society, not just see him as some monster without a conscience. That was the Dream. To look deeply and learn and grow from others. Was I being brave or crazy, I wondered as the lawyer drove me across town to the secure cell of the murderer of my sweet child.

I waited just inside the door of the local jail as the lawyer spoke with several police officers and sheriffs and deputies, until he tilted his head back to summon me over to him. I walked over to my lawyer and he quietly told me the ground rules. My lawyer, the public defender, and two security officers would be present. I would have to wait while the man was escorted to a table, where he would be shackled at the feet and he would pick up a telephone. I would speak to the man on the phone, looking through a Plexiglas divider.

As he spoke, my heart raced. Maybe this is a really bad idea, I thought. Should I back out? I fought to get here, I'd better stick it out. I can do it. It's what I'm supposed to do. Dandelions. Dandelions. Dandelions, I re-

12 Days Ago

peated over and over as I was escorted into the visitors' room.

The man entered his cubicle, clumsily sat, and picked up the phone. I felt nauseated upon gazing into the killer's eyes. He was a large, disheveled man with deep acne scars. He was wearing an orange jumpsuit with wet stains under his arms. I breathed deeply and tried not to gag. Dandelions.

I nodded to him and he stared at me with cold, lifeless eyes.

"You wanted to see me?" I said into the phone, not knowing where else to start.

"Yes. I wanted to say I'm sorry," the man said, with no emotion.

Excellent, I thought. Salvation.

"Thank you," I said quietly. "I'm sorry, too." I said, referring to the shooting of my child.

"That's what I wanted to hear," he said, devilishly grinning. "I wanted to hear you say that *you* are responsible for this."

"What?" I asked with disbelief.

"You heard me. You started all of this. You and your delusions of grandeur. You seem to be some sort of desperate housewife or something. You made up this story and never thought for one second how it would affect everyone else. You were just looking for your fifteen minutes of fame and now you got more than you bargained for, didn't you?" he said with a sneer.

"That's all," my lawyer said, standing and grabbing me by the arm.

"No wait," I said to my lawyer. Dandelions. Dandelions. Look deep. "It's okay. Let me answer him." I took

Coming

a deep breath and tried to imagine how his business had been hurt by the recent events. Ever since Jesus had visited me, the community had been thrown off kilter, and so many people lived on such a tight budget they could not afford any fluctuations in cash flow.

I stared at his chest, unable to lift my eyes to meet his. I again spoke into the phone. "I'm sorry your business has suffered," I said, "but did you hear the news? People all over the world have had the same Dream. I'm sure you had it. Jesus is coming. He wants us all to live in peace. He is coming to restore peace and joy to each and every one of us. Even you, if you're open to him."

"Jesus!" he said, puffing air and spittle out of his lips, spraying the phone. "Jesus does not pay my bills. Jesus does not keep creditors off my back. Jesus is not a customer. Jesus does not keep life from hassling me."

"But Jesus is Love," I said. "You just need to breathe deeply and let Jesus, let Love, fill your heart. I swear, you will feel his peace," I tried to explain.

"You're nuts, lady. Forget Jesus and forget you. I'm glad I killed your kid. I'm just sorry I missed *you*. You need a wake-up call. Life sucks and now you know how it feels," the man said with evil in his voice, pounding his fist on the table. And he slammed down the phone.

Look deep. Dandelions. Dandelions. My heart was racing and my mind was darting about the files in my head, searching for the proper response, but there was nothing. His words pierced my soul. The man's lawyer called an end to the interview and I was escorted from the room.

12 Days Ago

As the man was being escorted back to his cell, he raised his voice and I could faintly hear through the thick walls as he shouted, "I hope you die!"

Back in the lobby of the police station my lawyer straightened his shirt and tie and smoothed back his hair with his hand.

"I think that went well, don't you?" I said sarcastically, trembling from the verbal assault.

My lawyer smiled as he shook his head and suggested that he take me home.

Once again, people were gathering on my front lawn, so I asked my lawyer to drive around the block and drop me off there so I could enter through back door. When he dropped me off, he asked if I was okay, and I assured him that I was fine.

"Sticks and stones, that's all that was. He is a broken man, a sick, sad man. A goat. Baby's death was in no way my fault, and I know that," I said, trying to convince myself that I was all right.

He patted me on the shoulder and told me that I was exactly right and promised to keep in touch. As I cut through yards I started to pray that Baby's murderer would find love inside of himself, but I found myself hating him so much that I stopped praying. The death penalty option was suddenly looking attractive. I didn't really care about his fate. He made his bed, he could lie in it. Love your enemies was a thought that popped into my head. I don't want to, I argued with myself. I wanted revenge. Love your enemies. It brings you joy. I can't, I thought. You will not know peace unless you do, the nagging promised.

Coming

    I told my husband that the interview was interesting, but that I didn't want to go into detail, for which he was content. The rest of the afternoon and evening was filled with phone calls and camera people outside taking pictures of our house and scores of people in the yard with candles and rosaries. I felt increasingly anxious and frustrated and annoyed, and by the time I went to bed, I was just ticked off and went quietly to my room by myself without even saying good-night to anyone.

~ 11 Days Ago ~

It had been one week since Baby had died. One week. It seemed like she was just with me. I could still smell her if I closed my eyes. I could still feel her silky hair, her satin skin and her twinkling blue eyes. Everyone in my house had returned to work and school. With melancholy again in the air, I took a nice long, steamy shower.

As I was getting dressed, I found an envelope in my sock drawer. On the front of the envelope it said, "*Toof Fairy*." I had put the envelope into my sock drawer after exchanging it for money under Baby's pillow. When I opened it, I found Baby's little bottom tooth that had fallen out just a couple weeks ago; the tooth that had fallen victim to a kernel of popcorn. As I pulled the tooth from the envelope I clenched it to my breast. It was all I had to hold of my dear child. I sobbed uncontrollably and did nothing the rest of the day.

10 Days Ago

I guess I had no more tears. I knew my ducts would refill soon enough, but for now they were dry. I still had to be a mom for my other two children. They got ready for school, talkative and cheerful, as if nothing had happened to their little sister. I must admit, their ability to move on pained me, but then I remembered how slowly time passes when you are young. And although my children lost their sister just a week ago, it probably already seemed like years to them. I remembered as a child, how hard it was to wait for Christmas or wait until dinner or wait for anything adults tell kids to wait for…time moves so slowly. And now, I thought about how it was an advantage to be young. The recent past seems so far away to a child, that they can move on so much easier than adults. I had to act like I, too, was moving on.

Again, by eight-thirty in the morning the house emptied. My mother even borrowed my van and went back home to take care of some personal things and bring back some more of her clothes to our house. Although she promised she would be back right away, I pleaded with her to take her time.

10 Days Ago

I decided not to shower and went to the television to see what had happened while I was emotionally paralyzed the day before. I was hoping to find something interesting going on in the world to lift my spirits. I was not disappointed.

AMerica reported a huge influx of participation in places of worship throughout Europe. Protestant denominations were exploding with renewed interest. And after a recent steady decline, where Catholic priests were pulled from Africa to serve the dwindling faithful, European Catholics were coming to churches and not leaving. The Pope was planning on visiting the Aachen Cathedral in Germany.

Up until now, the Pope had been noticeably silent on the whole phenomenon. The Catholic Church handled alleged visions and locutions gingerly. But I assumed that the Pope also had the Dream and *that* was hard to ignore. His Mass was going to be telecast live the next day. I made a mental note to tune in. I was curious what his comments would be. I had thought maybe he would have tried to contact me by now, but what do I know? I smiled and thought to myself, the more important question is: *Who* do I know? And I found an immature "Ha!" coming from my lips, aimed right at the image of the Pope on the television. Why would Jesus pick such a juvenile prophet, I wondered with amazement.

I decided that I had better clean up and act my age, just in case I found myself on television again. I felt so much better after my shower, with clean jeans and an oversized, warm brown sweater. I actually put on make up and blew my hair dry. I grabbed a bowl of Life cereal and some orange juice and headed back to the television, balancing cross-legged on the couch as I ate.

The next story really made my spirits soar. A group of university students in Romania had formed what they called a Dandelion Coalition. They apparently met nightly, planning how they could best help others to get whatever they needed. They had, in a matter of days, grown to over two hundred volunteers, mostly students, but with others rapidly joining in. The group had organized a list of employers, grocers, landlords, department store owners and others who were willing to help anyone who was down on their luck.

Dandelion Coalition teams of three or four set out each day, combing neighborhoods. They went door-to-door, asking people what they needed. Each team had a checklist of needs and jotted names, addresses and phone numbers next to the needs. Once the needs of an individual were established, the students asked each person what they could do to help another, no matter how small. This list of contributions was as varied as one could imagine. It included driving others, sewing, small repairs, tutoring, haircuts, even singing.

The students wasted no time, text-messaging the information to their central command center, where names and needs were matched with those willing to donate to the Coalition. It was fascinating how the value of goods and services randomized. Apparently the Coalition did not attempt to qualify or quantify the needs and services. For example, if someone needed a sofa, they would get one and at some point help a child with their mathematics. If another needed a computer, they would receive one, to be asked only to sing to a lonely elderly tenant, if

10 Days Ago

that was their skill. When a donor felt like they had contributed all that they could for the time being, the Coalition was on task, filling the gaps.

Monetary donations had begun to flow in unsolicited, and a bank account was set up to hold the increasing funds. The students were on fire. In an interview, one student explained with broken English that everyone was deeply affected by the Dandelion Dream. He explained that rather than talking about it in coffee shops, a few students decided that the Dream was meant to incite action. When asked if he was afraid of what might be coming in the days ahead, the student replied that he did not have time to think about tomorrow, that there were people today who were hungry and cold, and they could not wait while he daydreamed.

People in need were crying literal tears of joy now that they were being heard and assisted. One single woman with three young children was hoping to be able to join the Dandelion Coalition now that she had enough food for her family. She wanted to be able to help, just as her family had been helped.

I thought back to when Jesus told me to find out what people need and help them get it. We are a human puzzle, he had said. God love the Romanians! That was exactly what the Dandelion Coalition was doing. Just then I knew that the Dandelion Coalition would save the world. Wow, I thought. Ambitious. Only college kids are young enough to have the energy, old enough to have the knowledge, and idealistic enough to have the drive to pull off such an ambitious task. The Romanian student made one final remark, urging others to start Dandelion Coalitions in their own communities, all

Coming

around the world. I thought that although I really wanted to be a part of it, I didn't have the energy just then and my optimism needed constant babysitting.

I spent the afternoon granting a few phone interviews, which was difficult because my mother had returned to our house, and she was a basket case. Going to her home had triggered emotions in her to which I had been insensitive. I was so enveloped with losing Baby, world events and the Dream, that I missed the possibility that her returning home by herself could trigger the anvil of grief to drop on her head. She was beginning to have a meltdown. After all, it was just a month ago that she lost her husband to a tragic accident. Then her only daughter became a lunatic, and finally her dear sweet grandbaby was murdered. How much is one expected to take, really? I let the phone ring while I sat with my mother, cradling a box of Kleenex. Some bags and boxes that she had brought from home barely made it inside the front door.

Strangers were still sprinkled across the lawn, praying and saying rosaries, holding signs that read "REPENT" and "THE END IS NEAR." My favorite sign read "GOD IS COMING AND SHE IS PISSED." My family barely even noticed these squatters anymore, walking past them like lawn furniture, even as they crowded towards us when we moved, or even as they fell to their knees when I opened the door. It became routine, as if we'd lived with this all our lives. It was no different to me than the person who had to push through a subway crowd every day on her way to work. At first I thought it was a temporary situation and an annoyance,

10 Days Ago

but I had come to expect, maybe even count on their being there.

The first thing I did each morning was glance outside my bedroom blinds to see if they were gathering yet. And the last thing I did at night was take one more peek and wave to those who were still hanging on. Many nights I even blew them a kiss. Occasionally, I'd put some food or hot chocolate out on the front porch for them, for which they seemed grateful. I felt a little as though I was treating them like pets, but I was enjoying their loyalty. Despite our lack of personal interaction, I do believe that their constant prayer was good for me, helping me to keep centered and focused in an otherwise absurd situation. I loved my pets. And I needed them.

But my mother was in agony. Back at her home she had seen all of my father's things, which she had barely had a chance to deal with before moving in with us. His voice, his hearty laugh and his smells flooded her brain when she entered her home. She missed him tremendously. When I tried to console her with the lovely visit I'd had with him in my kitchen that first day when Jesus came to me, and the craziness started, she just began to tremble and clamp her eyes shut and she told me to stop. Suddenly, she clenched her chest and began to suck air, unable to get a full breath.

No, I thought. Not her, too. Jesus, do not take my mother. I cannot go through this again. My mother gasped and looked around frantically, clenching the sleeve of my sweater as I tried to stand up. I quickly weighed the options: heart attack or panic attack. I knew they were hard to distinguish from each other. But assuming it was one over the other could be making a life-

Coming

or-death mistake. I tried to talk to my mom, tried calming her and stroking her hair and telling her to relax and breathe slowly. She just panicked more, until I scraped her off me and ran to the front door. I screamed into the solemn crowd, "Call an ambulance, quick!" which sent the peaceful gathering into a frenzy.

I closed the door to find my mother in a fetal position on the floor, clenching her chest and gasping for breath. I tried my best to pull her up onto my lap. I sat with her and assured her that help was on the way and that everything was okay. My tear ducts had apparently kicked back into gear; I saw mascara-tinted tears dripping onto my mother's face. I wiped her face with my sleeve and tried rocking her and repeating that everything was okay.

Four hours later, or maybe it was seven minutes, a paramedic entered the front door accompanied by one of the regular lawn-dwellers. They ran to my mother and me on the floor and the paramedic, now accompanied by other assorted firefighters and police, laid my mother flat on the floor and helped me up. He asked questions so quickly that I just answered robotically as they opened my mother's blouse, checked her heart with a stethoscope, and put oxygen to her mouth. They pulled me back to where I could not see what was happening. I desperately tried looking between emergency professionals, but I couldn't see my mother and I could not hear my mother crying or gasping any more. I realized she had died.

That's it. I give up. I do not want to do this any more. Jesus, I quit. I'm done. Get someone else. I don't like being on your team. With a burst of adrenaline, I

10 Days Ago

actually pushed two six-foot policemen to either side so that I could kneel down and say good-bye to my mother. One police officer fell over an end table by the couch, crashing a brass lamp to the floor and the other flew into a smaller, daintier female paramedic who was knocked flat. There was pandemonium as everyone was helping each other to their feet, but most important, there was my mother, being helped to her feet and escorted to sit on the couch. I ran to my mom and threw my arms around her. Almost as quickly, I apologized for my Jackie Chan maneuver. With my mother's pulse nearly back to normal and her breath slowing, people eased up a bit and began to poke fun at each other for being taken out by "just a mom," as my kids referenced my profession.

Although her situation was ruled as a panic attack, my mother was taken to the hospital for more tests and observations. After sweeping up the broken light bulb, I opened the front door and told everyone in the front yard what was going on. I asked them for just a few more prayers for my mother, but said that I was sure she would be fine. I was putting on my coat to run to the hospital when my children came in from school and I thought, oh my God, I'm losing it. I forgot about my children.

"Where are you going?" they asked.

"Grandma had to go to the hospital, but she's okay," I said, and my oldest daughter burst into tears. Apparently we were all dangling from our last nerve.

I took my coat off and told the kids that Grandma would be just fine, that she was just having a few tests done. Then I called my brother and told him the story and he assured me that I didn't need to go to the hospital. He would go and sit with my mother until she was released. He even suggested he take her back to his house, but I insisted that she come back home with me, where her things were and where my kids would feel better when they could give her a hug.

I made some popcorn and I flopped down on the couch and my kids told me about their day. Speaking so fast their brains could hardly keep up, they told me that the principal told them that school was indefinitely closed and that the principal would be leaving a voicemail on everyone's phone that night and sending a letter in the mail. I couldn't believe what I was hearing. No school? My kids explained that too many teachers and students were staying home after the Dream, and the school board had to make a decision. Even school board members were hard to find. My kids were ecstatic. To them it was like a snow day on steroids.

But my heart sank. I didn't think Jesus would want that. I didn't think he would want people to sit around and wait. Just then my husband called and said that his office was closing for the week and he was on his way home. He wondered if I needed anything from the store.

Jack Daniel's, maybe. Possibly even Prozac. This was all getting a little overwhelming again. I began fixing dinner and realized that I had to speak up about the situation. I could not let the world shut down.

After dinner, I went to the hospital and brought my mother home. All the way home my mom told me how embarrassed she was that she burdened me with her problem. I tried to reassure her that we had all been through too much. As we pulled onto my street, my

10 Days Ago

mother conceded that she was so proud of me. "You really think I'm doing what Jesus would want me to do?" I asked.

"Oh, I don't know about that," she replied, "but the way you took down a whole police squad was impressive!"

I looked at her and chuckled, then giggled a bit more, then began laughing so hard I could barely drive.

9 Days Ago

I decided to set up a press conference. My living room was too small and churches were too filled with people, so I got permission to use my kids' school cafeteria. I set the conference for two o'clock. I wanted to have as much press as possible for this important announcement.

The rest of the morning I stayed in my room and asked my husband to take the kids out somewhere for a while so that I could have some quiet time. My mother rested and read in the spare bedroom. All was quiet. I silenced the ringer on all of the phones and became cloistered. I prayed for God to give me the wisdom to know what to say to the press. I sat idly at the laptop. I suggested that now might be a great time for a little visit, a little encouragement, but there was no vision. No VW Bug coming down the street. It was just me, my vacant computer monitor and my wandering mind.

As I walked away from the laptop, I went to the bedroom window, and parting the blinds, saw my "pets" on the front lawn. Their numbers had increased and I didn't know if this was due to the excitement from the day before or if the word had already gotten around that I was going to make a public announcement. I smiled at them

9 Days Ago

and let the blinds snap back. I sat on my bed, and, grabbing a pillow to my stomach, put my head down and took a deep breath. Suddenly, I remembered Jesus telling me to breathe deeply and feel the energy, that with every breath I was pulling the spirit into me. I recalled the zing of energy that I had felt the first time, but life had been so crazy I had forgotten to be still and breathe. I pushed my stomach out as I took a deep inhale, focusing on the wind in my nostrils and imagining a subtle spirit filling my being. With slow exhalation, I pulled my stomach back in and felt the warmth in the back of my throat, and all of my muscles released, and I sank into my bed. I continued breathing deeply, not because I felt the zing. I didn't. But it felt so fabulous to relax. I didn't know how long it had been since my body had been given permission to relax and be still. I thought of nothing but my breath and the sensation that it caused in my body.

I had no idea how long I sat in that trancelike state. I felt as though nothing could jar me from the peace of those moments, not screams or fire or bullets, or even a whisper. The only thing that pulled me back into reality was words. I had the words for the press conference. I opened my eyes and ran over to my laptop and pecked out the statement that I would be offering to the media and the world. I felt confident and refreshed.

I went downstairs to read the statement to my mother and get her approval, although I had not planned on changing a word or even a comma, no matter what she told me. It was more of a compassionate action to help my mom feel connected and involved. On my way down the steps, I checked my watch and realized that I had

Coming

missed the Pope's address in Germany. Disappointed, I ran to the television and clicked it on to see if I could get the highlights.

News was coming out of Africa that a new committee of the African Union, African Countries United by Trade Economics, or ACUTE, had pulled government officials from every African country and aid workers from every organization involved in Africa, as well as natural resource specialists, to meet in Libreville, Gabon, on the west coast of the continent. The goal of the summit was "to find immediate solutions to chronic problems of the great African nations." HIV, famine, clean water, education, corruption, genocide…no issues were avoided. One issue at a time, input had been gathered as to the scope of the problem and what was needed in both the short term and the long term to improve any given situation, focusing on trade of natural and human resources. Africans were determined to first use their own resources to help each other and then, only when necessary, appeal to the world community for help.

An ACUTE spokesman said that once solutions were taking shape and Africa was empowered, their organization would work tirelessly to contribute to the world markets with whatever they could offer. He said that, as a continent, they felt they had been a drain on the world economy for too long. But they had every confidence that with their new cooperation they would grow to be an invaluable resource to all peoples of the world. The spokesman added that unbelievably creative solutions to the AIDS epidemic had been discussed and that remarkable strides were being made with many of the other so-

9 Days Ago

cial concerns. Their continent was rich with valuable resources. A full report was being compiled and would be released by the end of the month.

Wow. Progress in Africa. That was not something I had ever heard in my lifetime. Schools and community programs touted lovely tribal words which translated a deep understanding of peace and cooperation, but it always seemed like poor Africa was the poster child for poverty and social crisis. I had seen documentaries on the systematic raping of young women in one country. I saw women on the *Here's Hope Show* speaking of disgraceful female circumcision. Everyone had seen the benefit concerts that attempted to ameliorate the suffering of the AIDS orphans and the starving children. There were countries where uprisings resulted in atrocities that could not be fathomed by the human mind, forcing those who survived to be displaced from their homes only to live in squalor.

I could not imagine any vital world contributions coming from that continent, but I loved the prospect. A strong and equal world partner, I thought, might do more to relieve racial stereotypes in my own country than all of the speeches and school programs combined.

I turned off the television and practiced my speech with my mother. She was drained, I could tell, and she just told me softly that it sounded perfect. That was not like her. She always corrected dangling participles or tweaked vocabulary for that perfect meaning. I gave her a kiss on the cheek and she pulled me in and hugged me tightly and whispered in my ear that she had never been so proud. This time I knew what she meant.

Coming

I went to the school an hour early. I suggested that my family stay home and have a nice lunch together and enjoy their time off and watch me on television. I had called Father Michael, my parish priest, to accompany me just in case I needed a slight nod of encouragement. He humbly accepted my invitation.

With a tight mouth, a tight grey ponytail and a tight navy suit wrapping her generous frame, the principal was at the school cafeteria, orchestrating camera operators and news people. She was doing what she did best, administering. No one made a move without her approval. Maintenance workers were busy setting up a podium and running power strips and standing on ladders replacing light bulbs that had probably been out for most of the decade.

Father Michael and I were escorted into a fourth-grade classroom that was near the cafeteria, where I was told to relax. We were served some coffee and a few cookies that undoubtedly came from the endless source in the teachers' lounge. Remarkably, I felt relaxed and tried to calm Father Michael who seemed so jittery I was second-guessing my wisdom in bringing him along. He and I agreed that he would stand on the steps leading into the cafeteria, where I could find him if I needed him, but he would be out of the spotlight. He was a sweet, shy and humble man.

As I was recounting the story of my mother's panic attack and my karate moves to Father Michael, the principal burst into the room and called out, "It's show time!" The timid Father Michael noticeably paled, but what he lost in color, I gained in poise as I calmly en-

9 Days Ago

tered the packed cafeteria amidst flashing lights and quieting voices.

I took a few minutes to adjust to the bright lights, sipped from a glass of water thoughtfully placed on the shelf inside the lectern, looked around at the crowd, took a deep breath, and began.

"Thank you all so much for coming today. I feel like I must speak up, and although I am no expert, I appreciate your giving me your attention. As you all know, these are important times. Changes are happening in the world that are inconceivable. I have met no one who has not had the Dandelion Dream. No one. This is truly a remarkable world event that, as you know, I had forewarned with my maybe not-so-wise stunt." People chuckled. I continued.

"No matter what your religion, you must be awakened to the power of human cooperation. Advances have been made in the past couple of weeks that had been met with failure over and over in the past. How can this be? People are on fire with the message of the Dream. People are longing to help each other, to learn from each other, and to receive from each other. It is The Way. When you follow The Way of compassion and cooperation, miracles happen. Justice happens. Beauty happens. And our planet is being transformed." I took a sip of water and glanced at Father Michael, who had regained his color and smiled at me lovingly, nodding me on.

"What does the future hold? That is the question that is on everyone's mind. Is it all going to end? Just when we get things smoothed out, will it all be over? Is this a test? What will happen to me? Is there a heaven? Will I

Coming

make the cut?" I took a long pause and let those questions marinate in the minds of anyone listening.

"I cannot tell you for sure what the future will look like, but I can tell you with certainty that the only thing that will end is violence and selfishness and poverty. I know for sure that the world will be a garden, a beautifully restored garden of life. And that is my point in speaking to you today. We must live. We must work and learn and clean and shop and sleep and play. We cannot sit and tremble and wait. There is work to do; there is life to live. By isolating ourselves we are missing the joy of human interaction. I urge schools to reopen. I urge business to be business as usual. And although I am heartened by attendance in places of worship, I urge each person to make your life a prayer. By living and loving and learning, your life becomes a beautiful prayer, more profound than words can express. Continue to worship together, but return to life, keeping the Dream foremost in your thoughts. Thank you."

I took another sip and told the group that I could take questions, and the room burst into a shouting match that the principal had under control within fifteen seconds. She was impressive.

I handled questions with confidence, probably because Jesus had taken over my mouth at that point. I didn't even think about answers. They just spilled out of my mouth with such ease that I knew they couldn't be from me. Nothing stumped me, until I got a question about Baby's killer. I asked the crowd to focus on the positive, on the future, not on the past. At that point, I knew *I* had regained control over my mouth, because I was totally avoiding the subject, which Jesus would not

9 Days Ago

do. He would face it head-on, I knew he would. But I just couldn't. I was not ready. The man who took my baby made me sick.

I was escorted back to the fourth-grade classroom after I had satisfied every clever reporter looking for ambiguity in The Way. But love was always the solution. And the press gradually packed up their equipment and returned to their vans. I got my coat, and Father Michael grabbed a couple more cookies for the road. As I drove Father Michael home, he admitted to me that he had been a bit frightened of all the current events. Even though it was something he preached about happening, he had never in his wildest dreams imagined that it really could happen in his lifetime. But he told me that the calm, loving address I had just given made him relaxed, and he anticipated Jesus' coming like a kid before Christmas.

After dropping Father Michael off, I found myself humming an ancient Advent carol, "O come, O come, Emmanuel" and I suddenly appreciated the longing found in the minor chords of the tune.

~ 8 Days Ago ~

The day started out bad and went down from there. I flipped on the television hoping to be uplifted and there was Baby's killer at a video arraignment. He was still being held in the local jail, even though his lawyers had asked for a change of venue. A judge had decided to keep him where he was. The judge was afraid that any movement of the man might make my loyalists turn into an ugly, angry mob as they had done that first night.

So there he was, in an orange jumpsuit, shackled, looking into a camera with his lawyer by his side, entering a plea of "not guilty." My mind contorted as I tried to understand how his lawyer could possibly defend him as innocent under the circumstances. The police had practically caught him red-handed, and he made a full confession, not to mention the tirade I had endured at my visit!

I just wanted to hear the fiend admit to the whole world that he was guilty and ashamed. I wanted to hear him beg for forgiveness. I think I had once again abandoned death penalty retribution, but it was tough. I really just wanted him to have a heart attack and die. That way I would have a moral loophole, and my problem would be solved. He would be dead, and I would not be re-

8 Days Ago

sponsible. It would be perfect justice. I was consumed with what to do with this man.

In fact, with absolutely nothing else on my mind but determining justice, I contemplated day and night as to whether I could possibly forgive him. After all, he was a desperate man with unsound judgment. He probably had had no positive role models in his life and my compassionate act of forgiveness would be a beacon of God's saving power for the whole world to see. I had a plan. I would be a saint.

But it didn't work out that way. I found that I could not yet forgive him if he didn't repent. It was harder than I imagined it to be. I really hated it when I had great plans and they didn't work out. And I realized that my great plan was more about my sainthood than my compassion.

With school and work not yet back in session, I had a full house. I jumped up and clicked off the television so that the rest of the family would not be exposed to the murderer. I got a phone call, a voice message from the school principal, that school would resume on Monday, and all students and teachers were expected to attend. This was Thursday, too close to the end of the week to reorganize, I assumed.

My husband planned to go back in to work, even if they had a skeleton crew, to try to get the business back on track. He took his time going in, though, and probably left the house at about ten. He enjoyed being home with the family. But he realized that he could not stop working. We still had bills to pay and had to eat, and my new job was on a pro bono basis. Surely things would settle down soon and people would realize that Jesus

Coming

might not come for weeks, months, even years, and that they needed to *live*, not just wait in fear.

Not long after my husband left for work, he called from his cell phone in the car. "Hon, there's been a nuclear explosion somewhere near Iran. It's all over the news. It just happened. It sounds bad, really bad. You better check it out. I think I'm going to turn around and come back home for the day. If things settle down, I'll go in to work tomorrow. I'll see you in a little bit."

My heart raced. A nuclear explosion? How big? I felt sick. For years we had seen movies of what a nuclear war would look like. The intense nuclear wind. The instant cremation of thousands of bodies, not to mention the radiation poisoning of millions. Was this what Jesus was trying to pre-empt? Was he a day late and a soul short? Surely he knew when these things were about to happen. How could he allow such a thing when all was going so well?

I asked my mom to do a puzzle or something with the kids. I wanted to protect them from any horrific scenes they might see on television. And when my mother heard the news, she just shook her head and said, "We're all going to hell in a hand basket," which was something she had said daily after reading the newspaper for as long as I could remember. Still shaking her head, she said to my children, "C'mon kids, let's make the most of this imaginary snow day. Let's go sledding! We'll imagine there's snow and we'll slide down the hill in the back yard. What are snow days for, after all?"

I warmed at the sight of my kids bundling up, beaming at their crazy grandma. As they grabbed our saucer-shaped sleds from the garage, my mom winked at

8 Days Ago

me as they headed out to the back lawn, avoiding the omnipresent mob in the front.

I blew a kiss to my mom. She had taught me how to play. She had gotten down on the floor with my babies and played, and now, with the world teetering on the brink of destruction, she played. God love her.

I ran to the television and flipped on CNN. A midsize explosion was reported in northern Iran. It was unclear who was responsible. The explosion had happened only moments before, so camera crews were not yet on the scene. The bomb was believed to have detonated in the area of Dasht-e Kavir, or the Great Salt Desert. That's good, that's good, I thought to myself. Unpopulated. Officials from Tehran, the capital of Iran, were quick to issue a statement that the Iranian government had not done any nuclear testing, and they were beginning to insinuate that Israel could be responsible.

Just as quickly, the prime minister of Israel denounced the "despicable act of terror" and said that Israel was in full compliance with the treaty that they had laid out last week regarding cease-fires and progress toward peace in the Middle East region.

Newscasters were scrambling for new bits of information. The spokesman for the U.S. president was quick to report that, although tensions had been escalating between the U.S. and Iran, in no way did the U.S. have any part in the detonation of a nuclear bomb, and that the U.S. would be diligent in its search for the truth in who was responsible for this egregious act. Back and forth went the blaming and the denouncing like a ping-pong game. North Korea, China, Pakistan, even Venezuela was considered as a possible perpetrator.

Coming

My husband came in through the garage door, looking ashen and absolutely panicked. We watched all day in horror as accusations flew and pictures began to appear of a charred creation. Fortunately, there were only a small number of bodies, although any person lost to this type of destruction was absolutely vile. My husband and I held hands and worried that this could easily get out of control and that this would be the end: not a peaceful coming of Jesus, but a massive nuclear Armageddon annihilating the Garden and everyone in it.

I closed my eyes and pictured one head of state after another and sent vibes of the Dandelion Dream to them. They had to remember the Dream. It was not that long ago. It would end all of this quickly and nonviolently. "Remember the Dream. Remember the Dream. Remember the Dream," was my mantra into the late afternoon.

By dinnertime, mom and the kids had returned with soaking wet bottoms. Apparently the grass was not the best "powder" for sledding, so they had ventured off to get blocks of ice. It was not easy to find blocks of ice anymore, especially in the winter. But after driving to just about every gas station within a ten-mile radius, they stumbled upon some. They spent the whole afternoon sitting on their blocks of ice and sledding down the small hill in the back yard until it was nothing but mud. The backs of their pants were soaked and they were covered in muck, but they stumbled into the kitchen with frenetic laughter.

"A little disconnect from reality, mother?" I asked, winking, as I walked past her to begin making dinner.

"Isn't life wonderful?" she remarked, knowing something terrible was going on in the world, but that

8 Days Ago

maintaining the innocence of children was more important at the moment. And I thanked her for all that she did and all that she was.

By the end of the day, it was determined that terrorists had gone into Turkmenistan and were able to buy or steal (still not clear) weapons-grade uranium, smuggled from Russian caches. The terrorists were somehow able to assemble a weapon, either in Turkmenistan or Iran. The conclusion was drawn that the smugglers were on their way to Afghanistan or Pakistan when the nuclear weapon detonated by mistake, fortunately taking few lives, but throwing the world into a blame game that could end in absolute destruction of the entire planet.

I stayed up most of the night following the events and praying for Jesus to step in quickly. I thought of how totally crestfallen he had seemed to be at the destruction of life, and I imagined him holding his heart and sobbing at these latest events, which made me, too, cry for our world.

7 Days Ago

This day was truly a miracle. Among reports of damage to the desert region of Iran, with the grisly pictures of charred fauna and smoldering flora, the Nuclear Threat Initiative made an historic announcement. The NTI was an organization dedicated to reducing the risk of, and raising public awareness of weapons of mass destruction. They announced that an agreement was signed by the head of every nation...*all* nations...promising to destroy or dismantle nuclear, chemical, or biological weapons, effective immediately. Each representative agreed to weapons inspections and full disclosure of nuclear information. A threat of a nuclear war from any world nation would no longer exist. And even the terrorist organizations seemed to be losing steam as fewer and fewer attacks were being reported on international fronts, barring the recent fatal faux pas in Iran.

Although I never feared that a nuclear explosion in my part of the world would affect me personally, I knew that officials involved in this arena worried every day about that possibility and would think of me as a simpleton for being in such denial.

The Nuclear Threat Initiative spokesperson stated that the agreement had been made during a meeting in

7 Days Ago

Brussels, orchestrated by the International Atomic Energy Agency, or IAEA. The nuclear accident of the day before was happenstance, bringing a sense of urgency to the negotiations. World leaders, encouraged by the spirit of cooperation and collaboration spanning the globe, agreed to dismantle all weapons and signed the historic resolution which vowed to never allow a weapon of mass destruction to be deployed at the hands of the signers. Signatures were garnered by facsimile of non-participating countries, marked with state seals. Video from the meeting in Brussels showed much shaking of hands, patting of backs, bowing of heads, hugs and smiles.

It was hard to imagine a world without a constant threat of war. In fact, even the threat of crime seemed to be disappearing as well. My son, who was only eight, brought that to my attention in the evening. It was Friday night and he and his friends wanted to walk up to the neighborhood park and play some soccer. The park was only about a third of a mile from our house, but I never let him walk up there alone, even in the daylight. I always made sure he had a buddy when he came or went from the park, and I always knew when to expect him. I would watch anxiously out the window for him to return the block and a half he would walk alone after his friend split off to go his own way.

When I told my son he could not go to the park because it would be dark in a half hour, he looked at me like I was a helicopter, hovering a little too closely and totally unnecessarily.

"You know you can't walk home from the park in the dark!" I exclaimed. "And besides, I don't even like

Coming

you playing up there with your friends without an adult supervising."

"Are you kidding me?" he said, with disbelief, sounding more like a teenager than a second-grader. "Nothing bad has happened in this city for a couple weeks. Nothing. Ever since Baby got shot, it's like everyone realized how terrible that was, and everyone is being good. I'm not going to get shot, Mom. Don't worry."

I bit my lip. Just the thought of going through that again nearly made me faint. I knew he would not get shot. Although, it was just a month previous that it was not unheard of for several members of a family to die as a result of inner-city crime, not to mention the atrocities inflicted upon families around the world in wars and other conflicts. The mere thought made me sick. How could anyone go through what I was going through with my Baby twice, or more? I was certain that it was not something that got easier with practice. It was unthinkable.

But my son was right. Crime was basically now nonexistent, even in the major urban areas. Reports were coming out every day stating such. So what was I freaking out about? But how could I undo an undercurrent of fear in just a couple weeks? The dread was imbedded in my psyche. I didn't know if I could ever totally trust others to be fair and kind and respectful of life and property. I was conditioned to mistrust anyone's motive. I talked about being loving, but I loved at a distance, always wary of the other.

My mother chimed in, "You know, when I was a little girl, a murder happened in the city, and it was all

7 Days Ago

over the news for weeks. Murder was practically unheard of back then, truly a rare occurrence. We were never afraid. My friends and I walked everywhere, day or night. Of course, not so many people had cars, so if anyone wanted to go anywhere, they walked. But back to being afraid. I remember just last year I was walking in the mall, in broad daylight, and a huge man was walking straight towards me. I felt more and more uncomfortable as he approached. He did not do anything suspicious, other than be large, which was totally out of his control. Finally, I couldn't stand the tension and I ducked into a store and acted like I was interested in buying what was on display. I felt bad that he might think I was afraid of him, even though I was. He probably suspected so, because the display happened to be of treadmills and other contraptions for torturing the human body, but I had to look interested."

My kids burst into laughter at the thought of their grandma on a treadmill. I wondered if they pictured her, as I did, flying off the back of the thing, holding onto her purse, which was ever attached to her left forearm.

"Oh yes, very funny. Grandma can't run on a treadmill. Well, I'll tell you what, when you grow up walking on sidewalks, treadmills seem pretty ridiculous!" my mother snorted.

She had a point there, I had to admit.

My mom steered the conversation back to her childhood memories. The mall incident had reminded her of the time that she had been walking home in the dark, no older than six or seven. As she had looked up at an enormous man walking straight towards her, she tripped on an uneven seam in the sidewalk. She had cried at the stabbing pain in her scraped knee and asked the man if he could carry her home. He had happily obliged, bouncing her on his back like a pony ride until she had forgotten her scrapes by the time she arrived home a block later.

I would kill my kids if they did that, I thought. Wow, how could times have changed so quickly from one of basic trust and decency, to one of fear, suspicion and exploitation? No wonder Jesus feels an urgency to return, I realized.

Still, I could not let go of my fear and allow my son to walk to the park. Instead, my husband drove him, ran a few errands, and then picked him up an hour later. Interestingly, the other boy's parents were also chauffeuring, apparently unable to believe that all was truly safe.

But *trust*: what a concept! What a beautiful, wonderful concept!

⚘ 6 Days Ago ⚘

Jesus came. I was standing at the window of my bedroom, peering out at the lawn-dwellers and thinking of their faith and devotion and their kind support for me and my family. They were a quiet, peaceful bunch, praying and maybe just waiting. It was Saturday morning and my family was downstairs. We had finished breakfast, and my mom was doing dishes, my husband was reading the newspaper, and the kids were watching cartoons. It seemed like life had returned to a life with which I was familiar. I looked forward to a normal day.

I turned back into the room to make the bed and sitting right there on the side of my bed was Jesus. Startled, I jumped about a foot and a half, sucking oxygen. But upon my recognition of him, my mouth dropped open and I ran to him as if seeing a friend I had not seen in years. He rose to his feet and threw his arms around me, and we stood in an embrace for probably a full minute.

I felt warm tears streaming down my face as he held me. It was as if all stress that had been pent up inside of me completely melted and drained right out through my eyes. Jesus saw my tears and pulled me to himself again

Coming

and just held me for another few seconds, stroking my hair.

"I am so proud of you," he whispered into my ear.

"You are?" I asked.

"Absolutely! Look how the world is changing! You did it. I knew you could," he said with enthusiasm.

"Is this it? You're back. This is the big Second Coming?"

"No, not today, not just yet, but soon," he replied, smiling. "I just wanted to thank you from the bottom of my heart for having the courage to follow me. I know these last few weeks have been incredibly difficult for you. I know I asked so much of you and maybe that seemed unreasonable. But I knew you were creative and capable and the right person for the job."

Then his tone changed to one of extreme sadness. "I am so sorry that you lost Baby. I couldn't believe it! I mean, I am shocked every single time people choose greed, violence and evil over love and cooperation. It blows my mind that anyone thinks that these are viable solutions to any problem. What did killing Baby do for anyone? The man who did it got nothing, other than more misery. He heaped misery on your family and all who knew that sweet child. The whole nation, the whole world, was touched and saddened. Truly, many prayers have come to me asking for your peace in the midst of your terrible, terrible tragedy. I have come to you through neighbors and friends and even strangers, trying to bring you peace, and I heard your prayers. Please know that I was always with you. I never left you, ever, and I never will. I cannot."

6 Days Ago

My heart still ached at the mention of Baby's name. I listened to Jesus with every fiber of my being. He truly was shocked and sickened by Baby's murder. Free will, it seemed, was as disappointing as it was gratifying. Jesus was repulsed by all violence. He only wanted everyone to know the same peace that I felt when I was with him. He knew that people would feel the peace and joy if they looked to their hearts and believed in love.

"Thank you," was all I could say. What words are powerful enough to convey gratitude for healing amidst tragedy? I knew it was inadequate, but it was all I had.

"You are most welcome," he said politely, and with him squeezing my hand, we just sat on the edge of the bed in silence for a few moments, letting me absorb his strength.

"Jesus," I said, "could you teach me how to pray? I know you showed me how to relax and breathe and feel God's peace, but sometimes I just need words. I feel like I fall into begging for the same things over and over, while neglecting so many important problems."

"Try praying this way," he said calmly. "Our God, who is in all of creation, sacred is Your name. May wholeness come through the love that is shown on earth, as it is in perfection. Nourish my soul today and every day. And hold on to me as I reach out to others. Reveal through me all that is life, love, unity, until we do not know evil."

"That almost sounds like the Lord's Prayer…but not quite," I added quickly so that he wouldn't think I was unfamiliar with the most popular prayer in all of Christianity.

Again came one of those smiles that he had mastered. A smile that revealed both amusement at my ignorance and love for me despite my naiveté.

"It *is* the Lord's Prayer."

"But the words are different. How could it be?" I asked.

"Different times call for different words. I haven't heard anyone use the word "hallowed" in casual conversation lately, so I thought I would make it a little more 'user friendly.' But am I not the Lord? And did I not just pray?"

"Oh, of course," I said with shame. "How stupid of me. Could you say it again while I write it down?"

And Jesus proceeded to slowly repeat the new version of his prayer while I scribbled it on the back of a bank envelope that I found on top of my nightstand, along with other receipts and lint that I had emptied from my jean pockets. After we finished, I knew that I had something special, and despite its unholy appearance, I tucked the sacred words back into the top drawer of my nightstand under my lip balm.

"Thanks," I said sincerely, "that is beautiful."

"You are beautiful," he replied, which nearly took my breath away. My heart was so full it was about to burst.

Then gently changing the subject he patted me on the thigh and asked, "So, now what?"

I let out a quick puff of air and gave him a playful slap on the arm. "What do you mean, 'now what?'? I'm not in charge here. I've been wondering 'now what' for about a month. You tell *me* 'now what'," I demanded.

6 Days Ago

"I was just kidding. I mean, you're good. You've got great ideas. I just thought maybe you were on a roll," he said with a sweet, handsome smile.

"On a roll? I am flying by the seat of my pants each and every day. There is nothing rolling here," I guaranteed him.

"Well, you could have fooled me," he said. "I was just thinking…you were right on track in telling everyone to get back to work and school, back to their normal lives. I don't want people to stop living. I want them to *start* living in a way they've never lived before. Look at those people in your front yard, for example. Some of them have been there every day for weeks. That is no way to live, although I do hear their prayers. But I want their lives to be a prayer, as you said in the press conference. I want everything they do and everything they say to be a prayer...actions and words of love. I don't want people to fear my coming. I want them to rejoice in it. I want it to be the icing on their cake, not the grade on their test. How can we help them not to fear?" he asked.

"Dance," I said, as if in a trance, remembering how great I felt after dancing to the Aretha Franklin tune.

Jesus looked at me and shrugged, stood up and did a little soft shoe shuffle in my bedroom.

I laughed. I loved this guy. "No, I mean, everyone should dance. Dance is full of life. Dance is freedom. We should have a world dance party!"

Jesus leapt up, punching his fist into the air, and cried, "Yes!"

I smiled at his enthusiasm.

"I knew you would know what to do next," he said with a grin. And I wondered if the dance party was really my idea or his. I looked at him, voicing my suspicions.

"No, that idea was all you. I don't really meddle with people's thoughts all day. Your minds are miraculous, they don't need me. I just provide the loving framework, you do all the creating," he explained.

I grabbed his hand and led him back to sit on the side of the bed. I thought maybe we should quiet our frivolity, lest the whole family hear my hallucination. Okay, *vision*, if you must.

"Do you really think it's a good idea?" I asked, realizing what a privilege it was to actually get confirmation from Jesus himself, before doing something.

"I think it's brilliant. Tell the world to dance and rejoice. It will be so cool. I can't wait to see it. And then, be sure to tell everyone to get back to their lives and to let their hearts dance through each and every day. I will come soon, but I want the world to be alive and free when I come."

"Okay," I said, and I agreed that it could be fun. I wanted to do more planning with him and just talk and be with him, I so loved his company. But he had that look in his eye. "You have to go now, don't you," I said reluctantly.

"I do, but I'll see you soon. And remember, I never leave you. Ever," he reminded me.

"Just leave me alone in the shower," I said adamantly, and he chuckled.

"Hey, can I show you to my family before you go?" I asked, as if he were a rare Jewish artifact that I wanted to bring to Show and Tell.

6 Days Ago

He smiled softly and said, "They'll see me soon. I never leave them either, you know. Tell them I am with them."

He gave my hand a squeeze, and he was gone. I sat on the edge of the bed, alone, feeling slightly nervous about organizing a party, but also much at peace.

I called my husband into my room and told him what had just happened. I couldn't read his expression. I wasn't sure if he was jealous, or doubtful, but he gave me a hug, and I could feel that he truly loved me.

"I guess it's time for another press conference," he said, as if press conferences were as much a part of our daily existence as brushing teeth.

I got on the phone with the school principal, and she agreed to allow another conference. I think she liked the media exposure her school was getting simply by being the site of the press conferences. But I thought that I shouldn't tell her the topic of the conference. She seemed a bit stodgy, and I'm not sure she would be supportive of a world dance party. But she did agree to give me an hour at three o'clock, since everything was basically still cleaned up from the other day.

I called all of the local news stations and again, they were all over it. I even leaked to a few that I had had another vision, just to be sure that there was enough fervor in the air.

I was not disappointed. By three, the school cafeteria was as packed as could be. Order was called. This time, with my family by my side, I stood at the podium proclaiming that people needed to live. We needed to live in joy, not in fear, and that kicking up our heels would help kick the fear right out of us. I urged the communities

Coming

worldwide to have an impromptu dance party on Sunday. I called people to go out into the streets on Sunday to eat, drink and be merry. I pleaded with them to get to know their neighbors and have fun. I assured the public that Jesus would fully endorse the party and that we should listen to our spirit and let it soar. Life is to be enjoyed.

Reporters asked if I had conversations with Jesus recently, and I told them that I had. I told them that Jesus was dismayed that people were living in fear of his coming. And then I urged everyone to return to school and work on Monday. I told the public that Jesus was thrilled with the turn of events in the world and thanked each and every person for listening to their Dream and treating others with dignity and cooperation, rather than competition. Then came the question that always came. The big one. Did I forgive Baby's killer?

A silence dropped on the fairly joyful atmosphere. All eyes were upon me. I took a deep breath and my husband tenderly rubbed my back. My mind was racing, because I really did not know what to say. I didn't want to look like a hypocrite. I didn't want to look like a fool. But I couldn't lie either. It seemed that the silence was about to explode in my head when my daughter grabbed the microphone and bent it downward toward herself.

Standing on tip-toes, stretching toward the microphone, she said, "We loved Baby and we still do. That man really didn't take her from us. She is still with us every day. I know she is. I feel her. Sometimes I hear her. Listen, maybe you can hear her, too," my sweet daughter suggested.

6 Days Ago

As she spoke, a silence fell upon the crowded room, yielding to a burst of laughter and applause, and I knew I was hearing my cheerful Baby.

5 Days Ago

Party day. I set my alarm for six o'clock because I wanted to see if anyone in the world was dancing. Scuffing in my slippers quietly down the steps, I went to the family room to turn on the television and see what was happening. I was not disappointed. Apparently, news agencies all over the world and the Internet picked up my press conference, and parties began immediately. I watched on television as people all around the globe were spilling into the streets, farms and villages in celebration. In Australia, where it was Sunday at the time I made my announcement, people were out in the streets, milling about reluctantly at first, until more and more people ventured out of their homes and struck up conversations. Inevitably, someone would go inside to get their portable speakers and music began filling the air. People shuffled awkwardly, stiffly, until small children joined in and loosened the crowd as only children could do. The children jumped and spun as if it were a job.

In remote areas of Africa, villagers danced traditional dances and laughed and shared barbequed critters of one sort or another. In Asia, huge fireworks displays were seen, along with what seemed to be billions of people in the crowded cities of China.

5 Days Ago

I peered out my window to see if anyone was partying in my neighborhood yet and, to my surprise, found my front lawn empty. After all of these days and weeks, there was no one. It saddened me just a bit and I found myself missing my supporters. Trying to shrug it off, I turned back to the television.

On our side of the globe, people were just waking up and, it being Sunday, church bells were ringing. On the east coast a news team found a family who had gone to early services and were eating breakfast at a local chain restaurant. When the reporter approached and the family saw they were on camera, the overweight dad did a little sitting jiggle in front of his short stack, while the mother and children laughed at him.

The reporter panned the restaurant and asked, "What about the world party, people? Where's your manager?"

With that, the hefty manager appeared and said that he would follow the lead of his clientele as far as having a party atmosphere. The reporter, taking his opportunity, turned back into the restaurant and asked, "Who wants a party here?"

Adults looked at each other uncomfortably, but the children jumped up and squealed, "Yeah!"

"I think the patrons have spoken, sir. Crank up the tunes," the enthusiastic reporter said.

And with that, the reluctant manager turned up the volume of some easy listening music that was piped into the restaurant.

The reporter stared right into the camera, with the subtlest of expressions that looked like he might throw up. He walked back over to the manager and said, "Sir, no offense, but we're talking about a world *dance* party, here, not an elevator party."

At that moment, as if on cue, a young woman and her date entered the restaurant and, seeing the news crew, yelled out, "Come on people, let's dance for breakfast!"

She removed the nearly undetectable headphones from her ears and handed the manager her personal music gizmo, assisting him in dialing in a hip-hop song and the tempo picked up. Kids spilled off their chairs and jumped and danced. Elderly couples smiled and wiggled their shoulders to the music. Horns were heard honking as cars passed the restaurant.

"Now *this* is what *I'm* talking about," said the reporter into the camera. "That's all from here; now back to you, Jeff."

Jeff, back in the newsroom could hardly contain himself at the sight of uptight white Americans trying to cut loose on a Sunday morning. I wondered if Jeff himself would have danced in the restaurant. I doubted it. He seemed pretty stiff. He was, I surmised, a glass-house dweller.

With my home still quiet, I got myself a cup of coffee and cuddled back into the couch and watched the world dance party on television, thoroughly enjoying the coverage. I took pleasure in the way CNN had decided to cover the day. Sprinkled between the party scenes were updates on important social and political endeavors in each region of the world. The nuclear disaster that occurred a couple days earlier and the nuclear agreement that had been drawn, was followed by coverage of people in the Middle East region, dancing and embrac-

5 Days Ago

ing each other to the exotic sound of Persian reed flutes and ouds.

Scenes of vicious rebel revolution and bleak queues of desperate refugees in Africa were followed by video clips from the new African organization, ACUTE, giving updates regarding their mission. Then cameras would cut to energetic dancing to the pounding of djembe drums, with hopeful rejoicing erupting in the vast refugee tent cities as well.

Around the globe we went, with past troubles stamped out by updates of cooperation among governments and agencies, followed by citizens dancing, talking, laughing and sharing meals. It was beautiful. I could not have imagined a world like this in my wildest dreams and the cynic in me doubted that it could last. I wondered how long before the fighting and selfishness would begin. I wondered how long the Dandelion Dream principle would stay in the forefront of all domestic and foreign policies…how long before the world settled into its old ways.

I was jarred from my negativity by the telephone. It was my next-door neighbor, who was about my age and a good friend, asking me if I were going to the party starting up at the Value Time parking lot. It was the biggest space in our community and apparently people were showing up with music and donuts and skateboards and confetti and anything they had around the house that would lend itself to a party. My neighbor asked if her family could meet up with mine at the party, to which I responded, "Absolutely!"

Then my dear neighbor said to me, humbly, "This whole experience has been so hard to believe. But I just

Coming

wanted to tell you that I think Jesus sure knew what he was doing when he chose you. You are sweet and kind and a great mom and wife, but most of all, you are relatively normal and I just wanted to tell you that I am honored to be your friend. I'll see you up at the party."

Before I could tell her what her friendship meant to me, she hung up, leaving me holding a dead phone, but smiling at the kind words she had spoken. She didn't have to say "*relatively* normal," I thought, grinning. But I realized that kind words somehow infuse life into another and are just as important as kind actions. All of my cynicism and negativity was gone.

I ran up the steps two at a time yelling for my family to wake up because there was a party going on. We were skipping church and going to a party. After all, life and worship and community had become so intermingled lately that "church" was changing from a place noun to a people noun.

My family dressed quickly and went in all directions, packing up lawn chairs, some crackers, peanuts, string cheese and grapes. I brewed a pot of coffee, put it in a Thermos and found some Styrofoam cups. We got a couple blankets and threw on some jackets. Fortunately, it was a beautiful day, not a cloud in the sky and warm for the time of year. Jackets would be plenty warm, especially if we were dancing. We loaded up the car and as we pulled out the driveway, my son asked, "Mom, where are all our friends?"

He was referring to all of the people who daily gathered around our house and had just become a part of his life. I told him how I supposed they had gone home

5 Days Ago

to get ready for the party and that we would probably see them there, and for that he was happy.

The drive to the party was only a few blocks, but with all we had to carry, we thought it better to drive than walk. My mother, in her infinite wisdom, had suggested all along that we take less and just walk, but we couldn't stop packing and now we found ourselves circling the area, looking for a place to park until we ended up about a block from our home. As my husband pulled into the parking spot by the curb, my mother, who was sitting in the front seat, just turned around and gave me the "told you so" look that was so unnecessary.

We piled everything into our arms and walked to the party. We could hear music coming over loudspeakers. By now it was eleven o'clock in the morning and people were flooding into the Value Time parking lot from all directions. It looked like a hive, swarming with jubilant bees. As we approached, camera crews ran up to me and, as I stopped and put some of our stuff down, my kids looked at me with pleading eyes. "Go ahead, kids," I said to them, I'll catch up."

My husband somehow added everything I had been carrying to his own load and, not being one to enjoy the spotlight, went with the kids to stake out a spot. Reporters surrounded me, asking my reaction to the party, to which I could only say that I had just gotten there but that it seemed to be fun and that communities ought to celebrate together more often. When they were satisfied, they thanked me and roamed off through the crowd, looking for that newsworthy incident that could happen at any moment, good or bad.

Coming

I lost track of my mother and panicked at first. We had been together so much lately and I had been so concerned for her that it was almost like losing a child in a crowd. But then I remembered that she was a big girl and was probably enjoying a little freedom. I saw my husband waving for me on the left side of the lot and I eventually worked my way to him after being approached by all kinds of people, some asking for autographs. That was weird and I declined.

Our neighbors were situated by my husband, setting up their snacks and drinks, and we greeted each other with big hugs. Once seated on our blanket, I looked toward the center of the crowd and saw about three dozen children hopping and twirling, randomly grabbing partners by the hands and dancing. I even saw a police officer dancing at one point. I saw people that looked like they'd camped out all night with a cooler of beer and buckets of chicken wings beside their lawn chairs. I thought we had brought a lot, but some people had hibachis going, while others had brought folding tables with umbrellas. Still others were beginning to drag in speakers and drum sets and all kinds of equipment to a makeshift stage. Live music started with bands cordially taking turns, playing every kind of music from jazz to rock to hip-hop to blues and back again.

I ended up standing on our blanket rather than sitting on it, as the crowd closed in. Our lawn chairs were inhabited by strangers, but that was fine with me. I didn't see my mother for probably an hour and was starting to worry again when I spotted her dancing on the other side of the children with three other older women who I knew were also widows. It made me happy to see her having

5 Days Ago

fun. Friends and strangers stopped by our blanket. Occasionally, someone would grab my hand and pull me into the center of the crowd, and we would dance. Sometimes I knew them, sometimes I didn't. Once it was my husband, and I was shocked to have three-and-a-half minutes alone with him for a slow dance.

The parking lot swelled with people, and as far as I could tell, there were no disturbances. I saw a table set up at one end of the lot with a large banner over it that read "Dandelion Coalition," and it was swarmed with people signing up to help in one way or another. The sun warmed the faces of the crowd as the party went well into the afternoon. Feeling more like a summer day, I forgot that the sun set early and by four o'clock, we started looking for all of our belongings for the long trek back to the car. I signaled to my mother that we were going home, and she took her sweet time in coming over to help us pack up.

A police officer was breaking up the party with a megaphone as we were breaking camp. I felt the need to speak up. I went over to the police officer with the megaphone and, after a quick tutorial on how to use it without the deafening squelch, I thanked everyone for coming to the party. I urged them to go back to their routines, whether work, school or home, and to continue to live with joy in their hearts. I asked them to remember to look out for each other in our community and be grateful for our blessings.

When we got home no one was hungry for dinner. My children had slightly reddened cheeks from the unexpected warm sunshine. We all took baths and showers and collapsed into our beds, grinning from ear to ear.

~ 4 Days Ago ~

My house was so quiet. Supporters again quietly loitered on the front lawn. My husband went to work, the kids returned to school, and I helped my mom move back into her home with most of her stuff. She had decided that it was time, and she was again the strong and confident mother that I knew. By noon I found myself eating lunch alone. Life almost seemed normal. But now *normal* seemed peculiar.

The world party had been a huge success with not a single reported incident of crime anywhere in the world. People around the world had shared food and stories and music and did so without leaving their prints on the earth. Everyone cleaned up after themselves so that you could not even tell that there had been such a gathering of humanity. A beautiful, peaceful, joyful garden. It was taking place just as Jesus had hoped or predicted or orchestrated or whatever it is that God does.

The doorbell rang at two o'clock. My best friend entered the house before I even got to the door, and taking off her coat, told me that we had to check out the online guestbook that she had created for Baby. She had asked my permission to do so when the obituary was posted, but in the fog of those days I had forgotten all about it.

4 Days Ago

She told me that I ought to see some of the responses, and she had waited for things to get a little bit back to normal before coming over. Still, she was afraid of me reading them by myself, so she offered to sit with me.

We went to the computer and she showed me how to log on to the site. Up popped Baby's name and the dates of her short life, to which I closed my eyes and drew in a deep breath, as if preparing to be held underwater for a long time. My grief seemed a bit like drowning, never quite knowing if I would make it to the surface and rid myself of panic. My friend seemed to sense my distress, and she read the first entry. As I opened my eyes I noticed that she actually skipped many entries of friends and family and had scrolled down to a particular sentiment.

It was from someone in Chihuahua, Mexico who told me that she and her family were praying every day for the soul of my Baby and for courage for our family. I was shocked. How would someone in Mexico think to express sympathy to me?

The next entry was from the president of a gun carriers' support initiative, expressing their sorrow for the "egregious misuse of a firearm that resulted in our unfathomable grief." They hoped that I would not think less of their organization for supporting the right to bear arms and that they planned to continue to advocate for safe and responsible use. Another entry from a self-described "tough old single gal" in Laramie, Wyoming stated she would be sending me a small donation of five dollars to use in any way that I needed. She was embarrassed by the amount, but hoped that it would be helpful in some way. I kissed my forefinger and touched her entry on the computer screen as I filled with an overwhelming sense of gratitude for her sacrifice.

My friend then scrolled down quickly, skimming the entries, pointing out the names and countries with disbelief that people all over the world took the time to express their sympathy, love and solidarity with our family. We returned back up to the woman from Wyoming where we had left off and we took turns reading entries from Canada, Afghanistan, Poland, Uruguay, Malaysia, and South Africa, as well as all over America. Taking turns allowed each of us to recover before reading aloud again. We read slowly and carefully, thinking about the heart and soul that was poured into each word in hope of lifting me and my family. The compassion was overwhelming. It was more beautiful than I can express in words. And it was as humbling as it was heartening. I felt the power of love permeating the world.

After spending over an hour spilling many tears of sadness, gratitude and joy, I couldn't wait to share the website with my family later that night. But I, too, felt the obligation to get back to work and be productive. I bade my friend goodbye and hugging her tightly, thanked her for her small act that was indescribable in impact. Jesus had told me about average people who do ordinary things with great love and therefore live a sacred life. No doubt my best friend was a saint.

I spent the rest of the afternoon cleaning up the house and buying groceries, back in my routine of wife and mother, with a new sense of holiness lighting the ordinary day.

～ 3 Days Ago ～

As the world continued to spin, its inhabitants found themselves increasingly interconnected. The interconnectedness led to a tolerance, an acceptance and a deepened level of relationship that had never before been documented.

I learned that the Chinese government made a statement opening up all types of religious activity. The Chinese government had been a world leader in religious persecution. Not only had the government restricted and supervised Western religions, but also some Asian practices and rituals. Upon protests by tens of millions of Chinese people who were affected by recent mystical events, the government conceded to lifting its supervision of religious practices as groups of its citizens were gathering by the thousands to perform activities that sustain the spirit. What we might call "worship" or "public prayer" was suddenly, if only temporarily, allowed. It was a great contradiction to the human rights violations of the past. The authorities were taking a huge risk at undermining their own power to control the populace, allowing ideologies conflicting to the government's to be nurtured in places of worship.

Coming

Also announced this day was the repeal of draconian government restrictions on nongovernmental agencies in Russia. Restrictions on their activities, which had previously crippled their work under mounds of red tape and threats of great danger, had been lifted, allowing them to function with limited governmental interference. It was unclear where this newfound freedom was born, but this, too, meant an end to many of the human rights violations that had been seen in Russia. Journalists and other critics of the government were given wide latitude in their reporting. Was the government willing to become more transparent? How would this play out in the lives of those living in opposition to the current governmental system?

Also coming out of Asia from countries such as Burma, North Korea, Laos, and the Philippines were reports of more governmental leniency toward dissention. Some of the worst human rights violators, I learned, were backing off, beginning to give their people some freedom to congregate, even protest. I was so intrigued I spent until lunchtime reading the newspaper and surfing the net for any news I could grab on China and Russia and all of Asia. It was fascinating to me as I learned of some of the terrible things that had been going on halfway around the world that I hadn't even known about.

I felt a twinge of guilt for ignoring the atrocities that had apparently been a part of so many lives. I had been insulated and ignorant, but no more. Now my appetite was voracious for both the bad news and the good in the world. I promised myself and God, that I would no longer be silent as long as there were injustices in the world. In the past I had felt that the problems were too

3 Days Ago

big, that my voice was too small, but not now. I researched websites that were devoted to social justice and logged on, became a member or requested e-mail updates from over a dozen organizations that appeared to me to be doing excellent work in promoting peace in the world. Where had I been all my life? I said a quiet prayer of apology.

I ate my lunch while surfing late into the afternoon. Even after my children came home from school, they found me at the computer. Upon kissing them both and hearing about their day, I returned to my searching for information until my backside screamed for a little exercise. It hurt to stand up after sitting for so many hours. I had turned my house phone off, knowing that only my closest circle could try to contact me on my cell phone if necessary. My phone never rang, my children played "house" and I wallowed in the quiet.

The weather had turned seasonally chilly and I wished that I had a dog who would persistently bark at me until I conceded to a long walk in the fresh air, benefiting us both. But in the absence of any cajoling pet, and having the tendency to avoid anything that resembled exercise, I bundled up and just walked around my yard for about fifteen minutes, looking for signs of spring. I pushed some dead leaves in the garden aside with the toe of my shoe, searching for the new shoot of a crocus or maybe even daffodils. But the ground was bare and moist under the blanket of leaves. Still I knew it would not be many more days before I would see definite signs of new life. I knew things were starting to happen under the ground that I could not yet see. But I

Coming

could almost feel it, almost feel the pressure of new life trying to burst forth.

I couldn't help but think of the people of the world, under a blanket of hope, making preparations for new life. Changes were definitely happening and I wondered when this new life would explode. From the changes I had seen in recent days, I knew that the new season would not be a frightening one, but still the anticipation was driving me nuts. I wanted it to come. I wanted Jesus to return. I wanted to be off the job. I wanted a new heaven and a new earth and I wanted it badly.

I went back inside, missing Baby again, and meditated until my husband returned from work. As I arranged myself comfortably in my chair, I thought that maybe meditation, imagination, prayer, intention... maybe they were all really just the same thing. Maybe it all started in the mind of an individual and maybe by changing one's mind one could change reality. A prayer for healing could bring a miracle. Imagining a better life could make it happen. An intention to help could turn into an action of assistance. Maybe that's what was going on in the world. Since the Dream, everyone was united in their thoughts, in their intentions, and as a result, reality was shifting. Together, people were thinking of love and their thoughts became actions of cooperation. Only God, only Love, had that sort of power. It became clear as I sat in silent meditation, that peace was at the world's doorstep. I felt it within and I knew without a doubt that soon I would witness it all around me.

✥ 2 Days Ago ✥

This day was one of action for me. No more sitting around watching world events. I was ready to become a part of the change. I was excited. As soon as I saw my children off to school, I cleaned up the house a bit and went right to my computer.

I found helpful websites to assist the most politically ignorant among us. And I was the queen of ignorance. The first thing I did was check on current state legislation. I found a bill that I feared might actually oppress people, rather than help them. I also found a proposed bill that would allow a state income tax credit for the working poor, giving them an opportunity to keep more of their hard-earned money. That sounded like a fair plan to me, and after researching it some more, I sent an e-mail to my state representative urging him to support that bill and reject the other. It was pitiful, but I even had to look up who my state representative was! I had voted in the last election, but I just couldn't remember. I was informed on the websites that most politicians do read e-mails and letters from their constituents. I felt empowered to be a part of the policy-making process.

The next thing I did was bundle up and drive down to the campaign headquarters of a woman who was running for the U.S. Senate. I had followed her campaign and loved almost everything she stood for. I planned to vote for her. But today, I was ready to cheer for her. I wanted the whole state to know how important it was to elect her. I walked into the small storefront campaign headquarters and found the place humming with volunteers. They were young and old, men and women, people of all races. Everyone seemed busy. There were piles of paper and posters and bumper stickers. It was a mess. The candidate was nowhere to be seen, but I knew she had traveling to do and probably left the campaign details to her campaign manager. As it turns out, the campaign manager was just coming in from getting a hot cup of coffee. I was introduced to her and she sat down with me and talked about my interest in volunteering and my time availability.

I felt such a buzz of excitement as people were pouring themselves into the election of a single candidate. How different from the way I'd participated in politics in the past. I never failed to vote, but somehow I was never filled with the passion that I sensed in this office. I was thrilled to be a part of it. I ended up volunteering about three hours that afternoon, mostly stuffing envelopes. Even the mundane was exhilarating. As I left, I promised to be back every Wednesday afternoon for two or three hours. I drove home with a different perspective on politics. It was invigorating to be more involved and I felt that I had more than just a right to vote. I had a sense of duty to get involved.

The kids came home from school and we had peanut butter on celery sticks. I puttered around the kitchen while the children talked about school and I felt excep-

2 Days Ago

tionally blessed. Even with our tragedy, we had family, we had education, we had jobs, we had comforts. I yearned for everyone in the whole world to have what I had and to delight in living.

I told my husband about my busy day over dinner. He was supportive as usual, but seemed a little distant. I had noticed that ever since Baby died, we tended to grieve on different cycles. When I was feeling pretty good, he'd be down and vice versa. It was frustrating that we weren't on the same page, but then maybe if we were both down together it would have caused a dangerous dark vortex. Still, I was a little annoyed that he was not as excited about being an agent of change as I was.

I called my mother after dinner to make sure she was doing all right back in her own home. She assured me that she needed to be home and that she was planning on cleaning out my dad's things the next day and donating them to charity. I offered to come over and help, but she insisted that she do it alone. I understood. It would be something that would take courage and time and preferably solitude. She suggested in a way that only mothers can do, that I spend a little time cleaning out *my* guest closet. I sarcastically told her that it was my goal to not be able to actually close any of our closets. She told me that I was doing a good job at reaching my goal, and I said good-night, knowing she was back to her old self again.

As the stars brightened in the sky, my husband and I snuggled in bed. My suspicions about his quiet attitude were correct. Baby was on his mind.

"Honey," he said, "do you forgive that guy who killed Baby?"

Coming

No matter how many times I got that question, it always stumped me. I knew what I was supposed to say, but I couldn't say it unless I embraced it. But that night, I felt something stirring inside me. The door to my heart was not locked this time. I could feel it being pried open, but I wasn't sure what I would find. I stalled for time, stroking his cheek and looking at him in the eyes. He knew I was searching for an answer, and he waited patiently.

Finally, to my surprise, words came from my mouth. "You know, I don't *want* to forgive him. Something inside of me feels like if I forgive that man, I'm sending a message to Baby, wherever she is, that it is okay that she is gone…that it is okay that he did this to her, and us. That we are moving on without her. I'm so afraid that she would be devastated at the thought of being abandoned by her family."

"Do you really believe she would think that?" my husband asked. "I mean, don't you think that if she is with God and totally enlightened, which I'm sure she certainly must be, that she would understand? If she is so close to God, who is all about forgiveness, wouldn't she want us to forgive him?"

I thought about the killer's hurtful words. I thought about his murderous action. Then I recalled Jesus' teaching on love. I remembered how I had spoken up for the murderer the night he was arrested, trying to appease the irate crowd outside the city jail. But that night my brain was in such a fog that I didn't even realize what I was saying. Now I contemplated that the man who did this to us was just as human and needy as any of us. He needed financial stability. He needed a comfortable life. He just

2 Days Ago

chose a violent, hurtful way to meet his need. We all make choices, and who is to say that some of my choices in life were not hurtful? Sure, they weren't as violent, but I felt shame at some of the words and actions I had used in the past to meet my own agenda.

We all just need a way to work together to get our needs met, and the Dandelion Coalition understood this. People need choices. Desperate people do desperate things. We, and I mean *our society*, were not there for that man. We let him get too far into his desperation. We didn't stick together. But we must stick together. We are all connected. We are all one.

"You know, you're right," I said tentatively, then with conviction. "You are absolutely right. What was I thinking? I have not been thinking clearly. Jesus spoke to me about compassion and forgiveness. But I was imagining how I deserved to be the recipient of those things, not the source." I frowned as I thought of that horrible man, but slowly my furrowed brow softened. I could picture him without wanting to gag. I could speak his name without anger in my voice. I could hear his cruel words without letting them hurt my heart. I could forgive him for his desperate action. I decided that was how you know when forgiveness is creeping into your heart…if another's image is no longer vile, but neutral, possibly even acceptable. If you can pray for them and really mean it. At that point, I deeply understood what it meant to love your enemy.

Yes, I did forgive him. I did. I realized that I wanted him to feel peace and comfort. His unhappiness did not serve me. I could not be the one to wish pain on him, no matter what he did. Love felt too good to deny anyone

Coming

the privilege of resting in it. I could no longer hate that man. I just wanted him to feel the deep peace I was beginning to relish each day. In the past I had tried to forgive, to pray for him, but I couldn't. Now I asked God to touch him, to hold him and relieve his pain.

Immediately I felt thirty pounds lighter. I realized that I had been carrying the weight of blame and anger everywhere I went. Resentment had curtailed my enlightenment, and I finally realized that God's peace could never be possible without forgiveness. I regretted being so spiritually immature, especially with my current stature.

My husband could always read people well, and he read me like a primer. "Don't feel bad about not forgiving him sooner, honey. I think if you forgive too quickly, you end up just stuffing your anger and that's just as bad for you as denying forgiveness. Forgiveness takes time. But forgiveness is freedom. Don't you feel better since letting that guy go from your mind? He no longer has a grip on us. We are free."

He was right. I felt free and ready to move on. Not to say that I forgot what happened and was finished grieving over my sweet child. No, I assumed that would go on for a lifetime. But somehow, I felt like Baby was smiling at us, and urging us to live. I did feel free.

✨ Yesterday ✨

It happened again. I awoke in the middle of the night, this time to the single pulsing tone of some sort of horn. Not a car horn. It seemed to be some primordial sound undulating through my being. I rolled over and looked at the clock radio by our bed. Again, it was three-thirty-three, the same time that the Dream had come. The sound was not coming from the radio, but permeated the air. As I slowly focused, I realized that the room was filled with a fog, a kind of bright but dense fog. My husband woke an instant later, looked at me briefly with a perplexed expression, and then we both peered to the foot of our bed. The sound slowly faded.

This was it. I couldn't believe it. Jesus came. He was standing there in unbelievable glory right in our bedroom. He was glowing, but not so bright that we had to shade our eyes, even though we just awoke. We were transfixed. I could not take my eyes off Jesus. Yes, he was the same man that I had entertained in my kitchen. Same thick lashes, same charming smile. But he was absolutely captivating. He donned the white robes of kings, and they were brightest white I could imagine.

I tore my eyes off him and glanced at my husband who looked to be in a trance. His eyes were practically bulging out of his head, and his breathing was shallow. I looked back to Jesus, and he gestured for us to come to him. I didn't want to. I felt unworthy. Even though we had embraced many times before, he seemed more human then. Now, he was definitely God. No doubt about it. I could not bring myself to God.

My husband slowly pulled back the covers, and without taking his eyes off Jesus, he went to him and allowed Jesus to hold him in an embrace that brought tears to my eyes. I could only imagine the peace of that embrace. Immediately I, too, wanted to be a part of it, so I approached. Jesus opened up one arm and, while still holding my husband, he included me in the embrace. I wanted all time to stop right there. It was like nothing I had ever experienced or imagined. It was calm and beautiful and seemed to stroke my soul. It was as if every molecule of my body exploded out into the universe and intermingled with the molecules of every other living thing. I felt as if I was a part of everything and everyone. No longer did I have any flaws…I was perfect in Jesus' eyes and for the first time, also in my own. Tears spilled down my face. They were the kind of tears that come when something is so emotional, not precisely happy…just immensely awesome.

I could feel my husband crying tears of emotional release also, and I remembered the power I felt with Jesus' first embrace. Then Jesus spoke to us and told us to have a seat on the bed. I peeled away first and sat. Looking into Jesus' smiling eyes, I grinned as he patiently waited for my husband to stop holding onto him and sit. Eventually he did, and came to sit by my side. The fog cleared.

Yesterday

There we were, sitting at the foot of our bed, in the presence of the Messiah. I anticipated this moment for forty days now, but it somehow had not really registered. But this was definitely it. The Coming. I asked him if I could get my children and he quietly said that he was with them as well at that moment.

"Are you with everyone?" I asked, incredulously.

"Yes, everyone who accepts me. There really are only a few who continued with their selfish path, even after the Dream and all of your hard work. They cannot see me. They have shut their hearts," Jesus explained.

"What will happen to them?" I asked.

"They will be consumed only with themselves, living the rest of their days feeling tormented by their own selfishness. They cannot feel our peace. It is their choice. It saddens me very much."

My husband still looked like he was about to have a seizure. He was perfectly still and unblinking. I put my arm around him and rubbed his back to make sure he would keep breathing.

Then Jesus spoke again, this time directly to me. "I cannot thank you enough. Although we have lost a few sheep, most of the flock is intact. You did a wonderful job. Because of you, I have my sweet, dear ones with me. Because of you, the world has changed. Thank you for accepting the job. I know you didn't want it, but you were fabulous."

At that, my husband broke his trance and smiled at me. Now it was my turn to be in the trance. I could not believe that Jesus was thanking *me*, telling *me* he needed my help, congratulating *me* on a job well done. I felt in-

Coming

stantly humbled. I tried to speak, but only a small squeak worked its way out.

Then Jesus thanked my husband for his loving support, his behind-the-scenes encouragement that got him no fame, but was equally difficult. My husband, in his humility, dropped his head and just shook it back and forth. I don't know if he was renouncing the praise or trying to find a place for it all to settle into his brain.

Jesus walked over and sat in a wicker chair in our bedroom, leaning his elbows onto his knees and just looked at the two of us and smiled the most warm, wonderful, loving smile you could ever imagine. It loosened me up a little.

"Jesus," I said, "thank you for the compliments, but if it were not for the Dream, nothing would have changed."

"But if it were not for you climbing those buildings and bringing attention to my coming and your accurate interpretation of the dandelions, the Dream would have just been a strange phenomenon, and the fervor would have eventually vanished."

Now I felt a bit worthy of the praise. Maybe he was right, I thought. Of course he's right, he's God. Jesus laughed as if hearing my thoughts.

My husband now loosened up a bit, too. Sitting on the side of our bed, we slowly began asking questions. You know, those questions that you always plan to ask God when you die. Why is there suffering? Creation or evolution? Predestination or happenstance? Miracle or coincidence? Coke or Pepsi?

There we were, fully alive, in deep conversation with Jesus Christ. Jesus patiently answered any question

Yesterday

that we hurled at him. He explained everything to us. Jesus told us how he was having a similar conversation with everyone, no matter where they lived, at that moment, no matter what religion they practiced or whether they practiced any religion at all.

To some, he looked Latino, to others he appeared African or Asian, Jew or Arab, Inuit or Aboriginal. But for all, he came draped in the gleaming white robes of a celestial dignitary. We got so comfortable speaking with Jesus that we almost lost our sense of the mysticism of it all. At one point my husband even asked Jesus if he wanted to borrow some sweatpants and a T-shirt and Jesus threw back his head in laughter and leaned back into the chair, crossing his legs. All was translucent …nothing was a mystery any longer. We were totally satisfied. And we were all totally in love with each other.

The sun was coming up, but it was inconsequential to the light that was being emitted from every living thing. Jesus said to us that he was going to go, but that any time we wanted to see him or talk to him, we should just call on him and he would appear again. Things were different now. All was transparent. It was a new heaven and a new earth….all was connected and we would live in peace. He gave us each a hug and he disappeared right before our eyes.

My husband and I took several moments to just stare at each other in disbelief. Then at the same time, we said, "The kids!"

"Kids!" I yelled, running to their bedrooms. First, we went into our daughter's room. Our daughter was absolutely radiant, standing in the middle of her room, beam-

Coming

ing. I grabbed her, and we ran down the hall into our son's room. He, too, was gleaming brightness, jumping on his bed and laughing. We all jumped onto his bed and we listened as the children told us how Jesus had appeared to them. They were so happy; I had never seen them like it. They kept hugging us and talking so fast that I could hardly keep up.

After over an hour of sharing our experiences, I thought that maybe we should have some breakfast. I fixed eggs and toast and oranges. My husband drove over to my mother's house to pick her up. He didn't call first, because we were not sure if Jesus was finished speaking with everyone. So he just drove over and as soon as he pulled into the driveway, my mother came running out of the house in her robe and slippers. My husband got out of the car, and she ran up to him and threw her arms around him, and he told me later how beautiful she looked. All stress was gone from her face. She appeared younger and full of life, he thought. He brought her back to our house and we sat for the longest time, enjoying a good breakfast and babbling of Jesus' coming.

After breakfast my mother admitted, "Oh, I do wish your father was here to see all of this." At that instant my father appeared, again, right in our kitchen. My mother grabbed her chest and stopped breathing briefly, her mouth dropping open. My children, without hesitation, ran up to my dad, yelling "Grandpa, you're back!" They hugged him and I remembered how Jesus had told me that I would see my father again some day. I had thought that he had meant I would see him after I died, but here he was, among the living.

Yesterday

Daddy slowly walked over to my mother, with children dragging from each of his legs, and he kissed her gently on the forehead. Then he wrapped his strong arms around her in a long embrace. My mother sobbed with disbelief. The love of her life was back. After their embrace continued for some time, I went up behind my dad and put my hand on his back. He turned and gave me a huge hug and whispered in my ear, "Great job, sweetie! I am so proud of you. We are all so proud of you." With that, the tears flowed again, and he gently wiped them from my cheek.

My poor husband was back in shock, and my dad walked over to him and slapped him on the side of the arm. "What's the matter, kid, have you seen a ghost or something?" We all laughed as my dad threw his arms around my husband. My husband barely wrapped his arms around my dad, though, still in a bit of shock.

My dad explained how, since he died, he could see us, but we couldn't see him. He told us how everything "on the other side" was wonderful and peaceful and joyful and that if he started to miss us, he would just check in on us, and it would make him feel better. But now, he told us, that apparently anytime we missed him, we could call on him, and he could cross over and visit for a bit. He told us that he couldn't stay because he had to get back to "business" but to just give him a call if we needed him, and he would be back. With that he gave my mom another hug, a sweet kiss on the lips, and he was gone.

My mother had to sit, her knees weak, her heart pounding, her hands trembling. But my husband and I quickly looked at each other and I knew we had the same thought...

Baby.

As abruptly as the possibility of her coming back to us burst into our brains, she appeared. There she was, standing across the kitchen in green corduroy pants and a pink sweater, with her beautiful silky blonde hair and dimpled smile. Within a split second she was running to me calling, "Mommy!" and jumped into my arms. Her brother and sister ran over to me, too, and leapt on Baby, knocking us all to the floor. My husband fell on the scrum, and we all cried in disbelief. My sweet child again in my arms. Who could ever believe it? We lay on the ground in a big ball for what seemed like an hour, no one wanting to let Baby go again. But it was Baby who spoke up.

"I'm getting smushed!" she protested. We peeled off each other slowly, still being sure to touch our hand to some part of Baby to make sure she was real. She absolutely was.

She sat on my lap and told us in such a grown up way that she liked the other side. She said that she saw Grandpa all the time, that the angels were "super nice" and that she hung around with Jesus a lot and had lots of friends. She told us that she felt kind of "heavy" back in our house, and I realized that her soul was probably lighter than her earthly body, and it was a bit of a chore to re-enter our constraints of time and space. Maybe that's why they could only stay a while. Maybe it was too uncomfortable.

"Honey," my husband asked of her, "have you seen God yet?"

Yesterday

Baby threw back her head and put her hand to her mouth and giggled and giggled. "You're so silly, Daddy."

My husband looked confused. I knew he hadn't meant to be "silly."

Baby seemed to pick up on the seriousness of his question and sweetly explained to her father, "Daddy, I see God everywhere I look!"

Then Baby told my husband and me that she was glad we forgave that "dumb man." She said she was trying to tell us to do it, but that we didn't really hear her. I think that maybe it was Baby who had pried my heart open, allowing forgiveness.

We visited and kissed and hugged for probably about ten or fifteen minutes more until Baby announced that she had to go. I sent her off as if sending her to camp for a week. And she, just like my dad, assured us that anytime we needed her, to just call her and she'd come back for a little bit.

That's all I needed, I decided. Just a little bit, once in a while. Okay, maybe every day. But I had been able to move on with my life, in a way. I was putting one foot in front of the other, if not tentatively. But just a little hug once in a while would make everything so much easier. We were connected now in a way that was never before possible, and I loved it. The wide river between heaven and earth was now just a trickle, and that changed everything.

Once Baby disappeared before our eyes, we sat and talked about how very blessed we were to have each other and that we couldn't wait to go out and shout it to the world. We decided to walk down the street and see

Coming

what else was happening. The whole earth had new life breathed into it, and we felt like balloons ready to burst.

The entire community was out milling around by the time we got outside. Some seemed totally dazed. But most were ecstatic. Neighbors rushed into the arms of other neighbors, sometimes barely knowing them. People bubbled with stories of their unbelievable vision of Jesus and deceased loved ones. Some, who hadn't known they could summon someone from the other side, called out the name of a brother or wife or newborn son who had died, and there they were. People were falling to their knees in disbelief, while the rest of us, having already witnessed the phenomenon, stepped aside and let them have their joyful reunions.

The trees, the birds, the people...everything seemed to be emitting light. Even though it was daylight, the sole source of radiance was no longer the sun. There were no shadows, as illumination came from all directions. The trees, although still in their winter dormancy phase, were vibrant. Evergreens were greener than I could have ever imagined. I suddenly could not wait for spring to see the flowers. The light of God's love was visible in all of creation.

Obviously no stores or schools or businesses opened, but I knew that we would have to get back to the business of living. Soon we would all return to our normal lives, but now we would be living with a new sense of awe and working with a new sense of creativity. We would be responsible for the unfolding of the future, as we always had been, but we now felt an overwhelming accountability and pride in the results.

Yesterday

There was a kindness in the air that was palpable. I knew it would last. It wasn't the kind of niceness that happens after a local tragedy, where everyone is helpful at first, but then goes about their own business. I could sense this was a deep compassion in the air - the type of compassion that Jesus taught us. The compassion that brings forth acceptance and forgiveness and justice and humility. And peace. And sure, we would continue to make mistakes...we were still human after all. But I could tell that there was a collective responsibility felt toward others that would enable us to pick each other up, dust each other off, and get back on The Way.

We spent the day visiting with neighbors. The kids ran down the street for a while to see some of their friends. Everyone was out. Everyone was filled with joy. I knew the wonderful strides being made in world politics and economics would just continue at an even faster pace now that everyone had felt the peace of God. There was no turning back. No way could anyone ever again try to hoard goods or push someone else down to raise themselves up. It would not be possible. The world had changed, and I couldn't believe it happened in my lifetime. I felt amazed. I felt blessed.

As the sun began to sink, the darkness crept in, but there was still a light glow in the air from all that was alive. I just stood for a moment in silence, looking up at the stars that were beginning to twinkle in the sky. Living in the garden, I thought. How absolutely magnificent! To live more consciously with nature and others brought a feeling of balance within me.

I realized that when you reach out with compassion and touch another life, you are touched right back. It almost becomes like a game of "tag, you're it." You can't wait to touch another and a sense of urgency ensues. It becomes impossible not to play. You must run to others and touch them and you fill with joy at the touching.

We gathered the children and headed into the house to eat and to rest after such an amazing day. I could barely wait to see what the next day would bring. I could only imagine. A world at peace, every day, forevermore.

As we walked up our front lawn, there was a fresh new dandelion by the front doorstep. It was the kind of dandelion that had gone to seed and was a beautiful big puffball. "Look!" I cried excitedly and gently pulled up the stem so that the seedlings would not be disrupted.

"Ready?" I asked.

"Ready!" everyone declared in harmony. And on the count of three, we blew the seedlings in every direction and watched as the seeds of peace drifted skyward.

❦ *Today* ❦

I awake to the classical station on my clock radio playing Dvorak's "New World Symphony." I smile broadly at the synchronicity and roll over in bed, stretching. But my smile fades as I feel unusually heavy and lethargic. I almost feel achy. My husband rubs his face, sitting up on his side of the bed.

Something is wrong. I can just sense it. Everything seems darker. My room is a mess. It looks as if I took my clothes off from the night before and just threw them on the floor. I look again at my clothes. They are not what I was wearing yesterday. I distinctly remember hanging my jeans and sweater on the hook on my door before I went to bed last night. But the hook is empty and my black blazer is on the floor, along with the black dress that I wore to my dad's funeral over a month ago. What happened to our room? Who messed it up? Where is the glow? I start to feel a little nervous.

Cocking my head, I ask my husband quizzically, "Honey, what day is it?"

"Sunday," he says, with absolutely no enthusiasm in his voice.

"Sunday?" I ask with surprise. I know it is Friday, not Sunday. "Are you sure?"

Coming

"Positive, honey. You must have slept well after such a rough day."

"What do you mean, 'rough day'?" I ask, totally confused.

"The funeral, dear. And all of those people over here. It was a long day. It was rough for me. I assume it was even harder for you."

I feel weak. I feel nauseous. The frenzied symphonic melody coming from my radio fuels my anxiety. I begin to tremble. What is happening to me? Did I just have one of the most vivid, amazing dreams ever possible? No, it could not have been a dream. How could all of that been a dream? My mind is racing. It was all too real.

I ask one more time, "Honey, what's the date?"

My husband walks around the bed and sits next to me. "Are you okay, babe?" he asks with deep concern.

"Oh, I'm not sure," I say with a sickly voice. "Have you seen Jesus lately?" I ask, checking out the situation.

"No, not lately, dear," my husband says sarcastically.

I fall back onto my pillow and throw the covers over my face, my fists holding the blanket to my eyes, which clamp shut. Thoughts bounce around in my head like ten thousand monkeys. With great difficulty I try to quiet the chaos in my brain. I slowly pull the covers down from my head, but cannot yet open my eyes to reality.

"Oh man, I think I may have just had the weirdest dream ever. I dreamed that I woke up, and it was the day after the funeral, and there was a man knocking on our door. When I answered the door, the guy came in and told me he was Jesus. He didn't look like Jesus. He was

Today

just an average guy, driving an old orange VW Beetle. But he made my father appear, and then he told me it was time for his coming to earth and that he needed my help."

My husband chuckles.

I throw the covers back forcefully and sit up.

"No, it is not funny. It was so real," I say indignantly. I bite my lip to hold in the tears of disbelief, and I proceed to tell him all about the signs on the buildings and the appearances on AMerica and the *Here's Hope Show* and the universal Dandelion Dream and the press conferences, and then I come to the part where Baby was shot. I can hold back no longer. I start to sob.

My husband pulls me to his chest and reassures me that it was just a dream, that Baby and the other two children are safe in their beds. But I push away from him and continue telling him the rest of my dream. I cry as I speak, unable to control my emotions. I tell him in detail of all of the changes that happened throughout the world and about the world dance party and then I tell him about how Jesus actually did come. There was a new heaven and a new earth. I tell him how the earth was a clean and beautiful garden again and that we were all connected to each and every person in love, even with those who had passed on, and we lived in true peace.

My husband listens patiently and at the end of my ramblings he says, "Sounds like a great dream, except for that part about Baby. That would be so cool. Can you imagine something like that really happening?"

"Yes I can! I was there. *You* were there," I say emphatically. He just isn't getting it. "It was *so* real. Not

Coming

like a normal dream that is full of quirky events and bizarre timelines. No, this went day by day by day, and everything seemed perfectly normal. I can't believe it was not real. I cannot live anymore in a world with violence, greed, selfishness and fear. No way! I can't go back! I won't go back!" I cry.

I jump up from the bed and scurry to the window. I want to check and see if I have a lawn filled with the supporters that I have grown so accustomed to seeing. I could ask them what is happening. I could show them to my husband. I don't know if he is confused or if I am. I split the blinds with the fingers of my right hand as I had done so often before when I had waved goodnight to all of the people who had inhabited our front yard for weeks. There are no people. The rising sun is peeking through a hole in the dark clouds and it, once again, is the only source of light to the world. The trees seem dead, and the gloomy sky hangs heavy as it does on winter days. I am in absolute denial, and I am totally deflated.

But something catches my peripheral vision. I open the blinds wider with both hands and I press the side of my face against the window. I can't believe what I am seeing. My knees buckle. I gasp audibly for breath. My husband runs over to me to see if I am all right. With the mood of Dvorak's score brightening as if on cue, my husband supports me from behind with both his arms and peers over my head.

"Look!" I demand as I yank on the string and whip the blinds fully open. We both see it. It is real and right in front of our eyes. Turning onto our street is an old,

Today

orange VW Beetle, with several small dents and sun bleached paint.

"Jesus," I whisper softly, a smile creeping across my face. And I feel a chill race down my spine as my heart leaps in my chest with the hope of his coming.

*May the words of my mouth
and the meditations of my heart
be acceptable in your sight,
O Lord, my rock and my redeemer.
Psalm 19:15*

~ Afterword ~

Nineteen ninety-two was a year that would change my life only as it was about to be waved off with kisses and celebrations. The entire first ten months had kept me busy as a mother of four small children, ranging from three to eight years old. In November of that year, I met a woman with whom I became friends. We saw each other often. Our children played together. Six weeks later, just before the end of the year, her otherwise healthy eight-year-old son died swiftly from a virus.

I was shocked, crippled with sadness. I could not believe such a tragic thing was possible. Back home, after attending the funeral, I lay on my couch watching my own children play with such health, joy, and innocence. I felt at once blessings, guilt, grief, and fear. With my head pounding from emotional exhaustion, I closed my eyes to rest.

Within a few seconds, the story of *Coming* unfolded in my brain. I had the beginning, with Jesus arriving in an orange VW, a sketchy but framed mid-section, and a definite ending with the orange VW coming down the street. I had the title and I would dedicate the story to my friend's deceased son, who I believed whispered it

Coming

into my heart that day. I would donate profits from the sale of the story to organizations that worked for peace.

Leaping from the couch and bubbling with excitement, I told the plot to my husband. As I relayed the whole story, my melancholy lifted and my mood was completely altered. I was no longer drained and could see life as joyful and good. My husband and I decided to get a movie and have a date night at home.

I darted off to Blockbuster, now feeling elation rather than grief. The Blockbuster parking lot was packed. I had never seen it quite like that. I drove up and down looking for a spot. Suddenly, I spied a possible opening down the aisle to my left. As I pulled into the only open spot on the whole lot, there was an orange VW Beetle parked right next to it. I laughed aloud and pulled in quickly. Even in 1992, VW Beetles were an uncommon sight.

Inside Blockbuster I searched every face, looking for a clue as to which one drove the VW there. I looked at men and women, old and young. I ruled out no one. One young man, standing by a stack off to my right, made eye contact with me and smiled. As I grinned from ear to ear, I knew at that moment he would be my Jesus in *Coming*. I dare not think that he was truly a vision of Jesus. But I do believe that Jesus uses others to aid us. Possibly the man was merely a smiling conduit for Jesus' encouragement for me, and his face will forever be emblazoned in my mind. And it was then that I realized the story *had* to be written. It became bigger than an idea. It felt more like a mandate.

With young children and a busy life, I tried working on the book over the years, but only when the children

Afterword

grew up enough to leave me at home with several hours of unscheduled time could I complete the story. It took many years, but then maybe the timing never was mine.

Susan Marting
March, 2007

Quotations

*The following quotations
are the inspiration for much of this work.*

~

There is no limit to the partnership between humankind and the Great Mystery. Our faith and our intent, coupled with the Creator's boundless grace, make any situation that seems impossible a challenge we can overcome.
*Twenty-Sixth Meditation of the Twelfth Moon
("Earth Medicine — Ancestors' Ways of Harmony for
Many Moons" by Jamie Sams)*

~

The first step to better times is to imagine them.
Fortune Cookie

~

There is only one God and He is God to all; therefore it is important that everyone is seen as equal before God. I've always said we should help a Hindu become a better Hindu, a Muslim become a better Muslim, a Catholic become a better Catholic.
Mother Teresa

~

What does the Lord require of you?
To seek justice, and love tenderly,
and walk humbly with your God.
Micah

Believe nothing merely because you have been told it...
Do not believe what your teacher tells you
merely out of respect for the teacher. But whatsoever,
after due examination and analysis, you find to be kind,
conducive to the good, the benefit, the welfare of all
beings – that doctrine believe and cling to,
and take it as your guide.
Siddhartha Buddha

~

Life is a daring adventure or nothing at all.
Helen Keller

~

You're soaking in it!
Madge

~

Be like water, always seeking the lowest place,
yet strong enough to wear away stone.
Taoist proverb

~

Imagine all the people sharing all the world.
"Imagine" by John Lennon

~

For truly I say to you, if you have faith the size of a
mustard seed, you will say to this mountain,
'Move from here to there,' and it will move;
and nothing will be impossible to you.
Jesus of Nazareth

Let God be God in you.
Meister Eckhart

~

I like when this music happens like this: Something in
His eye grabs hold of a tambourine in me, and then I
turn and lift a violin in someone else, and they turn, and
this turning continues; it has reached you now.
Isn't that something?
Jalaluddin Rumi
("Love Poems From God" by Daniel Ladinsky)

~

You must be the change you wish to see in the world.
Mohandas Gandhi

~

Finding God within, you will find Him without,
in all people and all conditions.
"Inner Peace" by Paramahansa Yogananda

~

Can we all just get along?
Rodney King

~

And think not, you can direct the course of love;
for love, if it finds you worthy, directs your course.
"The Prophet" by Khalil Gibran

~

Wage Peace
Bumper sticker

Death is not extinguishing the light;
it is putting out the lamp because the dawn has come.
Rabindranath Tagore

~

God is big.
Helen Pennington

~

Money doesn't talk it swears.
"It's Alright Ma (I'm Only Bleeding)" by Bob Dylan

~

Call on God, but row away from the rocks.
Native American proverb

~

People usually consider walking on water or in thin air a miracle. But I think the real miracle is not to walk either on water or in thin air, but to walk on earth…
All is a miracle.
"The Miracle of Mindfulness" by Thich Nhat Hanh

~

If you want peace, work for justice.
Pope Paul VI

~

Injustice anywhere is a threat to justice everywhere.
I have a dream…
Martin Luther King, Jr.

About the Author

Susan Marting lives in St. Louis, Missouri with her husband and has four grown children. She believes that all of our children will one day know peace. Susan is grateful to Therese for the turning, to Mary for the leading and to God for pulling her in and holding her tight. And, of course, to Jesus, for being a verb.

Susan Marting thanks you much for buying this book. All profits from the sale of this book will be donated to organizations dedicated to the proliferation of peace. Discussion questions and more information can be found at www.integropress.com.

LaVergne, TN USA
23 April 2010
180305LV00001BA/1/P